# Frog in the Throat

# Frog in the Throat

E. X. Ferrars

FELONY & MAYHEM PRESS • NEW YORK

FROG IN THE THROAT

A Felony & Mayhem mystery

PRINTING HISTORY
First UK edition (HarperCollins): 1980
First US edition (Doubleday): 1980

Felony & Mayhem edition: 2021

ISBN: 978-1-63194-260-0

Manufactured in the United States of America


Library of Congress Cataloging-in-Publication Data

Names: Ferrars, E. X., author.
Title: Frog in the throat / E.X. Ferrars.
Description: Felony & Mayhem edition. | New York : Felony & Mayhem Press, 2021. |
   Series: Virginia and Felix ; 2 | "A Felony & Mayhem mystery"--Title page verso. |
   Summary: "Virginia and Felix's casual visit with friends turns mysterious when a
   neighbor reports the murder of her sister...and the body promptly goes missing"--
   Provided by publisher.
Identifiers: LCCN 2021045624 | ISBN 9781631942600 (trade paperback) | ISBN
   9781631942617 (ebook)
Subjects: LCSH: Women physical therapists--England--Fiction. | Divorced  women-
   -England--Fiction. | Thieves--England--Fiction. | LCGFT: Detective  and mystery
   fiction.
Classification: LCC PR6003.R458 F7 2021 | DDC 823/.912--dc23
LC record available at https://lccn.loc.gov/2021045624

The icon above says you're holding a book in the Felony & Mayhem "British" category. These books are set in or around the UK, and feature the highly literate, often witty prose that fans of British mystery demand. If you enjoy this book, you may well like other "British" titles from Felony & Mayhem Press.

———◆◆◆———

For information about British titles or to learn more about Felony & Mayhem Press, please visit us online at:

www.FelonyAndMayhem.com

# Other "British" titles from

# FEL♀NY&MAYHEM

## MICHAEL DAVID ANTHONY
*The Becket Factor*
*Midnight Come*
*Dark Provenance*

## ROBERT BARNARD
*Corpse in a Gilded Cage*
*Death and the Chaste Apprentice*
*The Skeleton in the Grass*
*Out of the Blackout*

## SIMON BRETT
*Blotto, Twinks and*
*the Ex-King's Daughter*
*Blotto, Twinks and*
*the Dead Dowager Duchess*
*Blotto, Twinks and*
*the Rodents of the Riviera*
*Blotto, Twinks and*
*the Bootlegger's Moll*

## CAROLINE GRAHAM
*The Killings at Badger's Drift*
*Death of a Hollow Man*
*Death in Disguise*
*Written in Blood*
*Murder at Madingley Grange*

## ELIZABETH IRONSIDE
*The Accomplice*
*The Art of Deception*
*Death in the Garden*
*A Very Private Enterprise*

## MAGGIE JOEL
*The Second-Last Woman*
*in England*
*The Past and Other Lies*

## SHEILA RADLEY
*Death in the Morning*
*The Chief Inspector's Daughter*
*A Talent for Destruction*
*Fate Worse than Death*

## LESLIE THOMAS
*Dangerous Davies:*
*The Last Detective*

## L.C. TYLER
*The Herring Seller's Apprentice*
*Ten Little Herrings*
*The Herring in the Library*
*Herring on the Nile*
*Crooked Herring*

## E.X. FERRARS
*Something Wicked*
*Root of All Evil*
*The Crime and the Crystal*
*The Other Devil's Name*

# Frog in the Throat

# Chapter One

I looked out of the window and exclaimed, *"Par exemple!"*

It is not that I am in the habit of bursting into French. My knowledge of the language got stuck at school level. But years ago I saw that outstanding film, *Carnet de Bal,* and in it a mayor, who is just about to marry his cook, looks out of the window and sees a very glamorous love of his youth crossing the street towards his house and he cries out, *"Par exemple!"* It had seemed to me an adequate thing to say in the circumstances. So it was what I said when I saw my erstwhile husband, Felix Freer, wandering up the garden path towards the front door of the house where I was staying.

I was staying with my friends, Helen and Andrew Boscott. They lived in the village of Stillbeam, near Wandlebury, in a rambling old house overlooking the river Wandle. I had known them for most of my life and had stayed with them more than once when I took a holiday from my part-time job as a physiotherapist. They were what I considered perfect hosts. They always left their guests to fend for themselves, get their own breakfast when they happened to want it, look in the refrigerator for something to eat for lunch, and only be sociable over a meal somewhat casually thrown together in the evening, followed by two or three hours of pleasant conversation. In the meantime, they went on undistracted with their own work, so that one did not feel one was being a burden to them.

Andrew was a furniture restorer, an immensely skilled craftsman, and worked in an old stable on the bank of the river, which he had converted into a workshop. Helen, in another part of the stable block, did tapestry work, some weaving and a small amount of dressmaking for very special customers. So far as I knew, their income had never been more than enough to live on in modest comfort, but they were both completely absorbed in their work, without any unsettling ambitions, and seemed to be two uncommonly happy people. I always found that staying with them, relaxing in the peace of their own contentment, was a perfect rest.

But there was no reason that I knew of why Felix should come to see them. They had never been specially friends of his.

It was in the late afternoon and they were still in their workshops when he arrived. I had been sitting in the living room, reading, having come in from the garden because it had been almost too hot to sit out of doors, and it had been the squeak of the garden gate that had made me go to the window. I saw Felix looking about him uncertainly as he came up the path, as if he were not sure that he had come to the right place. He was carrying a small suitcase. I went to the front door and opened it.

As if he were utterly astonished at seeing me there, he said, "Virginia!" and putting down his suitcase, kissed me on the cheek.

I did not invite him in at once. A deep instinct always warned me to keep Felix out of my life when, as sometimes happened, he showed signs of wanting to move back into it. I had gone through too much, making up my mind to break with him after three years of marriage, and the relative calm of the six years that had followed had been achieved by such a hard struggle that I did not dare take any risks with what I had gained just because, in a slightly perverse fashion, I was always quite glad to see him when we happened to meet.

"What are you doing here?" I asked.

"Well, I chanced to be in the neighbourhood," he said, "so I thought I'd just drop in on the Boscotts."

"You didn't know I was here?"

"How could I?"

I could think of several ways in which he could have found out. From my daily, for instance, if he had telephoned my home. She had been forwarding letters to me and would not have hesitated to give him my address if he had asked for it.

"I didn't know you knew the Boscotts well enough to drop in on them," I said.

"Perhaps I don't. Perhaps I shouldn't have come. But I remembered them as such nice, friendly people, and as I said, I happened to be in the neighbourhood. Aren't you going to ask me in? Do you want me to go away?" He was looking at me with a good deal of dismay.

I moved to one side to let him in.

"What have you been doing in the neighbourhood?" I asked. "Delivering a secondhand car?"

When I had last seen him he had been working for a very shady firm of secondhand-car dealers, whose managing director happened to be in gaol for fraud.

"No, I've given that up," he said. "They were going too near the edge for my liking. The older I get, the less ready I am to take risks. It's time I made something of my life."

His age, which was the same as mine, was forty-one and normally I did not feel that this was so very old. But I had just been thinking that he had aged a certain amount since our last meeting. There were threads of grey in his fair hair and an air of quiet distinction had taken the place of the boyish charm that had lasted him well into his thirties. He was a very good-looking man, of medium height and slender, with a triangular face, wide at the temples, pointed at the chin, with curiously drooping eyelids that made his vivid blue eyes look almost triangular too. He had thick, golden eyebrows and a wide, most friendly mouth. His mouth was among the few things about him that were not deceptive. He was a friendly man. It was that that could make him so dangerous. He always dressed conservatively and well, though it struck me that the checked jacket and tan slacks that he was wearing were a little shabbier than he would have cared to be seen in once. Carrying his small suitcase as if it contained his samples, he looked rather like the best sort of salesman, ever so slightly down on his luck.

"What are you doing now, then?" I asked.

"Nothing much at the moment," he said. "I'm giving myself a holiday before I start seriously looking for anything. I've got a little money put by, so I haven't got to worry, and I feel I need a good rest. I find I get tired much faster than I did when I was younger. That's inevitable, I suppose. We've all got to get used to it."

As I remembered it, Felix had been busy getting used to it for as long as I had known him. He was a man who really ought to have been born with a large income, he was so good at doing nothing. I know that most of us feel that we should be much the better for a large income which had come to us without the trouble of our having had to work for it, but I am fairly sure that that is true of far fewer people than believe it. Felix, however, would have been one of the few. He would never have been bored, would never have yearned for power, for responsibility, or to make his mark in the world. And he would have been generous and kindly and perhaps might even have become honest. It was a great pity that he was not rich.

"What made you choose Stillbeam, of all places, for your holiday?" I asked. I could not believe that there was not some object in the trip.

"Actually I've been staying in Wandlebury," he said. "Someone told me about a nice pub there, and I've been doing some walking and taking stock of things, doing some quiet thinking, you know, about the future. And I've been wandering around the antique shops, picking up a few odds and ends for the flat. I'm still in the old place in Little Carbery Street." He sat down. "You know, this is a very nice room. It's just right for your friends."

I was glad that he did not want to go on talking about the flat in Little Carbery Street. My early memories of it had been so joyous, my later ones, as I gradually began to find Felix out and to face the fact that I had married a crook, even if a very minor one, so full of sadness that I could hardly bear to think about the place. It was the only home that I had ever had into which, for a time, I had really put my heart. Since I had left it, I had never paid much attention to my surroundings.

"Yes, it's nice," I agreed.

The room was long and narrow and had once been two rooms, but Helen and Andrew had had the dividing wall removed. Where the wall had once been there was a step across the room, which somehow increased the feeling of length. The whole house was full of steps in unexpected places, treacherous until you got to know your way about. The ceilings were low, criss-crossed with dark beams. The windows were small, set deep in thick stone walls. I think the house dated back to the sixteenth century.

One wall of the room was covered in bookshelves. There was a big open fireplace with a crooked beam across the top of it and a log fire laid on the hearth, waiting for a change in the weather to be lit. The furniture was of a variety of periods, all of it owing a certain amount of its apparent perfection to Andrew's skill and none of it as old as the house, yet looking comfortably at home there. Even a low coffee table of some pale wood and entirely Andrew's work, did not seem out of place. The chairs were deep, with cushions in them in fine tapestry stitch, worked by Helen. There were a few pleasing watercolours on the walls. A glass door at one end of the room stood open, showing a slope of lawn and a glimpse of the Wandle, gliding among willows, at the bottom of it.

"Must be a bit damp in winter," Felix observed, "but very nice now, with the river and all. Very quiet. Very peaceful."

"You've brought in your suitcase," I said. "Were you counting on Helen and Andrew putting you up?"

He looked at his suitcase rather blankly, as if he were surprised to discover that he had it with him.

"Of course not," he said. "I just didn't think what I was doing."

"Is the holiday over then? Are you on your way home?"

"Not really. I'm just cruising about, looking for another pub. I don't much care for staying too long in one place. I thought there might be something attractive in the village here, but the only pub doesn't let rooms. Then I remembered your friends lived here, so I thought I'd look in on them. Perhaps they can tell me about somewhere nice in the neighbourhood. Nothing grand, just unpretentious and comfortable."

"Where have you left your car?" I asked.

"In the lane." He lit a cigarette. He had always been a heavy smoker and never seemed at ease without a cigarette dangling from between his stained fingertips. "Virginia, tell me honestly—I wasn't expecting to find you here—d'you want me to go away? I won't stay around if it's going to embarrass you."

I am not sure what I might have answered if there had not been the sound of a door opening and closing at that moment and Helen and Andrew had not come in.

❋ ❋ ❋

They both seemed very pleased to see Felix, though whether this was because they really remembered him after all the years that had passed since they had met him with me, or because they thought it was what I would want of them, I did not know. Helen was a small, dark-haired woman with a rather pale, pointed face and clear, deep brown eyes. She was wiry and vigorous and never seemed to get tired. She was wearing an embroidered blue smock, jeans and sandals. Andrew, who was about her age, was not much taller than she, with hair as dark as hers, but curly and untidy, whereas hers was neat and straight. He also had a sharply pointed face, but his skin was much darker than hers and the summer sun had given it a deep tan. He was wearing a sweat-stained white shirt and grey trousers, loosely belted, so that they wrinkled over his canvas shoes and looked as if they might be about to slide down over his narrow hips.

They had come in from their workshops earlier than usual, I supposed, because the three of us were presently going out for drinks to a neighbour of theirs and they felt that they ought to clean themselves up a certain amount for the occasion.

Helen told Felix what a good idea of his it had been to drop in on them, and Andrew said he was sure that Felix was thirsty and that it was not too early for a drink. Felix asked for a lager. In the heat of the afternoon it seemed as good a choice as any, so I asked for one too, but Felix would probably not have asked for anything stronger even if it had been snowing outside. He was a very cautious drinker. He was afraid, I had always thought, that whisky or gin would loosen his tongue and lead him to all kinds of regrettable self-betrayals.

He had so much to hide, poor man. He had all kinds of unimportant little secrets, most of them the result of the lies that he liked to tell about himself, in which it would have been undignified, if nothing worse, to be caught out. It would have been a pity for him, for instance, if he had told someone that he was an agent for MI5 and then presently had told the same person that he was, say, a professor of some very esoteric subject in a safely remote university. But really I am not sure how many people he succeeded in deceiving, as he had me in the early days of our marriage. I had believed then that he was a civil engineer, employed by a great firm who had sent him on important work all over the world, but who, as it had turned out later, had never even heard of him. I had sometimes thought since that time that I had been far more naïve and ready to accept him as he had said he was than most of the people he met, and that that had been partly why he had wanted to marry me.

Soon, sitting over our drinks in the cool, shady room, Helen asked him where he was staying, and of course, as soon as she heard that he was hoping that she and Andrew could tell him of some pleasant pub, said that he should stay with them. So at least part of his holiday would be free of cost.

But she went on quickly, looking sideways at me, "That's to say, if Virginia doesn't feel..."

She paused there. Although we knew one another so well, like most people she was not really sure of the relationship that existed between Felix and me.

"Oh, I've nothing against it," I said.

"But I really can't take advantage of you like that," Felix said, demurring insincerely, though the suitcase that he had brought in showed how confident he had been of the invitation. "It's awfully good of you, but I couldn't think of imposing on you in that way."

"It wouldn't be imposing in the least," Helen said. "We've lots of room and we love having people here. The house is much too big for just Andrew and me. Sometimes, you know, we hardly know who's staying here. You'd have to look after yourself, of course. Andrew and I are both frightfully busy at the moment. But you can come and go as you like and be perfectly free. So, of course you'll stay. Are you here because you've some special interest in the neighbourhood, or is it just by chance? If you're really interested in it, we've some books on local history, archaeology and so on, that you might like to look at."

"It's really just by chance," Felix answered, "though as a matter of fact..."

He hesitated. He had spoken so casually that I knew at once that what was coming was something important. But I was quite unprepared for what he said.

"I've got very interested recently in Basil Deering, the poet. Doesn't he live hereabouts?"

It astounded me. I had never known Felix take the slightest interest in poets or poetry. His reading had been almost entirely limited to newspapers, morning and evening, in which the financial pages and the sports news could keep him engrossed for most of his spare time.

Andrew replied, "Yes, he lives quite near. He happens to be a cousin of mine. A second cousin. Why? Would you like to meet him? It ought to be quite easy to arrange."

"Oh, I couldn't think of asking you to do that," Felix said. "He'd hardly want to meet a complete stranger and someone, at that, who doesn't know the first thing about poetry. It's just that his stuff somehow appeals to me. I can actually understand it, or I think I can. So I thought I'd rather like to see the sort of house he lives in and so on. Just impertinent curiosity, really."

"He'd probably be very flattered," Andrew said laconically.

I knew that his opinion of his cousin's verse was not a high one. It was light, jingly stuff with plenty of rhythm and rhyme, full of the simplest, most unexceptionable sentiments, refreshing in a way after the obscure and tortured prose that so often passes for verse nowadays, but difficult to take seriously. A great many people did, however, for his yearly volume of little poems, always published just before Christmas, sold remarkably well. But Andrew's taste was far too austere for him ever to be an enthusiastic member of Basil Deering's public. I had often thought that there was something very austere, almost with-drawn, about Andrew, though Helen's spontaneous warmth usually kept it concealed.

"Of course he'd be flattered," she said. "Who wouldn't be? I know he's successful, but his public hasn't exactly beaten a path to his door. He has to autograph a lot of books and that sort of thing, but I can't remember anyone ever coming here just to take a look at the house he lives in. And as it happens, we can probably fix it for you to meet him this evening. We're going over for drinks to a neighbour of ours, Barbara Gabriel, and Basil will almost certainly be there. In fact, I think Barbara told me he was coming. So all I have to do is telephone and ask her if she minds if we bring a friend. She won't, of course. New faces are always welcome in a little community like this. And you'll meet our other two celebrities there, the Fyffe sisters. Perhaps you like their books as well."

Felix looked vague and said, "I seem to know the name, but I'm not sure if I've actually..."

It was clear that he had never heard of the Fyffes, though their paperbacks had been in all the bookshops for the last few years. They wrote together as Carola Fyffe, the name Carola being a fusion of their first names, Carleen and Olivia. Actually Carleen's name was not Fyffe at all. She was a widow whose married name was Mansell, but everyone spoke of her and Olivia as the Fyffe sisters. They wrote historical romances, full of cloak-and-dagger stuff and lots of luscious adjectives, but with good plots and with what I had been assured by Helen, who knew much more about such things than I did, were extremely accurate historical backgrounds. It was Olivia who was mainly responsible for this. She had been a lecturer in history in London University and had given this up only when the books that she and Carleen had started to write had become so popular that the two of them had suddenly found themselves prosperous.

I had not met them yet, but I had seen the opulent-looking bungalow in which they lived together on the far bank of the Wandle. Helen had told me that it was Carleen who did most of the actual writing of the books, but that she always insisted that the really important work was done by Olivia.

"I'll go and telephone Barbara now," Helen went on. "You'd like to come with us, wouldn't you?"

Felix again demurred, but not to the point of stopping her doing what she had suggested.

After she had telephoned she took him to the room that she had assigned to him and they made up his bed together. I could hear them talking as they went about it, sounding already like old friends, although even in the old days they had never known one another well. By the time that they came downstairs again Felix seemed completely at home. But he had always had the knack of appearing at home wherever he found himself, and Helen was a very easy person to come to terms with. When the rest of us went upstairs to change for Barbara Gabriel's little party, he apologized for having brought nothing suitable to change into and settled down to wait for us by himself in the living-room, comfortably extended on the sofa, chain-smoking and gazing dreamily up at the ceiling.

I changed into a pale grey pleated dress I had brought in case of needing something more presentable than my usual shirt and slacks. I never tan well and in the blazing sunshine of the last few days my skin had turned an unbecoming shade of red. I did what I could to rectify the damage with make-up, feeling, unreasonably, that with Felix there I did not want to look my worst. Helen appeared looking neat and pretty in a white silk dress that looked far too expensive and individual to have been made by anyone but herself. Andrew had changed into a clean shirt and a moderately well-pressed pair of trousers and showed signs of having tugged a comb through his curly dark hair.

We set out soon after six. Felix offered to take us in his car, since it was still in the lane, but Helen said that it was only a few minutes' walk to Barbara's house and that we might as well go on foot. Andrew and Felix strolled ahead together, with Helen and me following them.

It was the most delightful of evenings. The sultry heat of the day had faded and the air, in spite of the heat that had lingered on, felt sweet and fresh, full of the soft scents of summer. It was very still. The leaves of the tall beech trees that lined the lane were motionless. The clear sky was gently tinged with the pallor of evening.

We turned to the right down the lane which led to the main road that passed through the village of Stillbeam, then we once more turned to the right, away from the village, then almost at once to the right again into another lane that took us over a humpbacked bridge across the Wandle and on to the house where Mrs. Gabriel lived.

Looking at the two men ahead of us, Helen said, "I hope it was really all right, Virginia, asking Felix to stay. You really don't mind?"

"Not in the least," I said. "I quite like meeting him occasionally to hear how things are going with him."

"I can't quite imagine what it feels like, meeting one's divorced husband. I mean, if you don't quite simply hate one another, in which case I suppose there are no problems."

In fact, Felix and I had never been divorced. I had suggested to him more than once that it would tidy things up if we went ahead with it, but he had an intense dislike of committing himself in any way and an almost pathological dislike to signing documents. So we had simply drifted apart, which had not seemed to matter, as neither of us so far had shown any signs of wanting to marry again.

"I know it's the kind of thing one oughtn't to say," Helen continued, "but I can't help feeling it's awfully sad you broke up. He's so charming really."

"Oh, he's never been short on charm," I said, "but by itself that's an unsatisfactory diet."

"But he's very good-natured too, isn't he?"

"After his fashion, I suppose he is. But don't lend him money and don't believe more than half of what he tells you."

"It's intriguing, isn't it, that he's so interested in Basil?"

"Very intriguing."

And indeed it was. It puzzled me very much, because there had to be something in it for Felix. I wondered if he could have concocted some curious scheme that he wanted to put to the poet which he thought might be profitable, though I could not imagine what it could possibly be. Did he think that with sufficient flattery Basil Deering might be led to give him a recommendation of some sort, say, to a publisher? Publishing would be rather a change after the secondhand-car trade, but I did not put it beyond Felix to think that such a switch might be made. At all events, the one thing of which I was quite sure was that Felix did not want to seek out Basil Deering for the sake of his poetry.

❊ ❊ ❊

We turned in at Barbara Gabriel's gate and went up the wide drive to her house. It was a square, Georgian house, built of red brick, not distinguished, yet dignified and charming. The garden was nearly all lawn, dotted here and there with apple trees and with a blaze of roses on either side of the fine doorway. The door stood open. Either because she had heard our footsteps outside or perhaps had seen us from a window, Barbara Gabriel came quickly to meet us before we had made up our minds whether to ring the doorbell or simply to enter.

I had met her once briefly. She was a frequent customer of Andrew's, and while I had been staying with the Boscotts had come over to their house to discuss an eighteenth-century sofa-table that she wanted him to restore. She was one of the fortunate people who could afford to pay his prices. Her husband, who had died about two years ago, had been chairman of a variety of companies and had left her a rich widow. She was fifty, as Helen, who knew her well, had told me, but in spite of her white hair she looked far younger. It was the kind of white hair, worn short, curly and cut with skillful casualness, which can actually give a misleading air of youthfulness to an ageing face. It seemed almost as if it were merely a whim of hers to wear it white. The skin of her rather large face was unlined and only very lightly made up. She was plump, but she moved with surprising buoyancy. She was wearing a gaily flowered cotton dress which might have looked better on someone slimmer, yet which gave her a cheerful kind of charm.

She took one look at Felix and decided that she liked him.

"I'm so glad Helen and Andrew brought you, Mr. Freer," she said. "I've only asked three or four people, just neighbours, but it happens I've something rather exciting to announce. Perhaps I ought to have made it a larger party, but I thought it would really be nicest to keep it intimate. A big party can come later on. We're in the garden. Come out and join the others."

She turned and led the way through a white-panelled hall and a lofty drawing room on to a shady terrace.

From the terrace wide steps led down to a formal rose garden, enclosed by a brick wall. A gate in the wall opened onto a meadow across which I could see, half-hidden in trees, the Fyffe sisters' bungalow. The sisters had arrived before us. Barbara Gabriel introduced them by their Christian names, and also the two men who were there, Basil Deering and a very erect, soldierly-looking man of about fifty whose name was Ralph Leggate.

Basil Deering was not at all as I had imagined him. For some reason I had thought that he would be short, stout, spectacled and bald. In fact, he was a big man with a square, strong face, a short nose with flaring nostrils, sardonic grey eyes spaced far apart under heavy eyebrows, thick, dark red hair and a quality of strongly sensual vitality that gave him remarkable attraction. I felt it at once, and as I did so, decided that he was a fraud. If this man really wrote the rather sickly verse for which Basil Deering was well known, it was done with his tongue in his cheek, because he had discovered that he had the knack of it and that it paid. I knew that this was Andrew's view of him, but I had been prepared to find him a shy, sincere little man who believed ardently in the depth and uniqueness of his own commonplace emotions, and not the man before me.

The Fyffe sisters were the youngest people there. They were both in their mid-thirties, with Carleen Mansell perhaps the older by a year or two. She was a small, timid-looking woman with hair of a faded brown, big, luminous blue eyes and a round, childlike face. She was wearing a frilly blue muslin dress, patterned with little white flowers, which somehow gave her a Victorian air. Remembering her books, I was sure this was deliberate.

The strange thing about her sister, Olivia, was that although there was a noticeable resemblance between her and Carleen, she should be so different. She was taller than Carleen and golden-haired and strikingly beautiful. It was a reserved yet arrogant beauty with something sombre about it. She also had blue eyes, but hers looked observant and analytical. Although she looked younger than her sister, in some ways she seemed the more mature. She wore a very simple black sleeveless dress. I noticed that Ralph Leggate could not keep his eyes off her.

There was an air of happy anticipation about Barbara Gabriel, but she wanted us all to have drinks in our hands before she made her announcement. The drinks turned out to be champagne.

"Of course this isn't a surprise to everyone here," she said when this had been attended to, "but this makes it official. Almost as official as if it was in a newspaper. Carleen and Basil are going to be married. There, isn't that marvellous? Let's all drink to their happiness. We all love them both, and of course they'll be staying on here amongst us, which is splendid for the rest of us. We'd hate to lose either of you. So here's to the best of everything for you both, my dears."

She drank and so did the rest of us. There was an appropriate congratulatory murmur. But I, at least, was very surprised. The heavily built, almost brutal-looking man and the small, shy woman seemed to me a curious match. But, of course, I knew neither of them, and I realised that there might be aspects of each which did not appear on an occasion like this.

Carleen blushed, smiled in a diffident way and in a gentle, precise voice thanked us all for our good wishes. Basil Deering cleared his throat, seemed to feel that he ought to make a speech, then laughed instead, put a proprietary arm round Carleen's shoulders, emptied his glass at a draught and held it out for more.

Ralph Leggate looked extremely pleased. He gave Basil Deering a slap on the shoulder, mumbled something about how lucky he was, then looked startled at himself, presumably for having displayed so much feeling. He looked that kind of man.

Olivia Fyffe looked faintly displeased. She must have known of her sister's engagement, yet for some reason seemed to dislike the way in which it had been announced. She wandered a little away from the rest of us and stood looking out across the rose garden to the bungalow among the trees. I thought perhaps she was wondering what would happen now to that joint creation, Carola Fyffe.

Helen and Andrew said some conventionally proper things. Only Felix looked oddly blank, as if he had been badly taken aback by events. I would have expected him to look as delighted as if he had known Basil and Carleen for years and had had a hand in bringing them together. Yet he looked with a kind of animosity at Basil, which was very unusual in him, as he nearly always worked hard at making a good impression on a stranger.

The party proceeded as such parties do.

I found myself sitting on a garden bench, next to Ralph Leggate. He was a very silent man, very difficult to talk to. Any question that I asked him he answered courteously, and there the conversation stopped. He never batted the ball back to me. But I learnt that he had been a farmer in one of those small African countries, the new names of which are so hard to remember, and that he had recently sold up and now lived in Stillbeam, in a house which he had inherited from his parents. He admitted to an interest in gardening and golf. I thought that he would certainly have been deeply embarrassed if he had realised how manifest his interest was in Olivia Fyffe.

Felix soon managed to get into conversation with Basil Deering. Whatever had caused that first blankness on his face, he had put it aside. I would have liked to know what they were talking about, but they were sitting a little too far away from me to be able to overhear them. Felix was wearing his sincere and earnest face, which probably meant that he was treating Basil to some fantastic flattery. Whatever he was saying, it seemed to amuse Basil. Perhaps praise of his verse did seem to him comic.

From time to time Barbara Gabriel shifted us about, though this was hardly necessary as all the people there except Felix and me knew each other well. It was about eight o'clock when Helen and Andrew decided that they had stayed long enough and the four of us said goodbye to the others and walked back again down the lane.

It was still daylight, but the first tinge of dusk was in the air. Andrew showed Felix the roomy garage, then left him to drive his car into it while he himself disappeared to his workshop, saying that he was uneasy about the work that he had been doing in the afternoon and wanted to check it. Helen went to the kitchen to fetch the cold meal that she had left ready earlier. She said that she did not need my help and left me alone with Felix, who threw himself down on the sofa, lit one of his cigarettes and seemed to retreat abruptly into his private thoughts. I was reminded of the look that I had seen on his face when he had first met Basil Deering.

Looking down at him, I said, "Well, did you get what you wanted out of him?"

He swivelled his blue, triangular eyes towards me without moving his head. "I didn't want anything out of him."

"Oh, come," I said. "This sudden interest in literature isn't very convincing."

"I can't see why not. People change, you know. Living alone, I read a lot more than I used to."

"How much do you really live alone?"

"Does it matter to you?"

"Not in the least. I'm just curious, that's all."

"That shows a remnant of interest. I'm glad. But probably I live alone far more than you believe."

"Anyway, why did you really want to meet Basil Deering? You can tell me that, can't you? We've always been able to say almost anything to one another, even fairly terrible things."

"As a matter of fact, I didn't specially want to meet him, but when Helen suggested it I thought I wouldn't miss the opportunity. I'd like to know certain things about him, but meeting the man himself wasn't important."

"What does that mean?"

"Perhaps I'll tell you sometime, when I've thought out a few things."

"Was he the sort of man you were expecting?"

"Yes, more or less."

"That's strange. I was expecting someone quite different."

"But you've never been specially strong on intuition, have you? Things have to be very cut and dried for you to feel you know where you are. I don't mean to boast, but I've always been rather better at seeing what's under the surface than you."

"I think you just knew a good deal about him before you came here," I said. "But I hope, whatever your real reason was for coming, that it won't lead to trouble between him and the Boscotts. They're relations and neighbours."

"Have you ever known me to be a troublemaker?" Felix asked.

As a matter of fact, I had not. He hated friction. He liked all the people round him to be on good terms, and sometimes, to improve this state of affairs, would pass on from one to the next totally imaginary compliments which he claimed that they had paid one another. Of course, this could sometimes backfire and lead to extraordinary misunderstandings, but at that point he always forgot that he had ever interfered. Whatever happened, he honestly meant well by everybody.

❋ ❋ ❋

Presently Helen called us into the dining room for a supper of cold chicken, salad and fruit. She had turned on the light that hung over the table, but had not drawn the curtains. Through the small windows the sky already looked the dark, rich blue of nighttime. Andrew came in from his workshop, seeming irritated. I understood almost nothing of his craft, but I gathered that he was dissatisfied with the way that he had placed a clamp on some joint and had decided that he must do it all over again tomorrow. We began to talk about the party and the engagement.

Helen said, "You know, I was surprised it's Carleen Basil's going to marry. It just shows how wrong one can be. I knew how often he went to see the Fyffes, but I took for granted it was Olivia he was interested in. She's so much the more attractive."

"But Carleen's the money-maker," Andrew said. "She could keep her writing going all right without Olivia, if she had to, but Olivia couldn't do anything without Carleen."

"That isn't a very nice thing to say," Helen retorted. "And why should Basil worry about money? He's got plenty of his own, hasn't he?"

"That doesn't mean he mightn't like some more. A wife with a splendid earning capacity must be quite an asset."

She shook her head at him. "I know you've never liked him, but you're really being unnecessarily horrid. He's never done you any harm that I know of."

"Actually I'm not sure he's as well off as he seems to be," Andrew said. "His poems sell well as poems go, but I've a feeling the money he inherited from his father isn't worth half what it used to be, what with inflation and all. However, you're probably right, I just don't like him, so I'm dubious about his motives, perhaps quite unfairly. Carleen may not be such a beauty as Olivia, or nearly as intelligent, but she's got her own kind of charm. Not a kind that appeals to everyone. All that childish sweetness, when you know she's really as tough as nails under the surface, it takes some understanding."

Helen was eyeing him curiously. "You do seem in a foul mood this evening. I thought you liked Carleen. Is anything the matter?"

"Nothing but that damned job I made a mess of this afternoon. Sorry. I didn't mean to cast a gloom over things."

"Speaking for myself," Felix said, "I don't really find the news of other people's marriages particularly exhilarating. But then I didn't make a notable success of my own, and I can't help thinking of all the terrible hazards ahead of them. But I should have thought you two would view the matter differently."

"I do," Helen said. "I was delighted to hear about it, but just a bit surprised, that's all. And another thing that surprised me was Barbara's enthusiasm about it. I've always thought she disapproved of Basil. I've heard her say very critical things about him. I'd never have expected her to give a party, even a little one, to celebrate his engagement. But again that just shows how wrong one can be. I wonder how soon they're thinking of getting married. I'd guess quite soon. There can't be any reason for people like them to wait. They know one another well enough, and if—"

She broke off as the front door knocker was violently hammered on the door.

Andrew stood up quickly and went to answer it.

A moment later he led Olivia Fyffe into the room. He was holding her arm, as if she needed support. In the light that hung over the table her face was a frightening, unnatural grey. Her eyes stared wildly.

"Please come and help me—please!" she gasped. She was panting as if she had been running. "I can't bear it alone. I found her dead. Shot! I've called the police, but I couldn't stay there in the house alone with her. I know that's wrong of me, but I just couldn't do it. So please come back with me and stay with me till they come."

She sagged against Andrew and would have fallen if he had not caught her.

# Chapter Two

We wasted some minutes, trying to get some more sense out of her, but she only said, "Please come—come and see for yourselves!"

She had shut her eyes, as if against some vision that she could not bear to look at.

I thought of the cool, controlled woman whom I had met at Barbara Gabriel's party and felt that there was something strange about this helpless collapse.

"You say you've telephoned the police," Andrew said.

"Yes, oh yes, at once," she answered.

"What about your doctor?"

"What would be the good of that? She's dead, I tell you."

Andrew and Helen exchanged glances. Helen's look puzzled me. She seemed to be searching Andrew's face for something that she was half-afraid to see there. In fact, it was almost expressionless.

He went on, "We'll go back with you, of course. But I don't understand, when could it have happened? Didn't the two of you go home together?"

"No, we didn't. But let's go now, if you're coming." Olivia started to her feet. "I've got to get back before the police arrive."

She moved unsteadily towards the door.

Helen went to her side and took her arm. "Yes, we're coming. But are you sure you can walk? Shouldn't we get out the car?"

"I can walk." Helen's concern only exasperated Olivia. "Let's hurry."

"You should have telephoned," Andrew said. "We'd have come at once."

"Don't you understand, I couldn't bear it?" Olivia's tone was one of despair at his inability to grasp such a simple thing. "Looking at her, thinking she was bound to get up and laugh at me in another moment, but seeing she never would! I ran out of the house. I didn't really know what I was doing. Then I thought of coming here..." She choked and almost flung Helen away from her in her haste to be gone.

I did not know if Felix and I were expected to go with the others, but he had no doubt about it. With a look of deep interest on his face, he followed close on Andrew's heels. So I went after him. In the lane we turned to the left, away from the main road through the village, crossed the Wandle by an old stone bridge, very like the one downstream, over which we had gone to Barbara Gabriel's house, and walked on rapidly to the Fyffe bungalow.

The evening was not as dark yet as I had thought from inside the house. The sky had still the deep turquoise shade of twilight, dotted with faint stars, and it was still easy to see one's way. A haze of midges hung above the river. It was a slow, rushy stream, grey-green in daylight, but now an oily black, its gentle movement silent and invisible.

The Fyffe bungalow was about a hundred yards beyond it. It was a long, white building, standing in a copse of tall chestnuts, in the midst of a wild garden. There was a scent of honeysuckle in the air. A short drive led from the gate to the front door. Olivia pushed at the door when we reached it, as if she expected to find it unlocked, but it did not open.

She stood still, looking at it helplessly.

"But I left it open," she said.

"The wind must have blown it shut," Andrew said.

"There isn't any wind."

"Some odd draught, then. Haven't you got a key?"

"No, I didn't think of bringing my handbag."

"Are any of the windows open?"

"No. I don't know. Perhaps. We'd better go and see, hadn't we? The French window into the drawing room may be open. Sometimes we forget to lock it when we go out. But that's where she is, in the drawing room, and I don't feel I can face going in...only, of course, I must. I've got to face it." She sounded a little more collected. "All right, let's go."

"Suppose I go," Felix said. "Then if I can get in, I can let you in here, if that's what you'd prefer. Where's the window? Round at the back?"

"Yes, the big window with the light on inside," she said. "Thank you, Mr. Freer. I'll wait for you here. Perhaps I needn't go back into the room at all."

He set off round the house. I heard his footsteps on the path, then they faded and there was silence. Olivia stood in front of the door, her head slightly bent, in the attitude of someone listening intently, waiting for the sound of his footsteps crossing the hall inside. But these were longer coming than, it seemed to me, they should have been. I began to worry. It was difficult to guess what Felix, alone in a house with a corpse, might think of getting up to. It was not beyond him to tamper with evidence if his odd mind found some reason for doing so. I ought really to have gone with him, I thought, but the fact was that, like Olivia, I had shrunk from having to walk straight into the presence of a dead woman.

Then a light came on in the hall and Felix opened the door.

"The drawing room, you said, didn't you?" he said. "The one with the French window?"

"Yes," Olivia said. "So it was open."

"Shut, as a matter of fact, but I managed to fiddle the lock. It wasn't difficult. You really ought to get something a bit more secure. You've some nice things in there."

He sounded perfectly calm, not like someone who has just been looking at the victim of a possible murder.

Olivia stepped inside and the rest of us followed.

The hall was a small one with passages leading off left and right, one, I supposed, to the bedrooms and the other to the kitchen. The walls were painted pale grey and the floor was covered in a dark grey carpet with one very fine rug on it, beautifully rich in colour. Two doors opened out of the hall. One was into an unlit room, which I later learnt was the dining room, and the other into one which was brightly lit and to which Olivia, after standing still for a moment, as if she could not bring herself to move, suddenly strode hurriedly.

In the doorway she stood still and started to scream.

The sound was horrible. At first there was sheer terror in it, then something like a laugh made it quaver wildly. Her thin body shook. She was apparently going into a good, old-fashioned fit of hysterics.

Felix, who had gone ahead of her into the room, slapped her face. He did it quite gently, but after her first shocked recoil, it steadied her. She moved forward into the room, while Andrew, Helen and I filed in behind her. And there was nothing there.

Nothing, that is to say, but a big, pleasant room with pale grey walls like the hall, the same dark grey carpet with some good rugs on it, light-coloured modern furniture, a piece of the kind of statuary that consists mostly of holes, a very long sofa, several deep armchairs, and on a low table a big silver bowl, full of roses. There was no corpse in the room, or any sign that there ever had been one.

Olivia walked slowly forward till she came to the middle of the room, then stood still there, looking down at her feet, as if that were where she had expected to find the body of her sister. Suddenly she swung round on Felix.

"What have you done with her?" she asked feverishly. "Where have you put her?"

"I haven't seen her," he answered. "The room was just like this when I got in."

"But she must have been here and you were a long time coming to open the door to us. What were you doing all that time?"

"As I told you, forcing the lock. I wasn't gone long really. I certainly hadn't time to move and conceal a body. If you don't believe me, why don't you search the bungalow?"

She looked towards the long, dark oblong of the window. "And outside, among the trees," she said. "You'd time to take her out there."

"Can you suggest any reason why I should have done so?"

She looked back at him, but with a change in her expression. It was confused and apologetic.

"I'm sorry, I don't know what I'm saying. I don't understand anything. It seems so impossible... But yes, we'd better search the house."

"And among the trees too, as you said," Andrew said. "Have you a torch? I'll take a look round out there, if you'd like me to."

"Yes, we've got a torch. I think it's in the kitchen. But let's look round first inside. Come with me, will you, Andrew? It's so crazy, I feel I'm going mad, and I'm scared of being alone."

She and Andrew went out of the room together.

I turned to Felix. "You *were* a long time, coming to open the front door. What were you really doing?"

"Having trouble with the window, as I told you," he said.

"And what else? Locks don't usually baffle you for long."

"Well, as a matter of fact, I took a quick look round the house, but it was a bit dark to see much for certain. All the same, I don't think they're going to find anything."

"Then what do you think happened?" Helen asked.

"Your guess is as good as mine," he said. "You know the lady much better than I do. Would you think she's prone to seeing things that aren't there?"

"I've always thought of her as a very well-balanced person," Helen said, "but really I don't know her very well. Perhaps she's too controlled. Repressed. She may have been nearer to a breakdown or something than any of us realised."

"Her sister's engagement somehow tipping her over the edge," Felix suggested.

We were all talking in lowered voices, not wanting Olivia, walking in suddenly, to overhear what we were saying about her. Yet, in fact, there was no need for caution. We could see the glimmer of a torch moving here and there among the trees outside the window and the two dim figures of Olivia and Andrew following the beam of light. Then they came towards the French window and re-entered the room.

"There's no sign of her," Andrew said, "but her car's gone from the garage and the handbag she had with her this evening seems to be missing."

Olivia dropped down on to the long sofa and covered her face with her hands. She spoke through her fingers in a muffled tone.

"You must all think I'm mad."

Because that was the possibility that we had just been discussing, we all stood round her in embarrassed silence.

After a moment she let her hands drop and flung back her head, looking round defiantly. "But I did see her, I did!"

"Are you really sure she was dead?" Andrew said. "Are you sure she hadn't just collapsed in a faint, or tripped over one of these rugs and knocked herself out somehow?"

"D'you suppose I didn't make sure?" she asked. "I told you, she'd been shot. There was a bullet hole in her temple. There wasn't much blood and it was quite a small hole and there were some scorch marks round it. I suppose they were scorch marks—I've never seen anything of the sort before, so of course I don't really know. But if they were, it means she was shot by someone standing close to her, doesn't it?"

"I suppose she wasn't playing some sort of gruesome practical joke on you," Felix said. "It's amazing what you can do with a bit of theatrical makeup. Was she a person who might do a thing like that?"

"Not at all." Olivia gave him a bewildered frown, then she gave a deep sigh. "Still, there must be some explanation of what's happened, I know that. But she'd never have done a thing of that kind to me. No, it wasn't any kind of joke. I felt for her heart, you know, and there was nothing there. And her eyes were open, staring."

Andrew was still standing only just inside the French window with his hands in his pockets.

"You told us you didn't come home with her after Barbara's party," he said. "Why was that?"

"I thought I'd let her and Basil come home together," Olivia answered. "I thought that was what they wanted. It was some time after you left, at least three quarters of an hour. And they came here across the meadow. There's that gate in Barbara's wall, you know, and the footpath comes right past the gate in our fence. And Ralph wanted to see me home and we started out to come round by the road, then he suggested we might have one more drink in the Hare and Hounds, so we went there and I suppose we were there for about twenty minutes, and then we walked here together."

"So Carleen must have got here something like half an hour before you," Andrew said.

"Just about," she agreed.

"Did Ralph come in with you?"

"No."

"And Basil had gone?"

"I told you—" she began frantically, but Andrew interrupted her.

"But you didn't search?"

"No, I didn't even think of it. But if I had, I'd have been much too scared to do it. I just made sure she was dead, and then telephoned the police, and then ran out to fetch you."

"Then what it looks like," Andrew said, "is that whoever killed her was hiding here in the house when you came in, and as soon as you left, bundled her body into her car, put her handbag in to make it look as if she'd just gone away, and drove off somewhere."

Olivia nodded. "Yes, that's what must have happened. Only you don't really believe it, do you, Andrew? None of you believes it."

"It's logical," Andrew said.

"Yes, but you're really only saying it to calm me down. You really think I'm making it all up, for some crazy reason of my own." She gave an abrupt laugh. "The things one learns about one's friends in a time of crisis! But I suppose all of us are inclined to think that most of our friends are mad. Only you're quite wrong. Carleen's dead. I'm not making anything up. She was murdered here in this room."

"Did you see a gun here with her?" Felix asked.

"No. No, I don't think so, but I didn't really look. I didn't think of it—"

She broke off as the front doorbell rang.

Andrew said, "That'll be the police. I'll go," and he left the room.

Getting to her feet, Olivia stood in the middle of it, looking quite in control of herself once more, thoughtful, withdrawn, beautiful, rather as she had looked at Barbara Gabriel's party.

❀ ❀ ❀

From the sound of it, several policemen came into the house, but Andrew brought only two of them, both in plain clothes, into the drawing room. One was a tall, gaunt man of about fifty, with thinning dark hair brushed smoothly over a pointed scalp, sharp features in a taut, narrow face and eyebrows so arched that they gave him a look of whimsical surprise. Only there was no surprise in the dark eyes under them. Rather, they looked resigned to accepting with a kind of placid and regretful scepticism whatever he might be about to hear. Andrew introduced him as Detective Superintendent Pryor. The other man, Sergeant Waller, was about thirty and was stocky, square-faced and fair-haired, with bold, shallow, blue eyes and clothes that looked a little too tight over his bulging muscles.

When Andrew had introduced Olivia and the rest of us, the Superintendent said to her, "You're the lady, I understand, who telephoned in to report a shooting. But I gather the body seems to have gone missing."

She gave him a thoughtful look, as if she were trying to make up her mind what kind of man he was before she answered. "Yes, that's exactly what happened."

"Would you mind telling me the whole story?" His voice was level and quiet.

She gestured at a chair and herself sat down again on the sofa. We all found chairs while a little silence settled in the room in which she seemed to be finding some difficulty in deciding how to begin. Then abruptly she started to talk, telling the Superintendent just what she had told us, though a good deal more calmly. He nodded occasionally, but for the most part sat perfectly still, with his long hands resting relaxed on the arms of his chair. Then he started to question her, asking her all the same questions as we had already asked.

She answered them concisely, but when she had told him how she and Andrew had searched the bungalow and the garden and found everything in order, except that her sister's car, a white Rover, and her evening handbag were missing, she added, "I don't think any of these people here believe me that I found my sister dead, but it's going to save you trouble if you do believe me. It wasn't a hallucination."

Like Andrew before him, the Superintendent said, "Then it looks as if whoever killed her was here in the house when you arrived and found her, and took the opportunity, while you went to your friends, of putting her body into her car and driving away. And since he needed her car, and since you saw no car in your drive when you arrived, it's reasonable to suppose that he arrived on foot. Now, with your permission, we'll take a look round ourselves. And will you please give Sergeant Waller the number of her car? We can put out a call for that straight away, in case it happens to have been seen."

She told the sergeant the number of the car and he made a note of it, then went out to give orders for a watch to be kept for it.

The Superintendent remained where he was for a moment, then with a sound of caution, as if he were afraid of rousing some storm in her, said, "Now suppose—just suppose—your sister wasn't dead, Miss Fyffe, and came to herself and drove away, is there anywhere special you'd expect her to go? Are you sure that none of her clothes are missing?"

Olivia responded with a sharp bark of laughter. The hysterical note was back in it, as it had been when she first came into the room, but this time she suppressed it.

"So you aren't going to believe me either," she said. "Everyone thinks I've suddenly gone insane. But no, I haven't looked carefully to see if any of her clothes are missing. I didn't think it was necessary. I didn't think that a dead woman would do any packing. And the only place I can think of where she might have gone, if she'd been going anywhere, is our flat in London. It's 37 Trenton Green Avenue, St. John's Wood. Search there, if you want to. You won't find her, but perhaps you'll find something that will tell you something about what's happened to her."

"The last you saw of her was when she left Mrs. Gabriel's house with Mr. Deering, is that right?" he asked.

"Yes."

"How long had they been engaged?"

"I'm not sure, actually. My sister told me about it three days ago, but I think it was longer than that. We weren't the kind of sisters who told one another everything. We lived and worked together, but we had our own private lives. But I noticed recently she was in an excited sort of state that wasn't like her. She was usually very quiet. And when she told me about the engagement I guessed that had been the reason."

"Did you approve of the engagement?"

She gave another brief laugh. "That's an old-fashioned expression. But if you want the truth, no, I didn't. I didn't think she'd be happy with Mr. Deering."

"Why not?"

"He isn't a kind man. She didn't understand that. She didn't understand how cruel a man can be. Her first husband was gentleness itself, and she took for granted that that was what she'd always find in a man she'd fallen in love with. But I didn't interfere. It wasn't my business."

The Superintendent said nothing for a moment, then he stood up.

"Well, it would seem the first thing is to trace your sister's car," he said. "If her body was removed in it—"

He broke off, turning quickly towards the door as the sound of the front doorbell interrupted him.

I heard voices in the hall, quiet at first, then suddenly loud, then the slam of a door as the front door was violently shut. Basil Deering strode into the room. He stared round at us all with a look of angry incredulity on his face, then fixed his attention on Superintendent Pryor.

"What the hell's going on here?" he demanded. "Police everywhere, with the nerve to ask me what I want here, trying to stop me coming in, telling me some fantastic story about my fiancée having been shot. Where is she?" He swung round on Olivia. "Where is she? What's happened? What are all these men doing here?"

Instead of answering, she looked at Mr. Pryor, leaving it to him to explain his presence.

He said, "We're here, Mr. Deering, because Miss Fyffe telephoned us, saying she'd found her sister shot dead. She told us she found the body here in this room. But while she was waiting for us, she left the house to fetch Mr. and Mrs. Boscott, and while she was gone the body appears to have been removed. There's no sign of it here now. And Mrs. Mansell's car and her handbag have disappeared also."

Basil Deering's face flushed a deep red and one of his fists clenched. I thought for a moment that he was going to strike Olivia. But drawing a deep breath, he let the hand relax. Looking back at the detective, he said contemptuously, "And you believed the woman? Haven't you realised yet she's practically a pathological liar? Nothing's happened to Mrs. Mansell. You've nothing to worry about."

"Can you suggest then where she might be?" Mr. Pryor asked.

"I'd guess she's gone to the flat in London," Basil Deering said. "It's my fault, I'm afraid. We walked back together from Mrs. Gabriel's house and somehow a quarrel of sorts blew up between us. Nothing important, but we'd been drinking champagne and she wasn't used to it. It seems I said something that hurt her deeply and when we'd been here only a few minutes she told me to leave. As I didn't think arguing with her would do any good, I did as she wanted. But later I thought that had been a mistake and that I ought to have stayed until we'd made peace. So I came back to do just that, hoping that perhaps she'd have calmed down and would want to make up the quarrel as much as I did. That's all. But unluckily she seems to have taken the stupid affair too much to heart and to have gone off driving somewhere, perhaps to London in a huff, or perhaps she's just driving around, trying to cool off. She may walk in at any moment. In any case, I'm sorry you've had this trouble."

"This quarrel of yours," Mr. Pryor said, "can you tell me what it was about?"

"Quite a small matter really, as I said," Basil Deering answered. "It was just about whether or not her sister should live with us when we got married. Mrs. Mansell seemed to take it for granted that she should, whereas I felt very strongly that it would be quite impossible. I understand they work together and are very dependent on one another, but after all my home is very near and when she moves in with me she can go on coming here every day, if she wants to, to keep the work going. But she said she couldn't leave her sister to live here alone, that it's too big for one person and too solitary and anyway, it's a valuable property on which she could raise a fair sum of money, and so on. And I realised I oughtn't to have argued with her. I ought to have left it till tomorrow, when she'd have seen things differently."

Olivia gave a bitter yet excited little smile, as if she found something stimulating in the thought of a quarrel.

"You needn't have troubled to fight over me," she said. "Nothing would persuade me to move into your house, and you know that. If you did have a quarrel with Carleen, it was you that picked it for the thrill it gave you to assert yourself. But perhaps just this once she didn't let you do it either, and that's why you shot her. You couldn't bear having her stand up to you. So you killed her and you were hiding here in the house when I came in, and I suppose if I hadn't run out of the house almost immediately I'd be dead too and my body would have been bundled into the car with hers and dumped somewhere. But where, Basil? Where have you put her?"

Her attack on him seemed to calm Basil Deering. His flush faded and he looked at her with a kind of pity.

"You really think I go to drinks parties in Stillbeam equipped with a gun?" he said. He turned back to the Superintendent. "What I've told you is the truth, but I wouldn't put any faith in a word this woman's told you. As I've said, she's a pathological liar and doesn't know fact from fiction. Usually she doesn't let her fantasies get so far out of hand as actually to call the police, but she spends a lot of her time in a dream-world of romance and violence. Her sister understands that and manages to make her use her imagination in a fruitful way, but the fact is, I think Miss Fyffe had a bit too much champagne herself this evening. Besides that, for all I know, she may have overheard the quarrel I had with Mrs. Mansell. She may have got back to the house before I left it and stood at the window, listening, and realised that my attitude to her wasn't the friend-liest possible. I think that may account for what really amounts to an attack on me, because as the last person to have been seen with her sister, I'd be bound to be suspected of the murder, if she could manage to persuade anyone that a murder had really taken place. And that would be irksome for me, if not truly a serious matter. I hope you don't still believe it, Superintendent. If you do, you're going to waste an awful lot of valuable time."

Something made me glance at Felix. As a terrible liar himself, he was always inclined to believe that everyone else he encountered was a liar too. But he could be quite acute in sifting truth from falsehood, recognising the small signs that betrayed invention, and I was curious to know what he was making of the mutual accusations. Which of the two, Olivia or Basil, did he find the more believable?

However, his face told me nothing except that, although he was deeply interested, he felt considerable distaste for the scene that the two of them were making. As I have said, he hated friction. Other people's quarrels filled him with embarrassment. He could hardly bear to let them make such fools of themselves in front of him. At the same time he was an intensely curious man, and at the moment his desire to know what was behind the scene that he was witnessing must have been very much at odds with a wish to escape from it.

Olivia changed the tone of it abruptly by bursting into tears.

"You fools!" she sobbed. "You stupid, useless fools! Standing there doing nothing when you ought to be looking for her! Of course she's dead! In God's name, why should I make up such a horrible thing? And what that man's told you about me isn't true. I'm not a liar."

Helen moved across to her side and sat down beside her. She put a hand on Olivia's shoulder.

"I think it's time you came home with us," she said. "You can leave things to Superintendent Pryor now, and you can't stay here alone. That's all right, isn't it, Mr. Pryor? We can go?"

He thought it over before replying, turning that resigned yet sceptical gaze of his on to Helen for a moment, as if he had only just become aware of her, then he gave a brief nod.

"I'll be in touch with you, Miss Fyffe, as soon as we've any news of your sister or her car," he said and walked out of the room.

There was a renewed sound of voices in the hall, then of the front door opening and closing, then there was silence, except for the sound of the police cars driving away.

Basil Deering gave an ironic laugh. "Feeling satisfied with what you've done, Olivia? You've not only got the police on the move, but here's Helen wanting to pick up the pieces. But in case Carleen comes back after you've left here, hadn't you better leave a note, telling her where you've gone to, or she may get quite anxious about you."

Andrew, after his long silence, suddenly exploded into anger. "Damn you, Basil, can't you leave her alone? Whatever's happened, can't you see she's coming apart at the seams?"

Basil shrugged his shoulders. "Just so long as you realise what you're letting yourselves in for. These Good Samaritan acts you and Helen go in for must get you into trouble sometimes. Good night, Olivia. Tell Carleen I came back to make peace with her, will you?"

He went out.

Olivia rubbed her eyes with her fists. Her eyelids were red, but her gaze looked stormy rather than sorrowful.

"That stupid, arrogant fool!" she muttered. "But he'll find out…" She turned to Helen and her look changed. "May I really come with you, Helen? You're quite right, I'd hate to stay here by myself. You see, I know, even if no one believes me, that it's no good waiting up for Carleen. But you've got two people staying with you already. How can you make room for me?"

"That's all right, we'll manage," Helen said.

"Then I'll just get a few things," Olivia said. "Wait for me, will you?"

She got up and left the room.

Helen looked up at Andrew questioningly, expecting him, it seemed, to be able to tell her what had really happened in that room earlier in the evening, but he turned away, looking as if he did not much care what the truth was. After a few minutes Olivia returned, carrying a small overnight case. Using the torch with which she and Andrew had hunted among the trees, the five of us set out in the darkness to the Boscotts' house.

❋ ❋ ❋

It turned out that Helen's idea of managing was to ask Felix to give Olivia the room that had been made ready for him earlier and himself to sleep on the sofa in the living room.

"It's really quite comfortable," she assured him, dumping an armful of sheets and blankets on it. "We often make visitors sleep on it and they don't complain. You don't mind, do you?"

Felix replied that he would happily sleep on the floor, if that would help, but Andrew said that they could still take in another guest or two before being driven to that. Meanwhile, he said what we all needed was brandy. He poured out drinks for us all.

Olivia, holding hers, said, "I think I'll take this up to my room, if you don't mind. I'd like to go to bed straight away. I don't suppose I'll sleep, though I'm so tired now, but my head's going round. I feel sort of dizzy and queer. I want to lie down."

"Perhaps we ought to get your doctor," Helen said. "He'd give you a sedative."

"No, no, I don't need anything like that," Olivia replied. "The brandy's all I need. Don't worry about me. And thank you both with all my heart."

Carrying her glass carefully, she went upstairs.

Helen and I made up Felix's bed together, then after finishing their drinks, she and Andrew also went up to their room, leaving Felix and me together.

I topped up my drink, but when I offered to do the same for Felix, he shook his head.

"You still seem to be drinking as much as ever," he said. "Lager, champagne, brandy—you've been nipping away at something ever since I arrived."

"No more than you have," I said, "except just for this last brandy."

"With me it's just a social obligation. I don't need it, as you do." He always made a point of asserting that I drank more than he did. I think he felt that in that one way he could claim a moral superiority over me. He had very few other moral pretensions. In fact, he generally accepted criticism of his various failings humbly, even if the criticisms never had the slightest effect on him.

"Today's been exceptional," I said.

I sat down in a chair by the fireplace. I was very tired, but felt too restless to want to go to bed yet.

Felix kicked off his shoes and lay down on the sofa that had just been made up as a bed for him, settling his head comfortably on the pillows.

"A bloody awful day," he said, "and it began so well. It was such a pleasant surprise, finding you here."

"I wish I knew your real reason for coming," I said.

"I've told you once already. If you didn't believe me then, you aren't going to believe me if I simply repeat myself."

"Well, now that you've seen a little more of your favourite poet, what do you make of him?"

"An unpleasant bastard."

That was going quite far for Felix. Normally he was capable of tolerating almost everybody, just so long as they showed a little liking for him. He numbered burglars, con men and forgers among his friends, and at the same time was capable of developing warm and sincere affection for little old ladies who, in the whole course of their innocent lives, had never even dreamt of fiddling their income tax or deluding the Customs. It is true his affection tended to be a little more warm and sincere for those who had money, but he did not absolutely require this of them when he carried their luggage for them, gave up his seat to them in buses, gave them a helping hand across the street, and generally did what he could to relieve the difficulties of their sad old age.

However, meeting him with one of his friends was always a problem. He had once introduced me to a respectable-looking, middle-aged man who had greeted me with the cryptic question, "Any orders?" It had turned out later that he was a pickpocket who would have been ready to obtain for me, out of friendship for Felix, a nice watch or handbag at a very modest price. But he might just as likely have been a genuinely respectable business man, or actor, or even a parson. Felix was an omnivore when it came to people, which I might have regarded as a high kind of charity if I had not felt that it came from his desperate need to be liked by everyone he met.

"So you believe Olivia about the shooting, do you?" I said.

"I didn't say that," he replied.

"But you didn't like the way Deering attacked her."

"Did you?"

"No. But she made a pretty vicious attack on him too. And he might be right that Olivia was lying, that it was all a kind of fantasy."

"Oh, she's lying," Felix said. "Anyone could see that."

"You mean you think Carleen isn't dead."

"Not necessarily. I know Olivia was lying, but I'm not sure what about."

"What makes you think she was lying at all, then?"

"It's just a thing I happen to be good at spotting."

"I'm afraid that may be just your habit of assuming that everyone's dishonest. It's sheer intuition, with no evidence to back it."

"Oh, I've some evidence," he said. "A little. Doesn't it seem a bit odd to you that when she found her sister dead she was calm enough to phone the police and only panicked after that and came running here? I'd have thought it more normal if she'd panicked straight away, come rushing round and got Andrew to do the phoning for her."

"Perhaps it didn't occur to her that the murderer might still be in the bungalow until after she'd phoned the police. Perhaps she heard something that suddenly made her think of it."

"In that case, why didn't she say anything about it? When she accused Deering of having been in the house, it was very much of an afterthought. And I can tell you something else, though this supports what Olivia said, they aren't going to find Carleen at that flat in London. Either she'll be home quite soon this evening, or she won't come home at all."

"How d'you make that out?"

"It was her evening bag she's supposed to have taken with her, wasn't it? And what do women put in their evening bags when they go out to have drinks with a neighbour? A key, a handkerchief, a comb. What else? It's very unlikely she'd have taken any money to speak of. But it's unlikely she'd set off for London without a reasonable amount, isn't it?"

"Perhaps she did take some money with her to the party. Perhaps she's the kind of person who'd never leave it behind in an empty house."

"Well, I'll tell you something else that strikes me as odd about what Olivia told us," he said. "When I got into the bungalow at the back and came to open the front door, I had to switch on the light in the hall. Now is it probable that if she was in such a state of panic that she didn't even shut the door behind her, she'd take the trouble to switch off the light? She'd almost certainly turned it on when she first arrived back at the house, but it was off when we got there. A small thing, but peculiar. And I don't feel sure we know the real reason why she came here at all. I'm not quite convinced that panic of hers was real. It was real when she went into the drawing room and started to scream. She had some awful shock then, and perhaps it's true that it was finding her sister's body missing. All the same, she's lying very hard about something, and I'd very much like to know what and why."

"And I'd very much like to know why you really came here, but I agree, it's no use asking." I yawned and stood up. "Good night. Sleep well."

"Good night, my love. You know you are my love still. I've never quite managed to stop loving you."

"I think you have, about as much as I've stopped loving you."

"But that isn't completely, is it?"

"Oh, I do my best to love my neighbour. That includes all sorts of strange people."

"What a bitch you can be," he said with a friendly smile. "Would it hurt so much to say you love me a little?"

"Who knows? It might. It might hurt quite a lot. Good night," I said again, and went upstairs to my room.

# Chapter Three

Next morning Felix brought me a cup of tea in bed. I guessed that he had taken one to everyone else in the house as well. He was an admirably domesticated man. When I came downstairs presently I found him, as I had expected, helping Helen to get the breakfast. He was at the stove, frying eggs. Helen, who was laying the table in the kitchen, where we always had breakfast, greeted me with a delighted smile and said, "Look what Felix has given me!"

She took a small object from the dresser and held it out to me. It was a charming little snuff box, made of white porcelain, decorated in soft shades of pink and with its lid edged with a band of silver.

"It's so pretty!" she exclaimed. "But I'm afraid it was horribly expensive."

"A trifle," Felix said. "I picked it up the other day in an antique shop in Wandlebury. It just caught my eye, it's nothing special. But I'm very glad you like it. You're being so good to me, I wanted you to have it."

I thought that I would not tell Helen that when Felix said that he had picked up the snuff box, he was almost certainly telling the literal truth. It had probably disappeared into his pocket while he was doing something innocent like turning over some flower prints that he had not the least intention of buying and the trusting shopkeeper had left him to himself. He was a deft and conscienceless shoplifter.

The discovery that he was had been one of the first bad shocks that I had had about him after our marriage. The fact that the lavish gifts that he often brought home for me had not been paid for had distressed me terribly, less, I have to admit, because of the immorality of the habit than because I was certain that he was bound to be caught. Yet oddly enough, he never had been. However, I had managed to stop him giving me presents of this kind, though he never quite understood why I should object to them. He never regarded shoplifting as criminal, but thought of it more as a kind of sport, what he called, "trying to beat the system." And often he stole things when he had more than enough money in his pocket to pay for them. I felt sure that he had not paid for the snuff box.

But I thought it best that Helen should not know this. I believe it is the law that you cannot be charged with receiving stolen property if you do not know that it is stolen, and apart from that, she was so delighted with the little gift.

Olivia did not come down to breakfast. Felix took a tray up to her, but when Helen presently brought it down again, nothing but the coffee had been touched. Andrew, who had come down a few minutes after me, had taken only a few minutes over his breakfast, then had disappeared to his workshop. Helen had stood still for a moment, watching him go, with an expression on her face that I did not understand. It was as if she wanted to stop him, but could not make up her mind to do so. Yet if she felt that this was not a time for thinking of nothing but his work, why did she not simply say so? She and I did the washing-up while Felix went into the living room to fold away the sheets and blankets on the sofa where he had slept. As soon as he had left us, she turned a slightly puzzled face to me.

"Virginia, isn't it a bit odd, Felix wants me to ask Basil here for a drink this evening?" she said. "I've said I will, but I can't help feeling it isn't the best sort of thing to do. I mean, in the circumstances. Of course, if Carleen's turned up, it'll be quite different. We can ask her too, and it might even help everyone to get back to normal. But if she's still missing, he'll be worried sick about her, however tough he pretends to be, and he won't want to sit around with us, being social."

"But Felix actually asked you to invite him?" I said.

"Yes, he seemed to want it very much."

"Then I shouldn't dream of doing anything about it."

"But I've said I will."

"You could forget about it."

"I don't like the idea of doing that," she said. "And it seems very important to Felix, for some reason. He's immensely interested in Basil."

A horrible suspicion entered my mind. Had Felix acquired some secret knowledge of Basil which he was hoping to use in extorting money from him? But I had never known Felix to sink to blackmail. All the same, if times were hard, might he not make at least a tentative experiment in it?

"Have you asked Andrew what he thinks about it?" I asked.

"No, but I know what he'll say. He'll be a bit sulky about it because he doesn't like Basil and doesn't see why they should have to have anything to do with each other just because they're related, but all he'll say will be, 'Do what you like.' Oh, I suppose I'll go ahead and do it. After all, Basil can easily refuse if he doesn't feel like coming."

But a few minutes later, putting the telephone down after speaking to him, she said, "He's coming. But I think he's more worried than he was last night. He says he's just been up to the bungalow, but that Carleen isn't there, and he's telephoned the London flat, but nobody answered."

As she spoke, the doorbell rang. Helen went to answer it and brought Ralph Leggate into the room. With a stiff nod to Felix and me, he sat down, regarding us all silently and expectantly, as if he were waiting to be questioned about what he was doing there, rather than meaning to ask any questions himself.

Helen said, "Of course you've heard about what happened last night."

"Yes, I ran into Basil when I was out for my usual walk this morning," he answered. "He told me about it."

The conversation might have died there without his ever telling us what had brought him, if Helen had not gone on, "We brought Olivia home with us. It didn't seem right to leave her alone in the bungalow."

"Quite right," he said. "Very kind of you."

"I expect you'd like to see her," Helen said, "but she isn't up yet. But I'll go and tell her you're here. She may be coming down soon."

"No, no, don't disturb her," he said. "I thought I might somehow be of use, that's all."

"I don't think there's much anyone can do till they find some trace of Carleen."

"In my opinion," he said, his voice suddenly loud and aggressive, as if to hold an opinion were something involving some degree of danger which put him in a fighting mood, "she's just gone to London to score off Basil. Simply that. He told me they fell out about whether or not Olivia should live with them. Absurd idea, of course, enough to wreck the marriage from the start. But Carleen and Olivia have always been very devoted to one another, so Carleen wouldn't take his objections lying down. I'm sure she's in that flat now, trying to teach him a lesson."

"He told me he tried phoning her there and nobody answered," Helen said.

"Because she'd have known who was phoning and had made up her mind not to answer."

"Oh, I don't think she's like that. She'd have got over her anger by this morning and realised how worried everyone must be about her. And after all it doesn't explain..." It did not explain what Olivia had said she had seen the evening before, but Helen did not seem sure that she wanted to refer to it. "I don't know how much Basil told you," she said cautiously.

"You mean about Olivia believing Carleen had been shot?" he said. It appeared the matter was of no great moment to him. "He didn't tell me the truth about it, of course. He's ashamed of it now and isn't going to admit what happened, but he's a violent man and he must have knocked the poor girl out when he got angry. And I dare say there were a few drops of blood somewhere which Olivia mistook for a bullet hole. I don't suppose she's ever seen a real bullet hole in her life. And if I'm right that that's how it was, it explains why Carleen didn't answer the telephone this morning. Not just cussedness, but fear. I shouldn't be surprised if we hear in a day or two that the engagement's off. I don't see Carleen settling down quietly to be a battered wife. Lucky she found the man out in time. Now I won't keep you any longer. Just tell Olivia I came, will you?"

"Basil's coming in for a drink this evening around six o'clock," Helen said. "Why don't you come too? You can see her then."

"Thanks, I will," he said and left us.

When he had gone Helen decided that she would invite Barbara Gabriel as well. It would be a repeat of yesterday's party, except that it was unlikely that Carleen would be there and there would be no champagne or celebrations.

Barbara Gabriel accepted the invitation, then kept Helen talking for a long time on the telephone, questioning her about what had happened the evening before, the rumour of which had reached her apparently from her gardener, who had seen the police cars at the bungalow when he was cycling home from the Hare and Hounds. I wondered if the extra people coming for drinks would spoil Felix's ploy with Basil, whatever it was, but he did not seem disturbed by it. It did not seem to be important to him to meet Basil again in a specially intimate atmosphere.

When Andrew came in later to make himself a sandwich for lunch, and heard who was coming, he looked surly, but shrugging his shoulders, returned to his workshop. A strong reaction came only from Olivia. She came downstairs about twelve o'clock. Her face had the grey, parched look of someone who has not slept at all. Sinking into a chair, she leant her head back wearily with an air of lassitude which seemed to make even the smallest movement an immense effort. But when Helen told her about the people who would be coming that evening, she started forward, staring at her incredulously.

"*Basil's* coming?" she exclaimed.

Helen nodded.

"But I won't meet him—I can't! Not after the things he said about me last night. Besides, I'm afraid..." Olivia choked over the word.

"Afraid?" Helen prompted her. "Afraid of Basil?"

"Yes, I'm terribly afraid of him," Olivia said. "Does that seem absurd to you? Of course, I'm not afraid that he'll do anything to me here amongst you all, but I'm afraid of what just seeing him may do to me. Because I think what I said about him may be true, and I hate him for it—I hate him with all my heart."

"You mean you really think he could have murdered Carleen?" Helen said, wide-eyed.

"Of course. He was there with her, wasn't he, and by his own admission they quarrelled, and he could have hidden when I came in, then driven her away in the car when I came here."

"But do you really think he went to Barbara's party with a gun in his pocket?" Helen asked. "That's what he asked himself."

"He must have, mustn't he?" Olivia answered.

"That's an odd kind of logic," I said. "He murdered Carleen, so he must have had a gun with him. That's all right so far as it goes, but you have to begin with the assumption that he did the murder, and I don't think you've any proof."

"And where did he put the car?" Felix asked. "He came back to the bungalow fairly soon after leaving it, so he hadn't much time to hide the car anywhere."

"He may have left it in his own garage, for all I know,"

Olivia said, "then got rid of it during the night."

"That would have taken a bit of nerve," Felix remarked.

"He's got plenty of that."

"But why remove the body at all?" he asked. "If he was in the bungalow while you were there, he'd have known you'd already reported the murder to the police."

"And then he came back just to try to make them believe that nothing I said was to be relied on. Wasn't that the real reason why he came back?"

"But he wouldn't have killed Carleen simply because they'd had a bit of a quarrel," Helen protested. "Lots of people spend their lives quarrelling day after day, yet they don't get around to committing a single murder."

"Well, you needn't believe me," Olivia said, "but I assure you he's an evil and dangerous man. He's capable of anything."

"Do you think it's possible your sister found out something about him and threatened him with it?" Felix suggested. "Threatened to tell his friends about it, or even to make it public in some way that would have alienated his devoted public. Wouldn't that have given him a motive for killing her? And if he'd been expecting something of the sort, it might even have given him a reason for taking a gun to Mrs. Gabriel's party."

"Did she look as if she had anything of the sort in mind when you saw her there?" Helen asked. "Didn't she look radiantly happy? And so did he, so far as he can ever look radiant, which I admit isn't very far. But he didn't look in the least like someone planning a murder."

"Dishonest people like him can control their faces," Olivia said.

Felix spoke quickly. "Have you any special reason for saying he's dishonest?" He was watching her face with a new intentness, as if her answer might be of great importance to him. "Do you *know* anything about him, or is it just a feeling you have?"

All of a sudden I remembered the suspicion that I had had of Felix earlier in the morning. I found myself wondering again if he was in possession of some secret about Basil Deering which he was intending to use to prise some money out of him. I had rejected the idea with horror when I had first thought of it, assuring myself that Felix had never sunk to blackmail. But now, watching him as he watched Olivia with what I guessed might be an unpleasant fear that he was not the only person who had this profitable knowledge and that he might have to go shares with her, I had a shocking feeling of doubt. I was certain that he did know something about Basil that he was keeping to himself, and why should it be so important to him if he did not mean to make something out of it?

"Oh, I know a lot about him," Olivia answered with a hard, little laugh. "But I'd just as soon not talk about it. And I definitely don't feel like meeting him this evening. I'm sorry, Helen, but that's how it is."

"Oh, it doesn't matter in the least," Helen answered. "You can stay upstairs in your room all the time he's here."

"I was going to say," Olivia said, "that I really think I ought to go home. It's wonderfully good of you to have let me stay here like this, but I've got to face things sooner or later, and really the sooner the better, don't you think? Then you can get back to work, which I know you're longing to do, and stop worrying about me. I'll go and pack and get out from under your feet."

"But not straight away. Anyway, stay to lunch. I'll get something in a minute. And meanwhile we can have drinks. Felix, pour them out, will you? I'll be back in a minute." Helen went quickly out of the room, leaving Felix watching Olivia with his new attentiveness, until he suddenly appeared to realise that he had been asked to pour out drinks and that he should be doing so.

He turned to the tray on the sideboard and on request poured out whisky for Olivia and me, then a small glass of sherry for himself. Then Helen returned and was saying that the easiest thing to do for lunch, if we didn't mind, would be bread and cheese, when Superintendent Pryor arrived, accompanied by Sergeant Waller.

Helen let them in and brought them into the room, then went to fetch Andrew. He offered them drinks and after a moment's hesitation the Superintendent accepted for both of them. The sergeant's bold blue eyes brightened slightly as Andrew handed him the whisky he asked for.

As we all sat down, the Superintendent said, "I came to see you, Miss Fyffe, to tell you there's no sign of your sister in your flat in London."

Olivia made a gesture as if she were contemptuously brushing his words away. "You didn't have to tell me that. I knew there wouldn't be."

"And I wanted to ask you," he went on without any change in the resigned expression on his sharp-featured face, "if you can suggest anywhere else she might have gone."

"Where she's been taken, you mean," she said.

"If you'd sooner put it that way."

"It's the only way to put it. And I can certainly suggest somewhere, though I expect you're too late to find her there now. It's Mr. Deering's garage. I've just been telling my friends I'm sure he took her there last night when I ran out of the house and came here, and that he left her there while he went back to try to persuade you I'm a chronic liar. But he'll have got rid of the car and the body by now."

The Superintendent drank a little of his whisky and nodded. "We thought of that, of course. It fitted the circumstances quite nicely. So we sent a man after Mr. Deering when he went home last night, to take a look in his garage and there was no white Rover there. If he did shoot your sister and remove her body, he hid the car somewhere else. Not far away, because he walked from wherever it was to your house in quite a short time, but we've found no indication of where it might be."

Olivia did not look much surprised. I doubted if she had ever entirely believed in her own theory. I thought it had probably been born simply of her antagonism to Basil Deering and her hope of involving him somehow in the crime, if there had really been one.

"However, I can tell you one or two things of some interest," Mr. Pryor went on. "A cyclist, coming down your lane towards the village, passed you in the lane on your way here. Do you remember him? His name's Vincent Hall, and he lives in one of those cottages further up the lane. He was on his way to the Hare and Hounds."

Olivia looked at him vacantly, then frowned.

"I don't remember anyone," she said. "No, wait a moment, perhaps I do. Yes, there was a cyclist who called out good evening as I got to the bridge, but I didn't see who it was and I don't think I answered. Was it Vince Hall? He's Mrs. Gabriel's gardener. But I wasn't in a state to notice anybody. I'd quite forgotten him till now. Why? Is it important?"

"Not necessarily, except that he says the time he saw you was about nine-forty. And your telephone call to the police station was at nine thirty-three, and Mr. Leggate says you and he left the Hare and Hounds soon after nine and arrived at your home at about nine twenty. So it took you approximately thirteen minutes after finding your sister's body to telephone us and nearly another ten minutes to get into the state of panic you described and come running here. Of course, none of these times, except your call to the police station, which was noted down, was precisely accurate. But the picture it suggests is a slightly curious one."

"I don't see why." Olivia looked perplexed. "I didn't make any note of the times myself, so I haven't any idea how long it took me to do the things I did, but I know when I found my sister's body it was a terrific shock and it took me a little while— you know, it wouldn't surprise me if it was even longer than you say—to convince myself that she was dead and that I couldn't do anything for her. Then when I'd phoned the police station I sat down to wait for you, and it was then the feeling began to work up in me that I couldn't bear it and I thought of coming to my friends here for help. I'm sorry I wasn't more practical and rational. I'm sure it would make things easier for you if I had been. But I believe lots of people do strange things when they're in a state of shock, isn't that true?"

"Perfectly true," he, said. "And, as I said, it isn't necessarily important. I was just interested to hear your comments."

"I didn't murder my sister during those twenty minutes I was alone with her in the house, Mr. Pryor, if that's what you're really interested in," Olivia said quietly. His apparent suspicions of her seemed to have jolted her into calm. "I realise you've got to check everything, but you needn't waste time on me. I'm glad, however, that you seem to be taking what I told you about her murder more seriously than you did last night."

"Oh, we've taken it seriously all along, Miss Fyffe," he answered. "Now if you don't mind a few more questions, may I ask you if you're aware that your sister recently made a new will?"

"I am," she said. "She told me about it when she told me of her engagement. She left everything she had to Mr. Deering. But how have you found out about it? I didn't think of it last night, but this morning I thought I ought to tell you about it when I saw you."

"When our men got no answer when they rang the bell at your flat in St. John's Wood," he said, "they spoke to the woman who has a flat on the same floor as yours, and it turned out she has a key to it. They explained that they were looking for Mrs. Mansell and that there was a possibility that she'd been taken ill, as it appeared she'd had an accident earlier in the evening. Well, this woman took them in, and, as I told you, there was no sign that your sister had been there. But on one of the desks in the flat there was a will, signed only last Tuesday in the office of her solicitor, a very brief will in which she left everything she had to Mr. Deering. We've been in touch with her solicitor this morning, and he confirmed that she'd done this, against his advice. He thought it was unfair to you, since it even included your bungalow. I gather that that was her property."

"Yes, her husband bought it four years ago, shortly before he died, and left it to her," Olivia said. "Our books were just beginning to do well at the time, and it was her suggestion that I should give up my job and move in there with her. Incidentally, the flat in London belongs to me. My work was in London and

I kept the flat on when I came down here, so I shan't be home-
less. And I don't think she was actually being as unfair to me
as you think, because it was her idea, if we can believe anything
Mr. Deering said, that I should move in with them and that
the bungalow should be sold. To be honest, I wasn't much upset
when she told me about the will, because I never dreamt that
she'd be dead in a few days. I thought that making it was just
a gesture. She could always change it, after all, if the marriage
didn't work out as she hoped."

"She was a wealthy woman, wasn't she?" Mr. Pryor asked.

"Moderately," Olivia answered. "She had what her husband
left her and what we were making out of our books, which will
go on for a while, I suppose, though we weren't such an over-
whelming success that it's going to last long if we don't go on
producing a regular book a year. All the same, Mr. Deering
stands to gain substantially now. That may have been his
motive. It may even have been why he took a gun to the party."

Felix drew attention to himself by saying, "Er…" Then he
went on, "If you don't mind my saying so, I don't think that can
be correct."

The Superintendent turned to him, lifting one of his
startled eyebrows, though his eyes retained their sceptical calm.
"How d'you make that out, Mr. Freer?"

"He'd have gained a certain amount, of course," Felix said,
"but not nearly as much as he would have if he'd waited till they
were married. I believe the law is nowadays that a spouse can
inherit without paying death duties, but as they weren't married
yet there'd have been quite a claim against Mrs. Mansell's estate."

I was always being taken by surprise by the odd pieces of
information that Felix managed to pick up. I wondered if it was
possible that he had investigated this matter in order to discover
how much he might inherit from me if I should suddenly die.
But he must have known that even if no death duties were
deducted from my estate, it would not amount to a great deal.
I had inherited enough from my mother to bring me in a small
income on which I might just have been able to live if I had

objected to working, but with inflation mounting as it had been doing for the last few years, my unearned income was worth less and less and what I mainly depended on was my salary as a physiotherapist. Luckily for me, I was interested in my job and much preferred it to the idea of filling my time with good works, golf or bridge, which I should have been driven to if I had had nothing else to do.

"I'll bear that in mind," the Superintendent said thoughtfully. "It's a point to remember if premeditation comes up. It certainly wouldn't have been the best time for a murder, from Mr. Deering's point of view. Meanwhile, we've still got to find Mrs. Mansell. I'll keep you informed, Miss Fyffe."

Andrew saw him and the sergeant out of the house, then came back to the living room, finished his drink and was about to return to his workshop when Helen told him that Olivia had made up her mind to go home.

"What, now?" he said. "I'll go with you, then."

"She's staying for lunch," Helen said. "But I think someone should go with her afterwards."

"There's no need," Olivia said. "I've only that small bag I brought to carry."

"But it won't feel very nice, walking into the house alone," Helen pointed out. "Andrew will go with you."

"Let me know when you want me," he said and returned to his workshop.

❀ ❀ ❀

Helen went to the kitchen, put out bread and cheese and made some coffee. The bread was soggy white sliced stuff, but the cheese was Blue Cheshire. We all sat round the kitchen table and ate almost without saying a word to one another. Afterwards Olivia packed her bag, Helen fetched Andrew in and he and Olivia set out together to the bungalow. Felix and I washed up the few things that had been used. Helen stood watching us.

"I do wish she hadn't insisted on going home," she said. "I honestly don't think she's fit to be left alone. I'm afraid I oughtn't to have asked Basil here, Felix. She'd have stayed if I hadn't done that."

"I'm sorry I suggested it," he said. "It was unthinking of me."

"I wish I knew the truth about what she saw yesterday evening," she went on. "Could she have made up a thing like that?"

"One thing she couldn't have done," Felix said, "is remove her sister's body herself. She had twenty minutes alone between the time Leggate left her at the door and the time she turned up here. Apart from the fact that she'd have found it quite difficult to lift and carry her sister, even though Mrs. Mansell was a small woman, that didn't give her time to hide the car where it wouldn't be found immediately."

"D'you mean you've been thinking she might have done the murder herself?" Helen asked, sounding startled.

"Haven't you?" Felix swabbed the sink with care as he came to the end of the washing-up. "Murderers have a way of turning out to be the victim's nearest and dearest."

"But she'd only lose by Carleen's death," Helen said. "She can't go on writing without Carleen, and she said herself their books won't go on bringing in much money for long, and she won't get anything under that silly will. She may even have to go back to teaching sometime soon."

"How d'you know she won't prefer that to what she's doing now?" I said. "Even at that party yesterday, before all this trouble happened, she didn't give me the impression of a happy person."

"No, I think that's true," Helen agreed. "I think we've all been very unobservant. I wonder if the truth is that she and Carleen had a quarrel last night and Carleen drove away, and Olivia's so overcome with guilt about it that she's taken to imagining things. Well, I think I'll go and get on with some work myself now. I'm making a dinner dress for the vicar's mother. By the time I've finished with her, I want her to be the best dressed vicar's mother in the country. I'll see you later."

Small, neat and purposeful, she went out of the back door and across the slope of lawn to the stable block by the river.

Felix and I went out through the French window in the living room and sat down, putting our feet up, in the long chairs that had been left outside it. The sun fell straight upon us out of a brilliant sky, but it was not as sultry as it had been the day before. A slight breeze touched my face. There was a faint rustling among the willows that overhung the Wandle and the surface of the water was rippled.

Felix lit a cigarette and lay back with his bright blue eyes, under their drooping lids, gazing up dreamily at nothing in particular. I felt very drowsy. I had not slept well the night before and listening to too much talk by too many people never agrees with me. I was afraid that Felix might want to go on discussing the problem of what had happened to Carleen Mansell, but he seemed, like me, to feel that we had had enough of that for the time being and was silent. I thought of perhaps fetching myself a book, but I was too lazy to move. Presently I fell asleep.

I did not know how much later it was when I was wakened by being prodded in the ribs. It might have been a few minutes, it might have been an hour. But I saw that the ashtray that Felix, being tidy about such things, had brought out with him and was on the around beside him, had a number of stubs in it, so apparently I had slept for some time. It was Felix who was prodding me.

"Wake up," he said. "Now that we're alone, there's something I want to talk over with you."

"What?" I asked, still only half awake. My skin was tingling as if I had lain in the sun for too long.

"I'm thinking of getting married again," he said. "I'd like to know your view of that."

I rubbed the sleep out of my eyes and pulled myself up higher in my chair.

"So that's why you really came looking for me," I said. "You want a divorce."

"I didn't come looking for you. I told you that. But when your Mrs. Something told me you were here, staying with the

Boscotts, I thought I might kill two birds with one stone. I mean, I could see both you and Deering. I remembered the Boscotts were connected with him, and I found out he lived somewhere quite close to them. By the way, just where is his house?"

"If you go on up the lane past the Fyffe bungalow you come to it," I said. "It's a plain sort of house, painted pink. But let's talk about this divorce."

"But I'm not sure I want one."

"How will you manage to get married again without one?" I asked. "Actually I've often thought it would be a good idea to get things tidied up between us."

He looked disturbed. "You know I hate lawyers."

"I don't think it's so bad if the case isn't defended and there aren't any children or financial complications. Total breakdown of a marriage one calls it, or something like that. Well, we could easily prove it's been total for a good long time."

"But we'd have to have a lot of lawyers and perhaps even a judge poking their noses into our private affairs. Wouldn't that be horrible?"

"Then what are you proposing to do? Commit bigamy?"

He gave a defensive frown and lit a new cigarette. "You know, I don't believe bigamy's treated as a very serious offence nowadays," he said. "But all I've said to you is that I'm thinking of getting married again and wanted to talk it over with you, and you go running ahead, talking about divorce."

"I'm not going to be an accessory to bigamy, even if it's your idea that it isn't a desperate crime," I said. "Tell me about the woman. Is she rich?"

"Fairly."

"That's a good thing. I'd like to see you safely married to a rich woman. It might be the making of you. How old is she?"

"About thirty."

"I'm glad she isn't too young. Are you in love with her?"

He stirred fretfully in his chair. "Look, I didn't start this discussion in order to hold forth about my private feelings. I just wanted to know what you'd think about the proposition in a general way."

"Well, what about her feelings then?" I asked. "Is she in love with you?"

"I'm not sure."

"Because if you're in love with one another and you can't bring yourself to face a divorce, why don't you just live together? That would be the easiest thing to do."

"I think she'd feel more secure if she was married. She needs security terribly. You see, she's a fearful alcoholic."

For the first time since our talk had started, I began to take him seriously. Early in our marriage I had made the mistake of assuming that Felix needed me because he had to have someone to depend on, and for a time, while I was still deeply, if unhappily, in love with him, I had tried to be the person I thought he wanted. It had taken me some time to understand that he was really a very independent person and that our marriage might have been more successful if I had depended on him far more than I had. He would have felt less inadequate, less of a drop-out in the difficult business of living. If the woman of whom we were talking was an alcoholic and he thought that he could help her, he might really, given a little encouragement, go deeper into a relationship with her.

"Doesn't it take an alcoholic to cure an alcoholic?" I said. "Isn't that the whole idea behind Alcoholics Anonymous?" But as I said it, I realised that it was not exactly an encouraging thing to say, and I felt suddenly afraid that Felix might think it was dictated by jealousy. I went on, "Anyway, I wish you both well. If she can support you financially and you can support her morally, that could be the foundation of a happy marriage."

He looked irritable, as if I had not said what he wanted. He stood up.

"I think I'll go for a walk. It's no good talking to you. You never take anything seriously."

"But I do—I do indeed."

"You're the last person to think I could ever support anyone morally."

"It's just that some years ago I learnt to face facts, painful though they were," I said. "And if you're going for a walk, remember there are people coming for drinks at your request, so don't be late."

He did not answer, but looking sour, walked away across the lawn to the path that ran along the riverbank and disappeared beyond a clump of willows.

# Chapter Four

In the circumstances it was unfortunate that Felix had not returned by six o'clock, when the Boscotts' guests were expected. I doubted if he had spent the whole afternoon walking. He was not a great walker. But he might have found some agreeable spot by the river where he had rested and then fallen asleep, or merely into one of his absorbing daydreams in which time had no meaning for him.

I had never known what kind of things he thought about when he was dreaming, whether it was of being immensely rich and owning yachts, castles and Caribbean islands, or whether it was of dazzling sexual conquests, or possibly of being the ruthless leader of some criminal gang whom he terrorized into obedience to him. In his everyday life he was not much interested in money, even if he was given to borrowing it from unwary people who certainly never saw it again, but his tastes were not extravagant and he probably spent less on himself than I did. As I remembered, he was an excellent lover, but not vain of his prowess, and he was too much of an individualist to enjoy belonging to any gang, even one which, unimaginably, he domi-nated. And he was on the whole a tenderhearted man, far from ruthless. But a person's dreams can be like the far side of the moon, unseeable except very occasionally from some psychological spacecraft. Felix's might represent the reverse of the man I knew, someone ambitious, avaricious and cruel. Whatever they were, I knew that he would be horrified at the mere thought of letting me into the secret of them.

I spent the rest of the afternoon reading and was wondering whether I ought to go upstairs to change before the guests came when Helen, wearing her slacks and working smock, came in from her workshop, saying that she did not intend to change.

"If we stay as we are," she said, "it'll be a sort of compromise between giving a party and going into mourning, which seems sensible, since we don't know which we ought to be doing. I'm going to make some snacks now. I've got some pâté and some cheese and so on. I don't think people usually really want to eat them, but it makes it look as if one's taken some trouble over them. You might come and help, if you feel like it."

So we spent a little time in the kitchen, spreading pâté and cheese on biscuits and decorating them artistically with olives and little bits of pimento. Then I went upstairs to comb my hair and put on a little make-up. I was beginning to worry because Felix had not returned yet, but I still thought I could count on him to appear before the other guests did.

However, Barbara Gabriel arrived before Felix. She was wearing the gay cotton dress that she had worn the evening before, but her face was solemn. It was a pretty face, I realised, so long as you only looked at the middle of it. The trouble about it was that it extended a little too far all round. Probably as a child she had had a charming chubbiness, but unfortunately chubbiness does not wear too well in the fifties. All the same, she was an attractive woman in a comfortable, reposeful way.

We sat out in the garden, which was in shade now, Helen and I on a bench against the wall and Barbara on the long chair where I had spent half the afternoon sleeping. Andrew sat on the grass with his legs crossed. He was wearing his remote, austere look, and for some reason I suddenly found myself thinking how little I knew him. I had known him ever since Helen had first brought him to see me when they were about to get married, which was twenty years ago now, yet as he sat there in front of us like a small, bony, inscrutable Buddha, I was utterly unable to guess from the expression on his face whether his thoughts were simply on the work which he had reluctantly left in the stable block, or on violence and death. I might be meeting him for the first time, so far as understanding him went.

Barbara Gabriel's thoughts were, or appeared to be, much easier to fathom.

"I think it's too bad of Carleen to play a trick like this on us," she said, "D'you know, I had the police round this afternoon, asking me questions about her? Of course they've got to investigate her disappearance, and it really isn't fair on them when there are probably all kinds of serious crimes being committed, even in a neighbourhood like this. You know, if one stopped to think about it, one would hardly dare to leave one's own home or even to answer one's doorbell to anyone one wasn't expecting. One's lucky, I suppose, that somehow one can't go on thinking about it all the time. It's always the other person it's going to happen to—I mean, the rapes and murders and robberies. Sometimes I'm glad I haven't any children. I'd spend my time being terrified of what could happen to them if I let them out of my sight. But when I was a child myself in Stillbeam I never thought about such things. I used to go to school in Wandlebury on my bicycle and often came home after dark and I had to be really late for my parents to start worrying. Sometimes I'd stop off on the way to have a chat with a boyfriend and I might get home perhaps as much as an hour late, and even then they'd hardly say a word about it. But now, if one was a parent, one would go out of one's mind and that would be so terribly bad for the child."

"Then you've always lived in Stillbeam?" I said.

"Not quite always," she answered. "I grew up in the house I live in now, but when my father died my mother couldn't afford to keep it going, so we sold it and moved into a flat in Wandlebury, then I went to London and did a secretarial course and got a

job with a big firm of building contractors, of which Nick—
that was my husband—was managing director. And we lived in
London for a number of years, till he retired, and just when that
happened we saw an advertisement in *Country Life* that my old
home was for sale, so we bought it and moved down here, and I
can't tell you what a thrill it was to be back. But poor Nick only
lived a couple of years to enjoy it. It was so sad, because he loved
the place as much as I did. Luckily, Stillbeam hasn't been spoiled
nearly as much as a lot of places. Of course, Wandlebury's spread
a good deal, but it hasn't yet swallowed up Stillbeam. And I must
say, compared with what I remember of it in the old days, we've
got far more interesting neighbours—Andrew and Helen, who
do such wonderful work, and Carleen and Olivia, and of course
Basil. By the way, is he coming this evening?"

"I think that must be him now," Helen said, as the sound
of the doorbell reached us through the house.

Andrew unlocked his crossed legs, stood up and went to
answer it.

But it was Ralph Leggate who had just arrived. He came
out to the garden, apologizing for being late. He was not so very
late, but it started me wondering not only when Felix was going
to appear, but also whether Basil Deering was going to appear
at all. I could easily imagine that he was the kind of person who
might change his mind about visiting friends without bothering
to telephone.

I did not blame him for deciding to stay at home. With
Carleen still missing, it was unlikely that he was in the mood for
company. But a telephone call to the Boscotts would not have
cost him much effort. It was a minor matter, but I added it to
the list that was growing in my mind of things about him that
I did not like.

Ralph Leggate commented at once on the fact that Olivia
was absent.

"Yes, I'm sorry about that," Helen said. "After all she went
home and said she didn't feel like coming out again. One can
understand that, can't one?"

"Of course," he said, "but if I'd known she wouldn't be here I'd have gone to see her. It can't be good for her, being alone."

"It may be what she really wants," Helen replied. "If I'm in trouble of any kind I never want to see anyone but Andrew."

"But since you've got him," Barbara said, "one can hardly call that being alone. I think I'll look in on Olivia presently and make sure she's all right."

Ralph Leggate looked vexed, as if this did not fit in with his own plan for looking in on Olivia. Nursing the drink that Andrew had brought him, he sat down on the bench beside me, while Helen sat down in the long chair in which Felix had passed most of the afternoon. I was beginning by now to be seriously worried about him. He was not normally discourteous and his lateness was not characteristic of him.

"I had the police round to see me this afternoon," Ralph Leggate said. "They wanted to know when I'd last seen Carleen and then if there was any special reason why Olivia and I had gone to the Hare and Hounds instead of my seeing her straight home by the short cut across the meadow. I said that there had been a special reason, but that I didn't choose to tell them anything about it. They didn't press me. I suppose they guessed what it was."

"I can guess," Barbara said with a curious note of mockery in her voice. "I've seen it coming for some time. What happened? Did she turn you down, Ralph, or didn't you get around to asking her? Aren't we going to have a double wedding in Stillbeam?"

He and she exchanged a long look. What took me by surprise about it was its intimacy, and I found myself wondering suddenly if they had ever been lovers, or even still were, though with their relationship dangerously disrupted by the presence of Olivia Fyffe.

"I didn't ask her anything," Ralph said, looking away from Barbara across the garden and speaking to no one in particular. "I might have—I almost did—I wanted to tell her a few things about myself. I felt it was time I did. But she was in a queer mood, so I said nothing. It's my guess she was more upset than she wanted to admit by Carleen's engagement. I think she saw it as the end of their working together."

"Why?" Andrew asked. "Basil wouldn't have interfered. He'd never have discouraged anything as profitable as that partnership."

"You can't be sure," Helen said. "He may not think about money nearly as much as you think, Andrew. You've always been unfair to him about that. And he may be more jealous than you realise. He told us himself he quite definitely refused to have Olivia to live with him and Carleen."

Barbara was still watching Ralph with a probing, doubtful glance.

"So you said nothing to Olivia," she said. "Nothing at all?"

"Oh, we talked, of course," he answered. "We didn't sit like mutes."

"You sometimes do," she said. "But this time it wasn't about anything special?"

"No, just this and that."

She stirred and seemed to relax more easily in her chair. It was at that moment that I heard footsteps on the path that led round the house and Felix appeared.

I had a shock when I saw him. I had hardly ever seen him so pale. When he spoke, apologizing for being so late, it was very quietly, as if he were afraid that if he spoke much above a whisper his voice would somehow slip out of control and betray something about himself that it was vital to conceal. I knew that trick he had of speaking in a hushed, toneless way and it usually meant that he was feeling guilty. There was sweat on his forehead, which could hardly be accounted for by the mild warmth of the evening. In fact, he looked like someone who has recently vomited. Dropping down on the grass beside Andrew, he said, most unusually for him, that he would like whisky.

As Andrew went to fetch it, Felix looked at me and held my glance with an intentness which I felt sure was meant to tell me something. Unfortunately, I had not the slightest idea what it was.

He explained that he had gone for a walk along the riverbank, had found an attractive spot to sit down for a little, then
had fallen asleep. I did not believe him. I noticed that his
hands were shaking and his way of gulping the whisky that
Andrew brought him was quite unlike him. Something very
disagreeable must just have happened to Felix, something far
worse than being startled out of a doze by, say, a wandering
cow. And he wanted to tell me about it, that much I understood of what his glance had tried to convey to me. But there
would be no chance of his doing so until after Ralph and
Barbara had left, and after they had gone we should have to sit
down to a meal with Helen and Andrew, so unless it could be
told very briefly it would have to wait until a good deal later
in the evening.

Ralph and Barbara left together at about a quarter to eight,
Barbara saying that she was going to look in on Olivia and
Ralph showing some irritation at this, then saying that he would
go with her. We had another round of drinks after they had
gone, then Helen made omelets, with Felix coming to himself
enough to help her by mixing a salad while I laid the table.

As we sat down round it, Helen looked at him in a worried
way.

"Are you feeling all right, Felix?" she asked.

"Well, not too good," he answered. "I think I may have
picked up a bug of some sort. I hope I don't pass it on to you."

"Shall I get you an aspirin?"

"Oh no, it's nothing to worry about."

But he was very silent during the meal and for once, when
it was over, he did not offer to do the washing-up, but took me
by the arm in a quite marital kind of way and said that it would
be nice to go for a short walk before it got dark, wouldn't it? As
we left I saw Andrew looking after us with a steady, inquiring
gaze. I guessed that he was as aware as I was that Felix was not
behaving like his usual self.

It was almost dark when he and I set out. The light
breeze that there had been in the afternoon had dropped and

the evening was very still. There was a greenish tinge in the darkening sky, in which stars had begun to glitter. Outside the gate we turned to the left and walked slowly on till we came to the humpbacked bridge over the Wandle. There Felix paused, let go of my arm and leant against the stone parapet. I did the same, looking down over it into the shadowy depths of the slowly moving water. It had a faint and not unpleasant smell of mouldering vegetation. I did not ask Felix why he had brought me there, but left him to say what he wanted.

He spoke abruptly. "Deering's dead."

I started and looked quickly into his face. He was looking with deep anxiety into mine. Even in the dim light I could see that much. As I did not speak, he nodded his head solemnly.

"It's true, Virginia."

"How d'you know?" I asked.

"I found him."

"By the river, d'you mean? Had he fallen in, or what?"

"No, no, in his house," he said impatiently, "with a bloody great knife sticking out of his back."

"What were you doing in his house?"

He sighed sharply. "I suppose I'd better explain."

"I think it's time you did," I said. "Have you called the police?"

He shook his head. "You know, you're a cold-blooded creature. I tell you I've found a man murdered and all you can say is have I called the police."

"Isn't that the usual thing to do?"

"You might at least sympathise with me a little. I nearly fell over him. It was a perfectly horrible experience."

"But what were you doing there? Had he asked you in?"

"You'll be asking me next if I murdered him. No, as a matter of fact, I was sure he wouldn't be there. I thought he was coming here for drinks. I'd arranged that with Helen. I thought the house would be empty."

"Then how did you get in?"

"I forced a window. It wasn't difficult."

"But why?"

"I said I'd explain, didn't I?" He took hold of the stone parapet with both hands, as if that gave him a feeling of support. "You know I told you I'd got out of the secondhand-car business."

I did not see how that could connect up with his discovery of Basil Deering, dead, even if his story of doing so was true, of which I was not entirely convinced, but I nodded.

"I'd got tired of selling cars that I knew had had their mile-ometers turned backwards and a spray job done to cover up the cracks," he went on. "It's difficult to keep your self-respect doing that sort of thing. Besides, I knew the police were on to us and trouble was looming up ahead."

"So it wasn't only that you had an attack of conscience," I said.

He frowned. "I've as much conscience as you have."

"I know you have," I agreed, "but it moves in a mysterious way, its wonders to perform."

"Look, do you want me to tell you what happened, or don't you?"

"Yes," I said. "I'm sorry. Go on."

"Well, when I left the garage I had to find another job, hadn't I? And just then I got talking to a man I'd met in a pub. I'd known him for some time, actually, though I never knew what he did. I generally find it's more tactful not to ask about that kind of thing. But when I told him I was looking for a job he told me about his. He was a private detective, working for a very obscure little firm called Canning Brothers, who needed a new man and he thought they might be able to use me. The pay wasn't much, he said, but they were quite decent people to work for. It didn't attract me much at first, but then I thought why not, it was something I'd never tried before and I'm ready to give most things a try. So he fixed up an interview for me, and I've been working for them for about six months now, learning the job bit by bit. It's quite interesting work really, though a lot of it's very sordid. I could tell you things that would shock even you."

Thinking of Felix as a private detective was more than enough of a shock to be going on with. But it had always been his contention that I was never shocked by the behaviour of anyone but himself, and there may have been some truth in this, because even now he was too close to me for me to be able to play the part of detached onlooker, which was the way that I liked to think, no doubt mistakenly, that I viewed the utter strangeness of the human species.

"Well, and then?" I said.

"Then, by degrees, after being sent trailing along with the other chaps, learning the job from them, they've begun to give me jobs on my own and they seem to be quite satisfied with me. It seems I've a natural talent for the work and there's some satisfaction in that. But this job down here is the first time I've been given something really responsible. And look what happens!"

"Felix," I said, putting a hand on his arm, "is this all quite true? Did you come here to investigate something to do with Basil Deering?"

"Of course I did. I practically told you so when I first got here, didn't I?"

"Yes, but I didn't believe you. I couldn't make any sense of it. I should have remembered that you sometimes tell the truth, or anyway, part of it. If you'd told me all this sooner, it would have made things simpler."

"My job's a very confidential one," he said stiffly. "That's the very first thing you have to learn about it. You don't discuss the affairs of your clients with anyone."

"I'm not just anyone."

"No, you're a very dangerous woman. You'd probably have taken the job over and tried to tell me how to do it."

I had never in my life thought of myself as dangerous to anyone, though at times I had wondered if by marrying Felix I had really done him harm. Someone more pliable than I could ever manage to be, someone with more flexible ideas about right and wrong, might have made him a far happier man and so perhaps a better one.

"And I thought you followed me down here to sort out the business of divorce," I said. "I thought your interest in Basil was entirely bogus."

"No, as a matter of fact, I just thought I might be able to make use of you," he answered. "I remembered that the Boscotts were somehow connected with Deering, but I wasn't sure if they'd remember me after all these years, or how they'd react if I simply turned up here without warning, so I phoned your home to see if you'd give me a reintroduction to them, and your daily told me you were actually staying here. That made everything simple. I knew you wouldn't believe me about my interest in Deering and that you'd think I'd come here looking for you—which in a sense I had, of course, because I've been wanting an opportunity to ask how you'd feel about my getting married again. Anyway, it all fell out very conveniently till I walked in on that bloody man's murder."

"Now listen—wait a minute," I said. "You broke into Basil's house this evening and you found him dead, with a knife sticking out of his back?"

"Isn't that what I said?"

"And you never even thought of calling the police. You came back to have drinks with the Boscotts and you stayed on quietly for supper, and even now you haven't done anything about it."

"How could I?"

"How d'you mean, how could you?"

"How could I explain what I was doing there? I forced a window and I'd been prowling around the house for a bit, looking for one or two things, before I found him. And besides—" He stopped suddenly, as if he had almost said something that he did not want me to hear.

"What?" I asked.

He did not answer for a moment, then reluctantly he put a hand into a pocket and brought it out again, holding something white. Opening his palm, he held it out to me. In the dusk I could only just make out what it was. It was a frog, carved in what I supposed was ivory, and about three inches long, with its crouching body flattened to the ground, but its head raised in a questing, listening attitude. The carving was very simple, carried out with a few bold strokes.

"It's Chinese, I think," Felix said, "not specially valuable, but so charming, isn't it? I couldn't resist it."

"You mean you stole it." He could still scandalize me.

"It really isn't valuable," he said defensively.

"But Basil may have been specially attached to it," I said. "It may have sentimental associations or what not. Or he may just have liked the thing."

"That can't make much difference to him now."

"But I thought you made a point of not helping yourself to the belongings of friends."

"He wasn't a friend," Felix said sharply. "Anything but!"

"Well, whatever he was, you didn't want the police to find it in your possession, I can understand that," I said. "But why didn't you simply put it back where you found it after you found him dead. Wouldn't that have been the safest thing to do?"

"I simply didn't think of it. I wanted to keep it."

"But you still haven't told me why you wanted to get into the house."

He looked down at the frog and stroked it with one of his shapely fingers, a thief's finger, delicate and adroit. I had always loved his hands for their sensitiveness and their look of supple strength.

"Deering was a blackmailer," he said. "He had letters that he was holding over a client of Canning Brothers. It was my job to find them. That's what I was looking for when this little chap caught my eye on a shelf among a lot of other odds and ends, and I thought no one was going to notice it if I nicked him."

"And did you find the letters?"

"Yes."

"Can you tell me what they are?"

"I've told you so much, I suppose I may as well tell you the rest. The client, now happily married with a couple of children, went through a homosexual phase. He wrote these letters to a boy who got to know Deering sometime and talked about the affair to him and sold him the letters. And Deering's put the bite on the man ever since. Not that the law would have worried about him these days, but he happened to be particularly vulnerable. He's in the church, and if the letters had been sent to his bishop, which was what Deering threatened, that would have been the end of him."

"So that's where Basil's money came from," I said. "Were there any other victims?"

"Oh yes. I don't think he was really a professional black-mailer, he just made use of what came his way, but he'd a file of letters and photographs which I'd have liked to destroy. But I didn't know how to set about it and I was scared of staying around too long, so I went to his drawing room to let myself out by the French window and I found his body there in the middle of the room. After that I cleared out as fast as I could and vomited in the garden. Violence never did agree with me. But I did bring just one thing away with me from the file besides the letters I was looking for."

He put the frog down on the parapet and felt in his breast pocket for his wallet and took out a photograph, which he handed to me. It had grown too dark for me to see what it was, except that it was of two figures, one of them a dark, straight figure, the other dressed in floating white.

"Just a minute," Felix said, brought a small torch out of his pocket and directed its narrow beam onto the photograph.

It was a wedding photograph, a little creased and faded, taken, I judged, by a cheap photographer. It was of two young people, neither of them much more than twenty, the man tall and erect with very square shoulders, the girl pretty in a plump, round-cheeked way, with her veil thrown back from her face to show a frame of dark, curly hair. The dark hair made me uncertain for a moment, but then I exclaimed, "It's Ralph and Barbara!"

"You think so too, do you?" Felix said sombrely.

"Oh yes."

He put the photograph back into his wallet. "And I can't think of any reason why Deering should have kept it in his file unless it's evidence that Mrs. Gabriel's marriage to Gabriel was bigamous."

※ ※ ※

We had talked about bigamy only that afternoon and I had told him that I would not be an accessory to it, but at the time it had not seemed serious. Now I felt very disturbed.

"You're guessing," I said.

"Yes," he admitted.

"They may have had a divorce since that was taken."

"In that case, why did Deering keep it?"

"Perhaps he was at the wedding himself and kept it as a souvenir."

"You don't believe that."

"No, I suppose not. And I haven't heard anyone talk of Ralph and Barbara ever having been married and divorced, which is the sort of thing people do talk about if it hasn't been kept secret."

"Of course, it's odd, if I'm right about them," Felix said, "that they should have settled down so near each other in a little village like Stillbeam. You'd think they'd have taken care to avoid one another."

"They both grew up here," I said. "Barbara was telling us this evening that when she was a child she lived in the house she's living in now, and I believe Ralph inherited his house from his parents. And they may have felt sure they'd covered their tracks. I wonder how Deering got hold of the photograph."

"It could have been by chance. It may have caught his eye in a photographer's window."

All at once, as clearly as I had seen the photograph in the beam of Felix's flashlight, I saw a picture of Basil Deering lying dead with a knife sticking out of his back, and of Felix standing over him, then rushing out into the garden to be sick.

"You were taking a frightful risk, breaking into the house," I said. "Hadn't he any servants? Mightn't there have been someone there?"

"No, I found out about that yesterday evening at Mrs. Gabriel's," he answered. "I got chatting to him about how he lived and found out he had a woman who came in from the village every morning to clean, but who left once she'd washed up the lunch. Then he cooked for himself in the evening. He was quite an enthusiastic cook, I gathered. We even swapped one or two recipes."

"Men aren't what they were," I said. "They used to be so dependent, but now quite a lot of them can look after themselves. But d'you realise, Felix, if you don't get in touch with the police and tell them what happened, that unfortunate woman is going to walk in in the morning and find a corpse. Really, you can't let that happen."

"I've got to," he said stubbornly. "What else can I do? If I'd telephoned them at once, it would have been hard enough to explain what I was doing in the house, but by now it's become absolutely impossible. No, I wanted to tell you what had happened because I wanted to know if you agreed with me that that photograph is of Leggate and Mrs. Gabriel, but I don't mean to get mixed up with the police any more than I can help." He gave me an anxious look. "You haven't any idea of telling them yourself, have you?"

Unhappily, I shook my head.

He touched my shoulder gratefully. "I knew I could trust you. In a pinch you've never let me down. We may as well go back to the house now."

"What about him?" I asked and pointed at the ivory frog on the parapet.

"Oh," Felix said. "Yes."

He picked the frog up, weighed it in his hand for a moment, then with a sudden movement, flung it some distance away into the river. In the dusk, which was almost darkness now, it disappeared from our sight even before it hit the water, but there was the sound of a small splash as it did so, like the plop of a fish leaping up to snap at a midge above the surface.

"Pity," Felix said. "Such a nice little thing, but I wouldn't like to risk having it found on me, and—"

Abruptly, he paused. I heard him draw in his breath. Looking at him, I saw a very odd expression on his face.

"What's the matter?" I asked.

"What?" he said vaguely, as if he had not heard what I had said.

"I asked, what's the matter?"

"Nothing. Just a twinge of guilt, perhaps. If I hadn't taken it, it wouldn't be lost to the world for ever, would it? It'll never be found now."

His tone was totally unconvincing. Whatever thought had startled him, it had had nothing to do with guilt. He took my arm once more and we walked slowly back towards the Boscotts' house.

We found them in their living room, watching television. It was a programme about deep-sea diving. I was glad of the semi-darkness of the room, because the shock of what Felix had told me was just beginning to get through to me and I felt sure that it must show on my face. Sitting down and trying to control a tendency to shake, I fastened my gaze on the screen.

I saw shoals of small fish swimming in and out of caves in a coral reef, and waving tendrils of weed and strange objects like great flowers attached to the coral, opening and closing their hungry mouths in the silent depths. A diver, as dark and sinister-looking as any shark, glided smoothly amongst them. I found myself thinking of the small ivory frog squatting in the mud on the bed of the Wandle, with its head raised, looking upwards so curiously, but never to be discovered by any gracefully moving diver. It might stay there for centuries, for ever.

The programme came to an end and the one that followed it had a lot of noisy motorcycles in it. Helen switched it off, turned to Felix, who had sat down on the sofa, put up his feet and lit a cigarette.

"How are you feeling, Felix?" she asked. "Any better?"

"Oh—oh yes, thank you." Apparently it took him a moment to remember that he had been supposed to be feeling unwell when we started on our walk. "Much better. The walk did me good. But I think perhaps I'd better go home tomorrow. If it's a bug, I don't want you to catch it from me."

"Andrew and I never catch anything," Helen said. "You needn't be afraid. And if you aren't feeling too well in the morning, you oughtn't to travel. I think perhaps I ought to take your temperature. You aren't looking too good."

That was true, but when Helen, overriding his protests, insisted on putting a thermometer into his mouth, it showed that his temperature, as might have been expected, was normal. However, he accepted her suggestion without any argument that he should go to bed early, said good night and went upstairs to the room that Olivia had occupied the night before. He would soon recover in the morning, I thought, once he had put enough distance between himself and Stillbeam.

But he did not leave Stillbeam in the morning.

We were all at breakfast in the kitchen when the front doorbell rang and Andrew, going to answer it, found Sergeant Waller on the doorstep. As I looked across the table at Felix, I had a sinking feeling in my stomach. The body of Basil Deering had been found, I took for granted, and the police had come straight to where Felix was. But even before the sergeant had begun to speak, I had had second thoughts. For if that had happened, wouldn't someone more senior than the sergeant have come to the house? Superintendent Pryor at the least.

The sergeant's baleful, blue stare took us all in, but his tone was mild.

"We thought you should know, since you're among the people she saw last," he said, "that the body of Mrs. Mansell has been found. It was in her car, the white Rover, which was discovered on the rocks at the bottom of the cliffs outside Lynechurch. That's about ten miles from here. The tide was high when the car was driven over and it would have been submerged for a time—it's full of weed and muck now—but it got caught on the rocks and never got into the deep water. It should have been found earlier, but not many people go there now since there've been landslides and the cliffs are known to be dangerous. But a young couple were up there yesterday evening and saw the car and reported it."

"So it may have been suicide," Andrew said.

"That isn't likely, sir," the sergeant answered. "Mrs. Mansell had a bullet in her brain and could hardly have done any driving."

# Chapter Five

I know my mind ought not to have worked in the way it did, because the first thought that came into it when I realised that the sergeant had not come to tell us of the discovery of Basil Deering's body, was that the whole story that Felix had told me the evening before had been imaginary. This was my legacy of three years of marriage to him. If any doubt happened to be cast on anything that he had told me, I automatically assumed that it was he who had lied. But he would never have thrown the ivory frog into the river if he had not been seriously frightened of something.

At that point common sense intervened. I realised that the sergeant knew nothing about the murder of Basil Deering simply because the time was only half past eight and the woman from the village who came into Basil's house to clean had not arrived yet. But soon she would be telephoning the police and perhaps we should have another visit from them then. Until that happened there was nothing to worry about. All the same, I dared not look at Felix. The bold eyes of the sergeant struck me as observant, and I did not know what he might read on my face if I so much as glanced in Felix's direction.

The sergeant wanted to check up a few of the things that we had told him and the Superintendent about the evening when Carleen had gone missing. What time had we left Mrs. Gabriel's house? Andrew said eight o'clock. Had we all been together for the rest of the evening? Andrew said we had. What time had Miss Fyffe appeared? None of us was sure about that, but Andrew thought it had been about a quarter to ten, or perhaps a little earlier.

"Wasn't there a cyclist who saw her running here?" he said. "I thought he told you."

"Just checking up, sir," the sergeant answered.

He asked one or two more questions about the mood that Mrs. Mansell had appeared to be in at Mrs. Gabriel's party, about how long each of us had known her, about Mrs. Mansell's relations with her sister, and about whether she had ever spoken as if she were afraid of anybody. Neither Felix nor I had anything much to say, and Andrew did most of the answering for himself and Helen. But when the sergeant had gone she turned on him with a bewildered expression on her face.

"Why did you tell him that lie, Andrew?" she said. "It wasn't necessary."

"What lie?" be asked, sitting down at the table again and going on with his breakfast.

"You said we all spent the evening together after Barbara's party," she said. "But you went to your workshop for quite a while."

"Oh," he said. "So I did. It slipped my memory."

"Don't you think we ought to tell Superintendent Pryor?" she said. "He couldn't possibly think you popped out during that time and shot Carleen and got rid of her body and the car, and I'm sure it's a mistake to tell any lies one hasn't got to."

"If you'll take my advice," Felix said, "once you've told the police something, true or not, stick to it. I've been told that by a man with a lot of experience, an eminent criminal lawyer, as a matter of fact. I'm sure he knew what he was talking about."

I had no doubt that he did, though I thought it probable that he was not a criminal lawyer, but simply a criminal, and not such a very eminent one at that. Felix's more dubious friends were mostly on the lower rungs of their profession. Nevertheless, I thought that his advice was good.

"I'd leave things as they are," I said. "There are only the four of us who know that Andrew was out of the house for a little while."

"Just so long as we all remember that," Helen said, looking uneasy. "I'm not at all happy about it."

"Because you're such a terribly bad liar yourself," Andrew said, smiling at her. "But this is such a simple little matter, it shouldn't be beyond your capabilities."

"All right," she said, with a sigh, "but I wish you hadn't done it."

"So do I," he said. "It was stupid. I was thinking about poor Carleen and not really about what I was saying. I expect the police are going to come up with the proverbial tramp, or at any rate someone who broke into the house while we were all at Barbara's to see what he could steal, got surprised by Carleen, shot her, hid when he heard Olivia coming, then bundled Carleen's body into the Rover when Olivia ran out, and drove off to those cliffs and sent the car over the edge. Then he just walked away, and he may be anywhere by now, miles away."

"Having stolen nothing from the bungalow?" Felix said.

"We don't really know if he did or not, do we?" Andrew said. "Olivia wasn't in a mood to go round checking everything carefully when we last saw her. But I think that's really the most logical explanation of what's happened. None of us who saw Carleen that evening could have done it. You three have perfect alibis and mine's got only one small hole in it. And Basil might conceivably have shot the woman he'd just got engaged to, for some mysterious reason, but if the police checked that he hadn't put the Rover in his garage, he couldn't have got rid of it in time to come back and start bullying Olivia. She could have done it after she'd said good night to Ralph at her door, but she only stands to lose by it, and like Basil, she hadn't time to get rid of the car. Ralph could have got rid of the car—we don't know where he was that evening after he'd left Olivia—but unless she's lying to protect him and he actually went into the house with her, he couldn't have done the murder. Anyway, I can't think of any possible motive for him."

"I can," Helen said. "Suppose he didn't know about the will Carleen had made, leaving everything to Basil, and thought Olivia would inherit all Carleen had when she died. Then if he married Olivia, they'd be quite rich. He may be expecting to marry her. Anyone can see he's terribly in love with her."

"But I repeat," Andrew said, "if he shot Carleen, Olivia must have seen it and be covering up for him, and she did know about the will, so she'd nothing to gain by letting him kill Carleen."

"There's one person you haven't mentioned," Felix said. "What about Mrs. Gabriel?"

For a moment Andrew looked simply astonished, then he laughed. "Yes, of course, I've been forgetting Barbara. The kindliest soul alive, not fearfully bright but not in the least abnormal. And about Carleen's best friend in Stillbeam. But perhaps that's against her. Who knows what their relationship really was? And so far as we know, she hasn't a shred of an alibi." Then his face became serious once more. "We'd better not lose our sense of proportion. It's always tempting to spin fairy tales, but Barbara isn't a murderess."

"Is she an honest person, would you say?" Felix asked.

"Honest?" Andrew said, puzzled. "What about? Money and that sort of thing? Certainly. But if you just mean honest with herself, I'd say no, I shouldn't think she shines at it. To get far with that, you've got to have a reasonable amount of intelligence, and as I said, she isn't very bright."

"I really meant, is she the sort of person to have any dark secrets in her life?" Felix said.

I wished that I could stop him. He was thinking about the photograph in his wallet and the fact that Barbara Gabriel had possibly been married at one time, and perhaps still was, to Ralph Leggate and that she had had the wit to keep this hidden for many years from everyone except Basil Deering. But if Felix was not careful about what he said, the very fact that he wanted to hide, the fact that he had been in Basil's house the evening before, might somehow slip out.

I said, "You're suggesting Barbara had some dreadful secret and Carleen knew it and was blackmailing her, and so Barbara killed her, managed to lift her body all by herself, drive it off to those cliffs and then walk ten miles back through the darkness. Quite a feat for a woman of her age. And of course, that may not be her last murder. Others may know her secret, so perhaps it's only the beginning of an epidemic of slaughter in Stillbeam."

Felix gave me a curious look. However, he remained silent, which was what I had hoped for.

Andrew laughed again. "Carleen as a blackmailer—no, there are some things that won't do. I repeat, we'd better not lose our sense of proportion. There's no reason, for one thing, why the murderer should have been someone at Barbara's party. There are other people in Stillbeam, Wandlebury, London—oh, anywhere—who are just as likely to be guilty as any of us. But to return to my theory about the thief whom Carleen surprised in the house, I think that's the only logical solution and it's what the police are going to come round to, if they haven't already."

After that he went to his workshop.

❄ ❄ ❄

I had realised long ago that Andrew was an obsessional worker. Without his craft he would have been lost, a man who had no other hold on life. All the same, it seemed to me that he was rather overdoing it at the moment. But I knew that if he was troubled in any way, or if he had some special reason for satisfaction, all his feelings found expression through his small, square, clever hands.

He was not in the least creative, he had once told me. He seldom felt any urge to design furniture, but only to make it. All the best designs, he held, had already been thought of by other people and his skills were directed simply to carrying them out. He was a man who might have been far happier in an earlier century, when a fine craftsman was not regarded as a bit of a freak.

It shocked me a little to realise that this was how I myself had always regarded him and Helen. What they wanted in life was so different from what most people want that it was easy to slip into thinking of them as dropouts of a kind. Certainly they were lacking in the average amount of competitiveness and money came low in their scale of values. I had wondered sometimes if having more money than they actually needed would subtly have undermined them both. They charged very high prices for what they did, but were so slow and painstaking about their work that cheques arrived at rather rare intervals, which occasionally worried them, though never very deeply.

When Andrew had gone, Helen lingered for a little until I said that Felix and I would do the washing-up. She asked me then if we would mind doing a little shopping for her in the village and made out a list of the odds and ends that she wanted from the grocer, saying that we should have them charged to her account. She left the list on the kitchen table, put out a shopping basket for us and followed Andrew out to the stable block. As I started to stack the dishes by the sink, Felix picked up the list and frowned at it.

"There's nothing here you couldn't get by yourself, is there?" he said.

"I don't expect so," I answered. "Why? Don't you want to go out?"

"I think it's time I left," he said.

"Go back to London, d'you mean?"

"Yes."

"But you can't do that. You can't just leave without even saying goodbye to Helen and Andrew."

"You could tell them I had a telephone call from my office, telling me to come home immediately, and how I hadn't wanted to disturb them when they were busy. Then I could write them a nice letter of thanks and send Helen some flowers."

I filled the sink with hot water.

"Apart from the fact that I've no intention of telling them anything of the kind," I said, "I think it would be very stupid of you to do a bolt just at the minute. It would look highly suspicious."

"But I've got to get back to the office," he said. "They'll want to hand on these letters I've got to the client."

"Then why don't you telephone and explain what you've got yourself mixed up in, and send the letters by post?"

"I'm not mixed up in anything, I just happened to be in the wrong place at the wrong time. But if I stick around I may get seriously mixed up in it. That's the kind of awful thing that happens to me."

"D'you mean you're afraid you may have left some finger-prints somewhere in Basil's house, or something like that?"

He was drying the cups and saucers as I put them on the draining board.

"Why haven't these people got a dishwasher?" he muttered. "I know they're crazy on doing everything by hand, but they've got a vacuum cleaner for their carpets, haven't they, and I bet Helen presses her seams, when she's dressmaking, with an electric iron. It's just deliberately eccentric not to have a dishwasher."

"Don't try to change the subject," I said with determination. "Are you afraid you've left some fingerprints in Basil's house?"

"Well, I was wearing gloves, but I did take one off to handle that frog. I wanted to *feel* him, if you know what I mean. And it's so damned difficult to be absolutely sure about what one's done. The more I think about it, the less sure I am about anything. Think of the train robbers at Letherslade Farm. They were all sure they'd worn gloves all the time they were there, yet the place was thick with their fingerprints. Then there's something else..."

"Oh Lord," I said in dismay as he stopped. "Is there something more you haven't told me?"

"Not exactly, no. It's just a thought that's crossed my mind. You see, I had to walk back here in daylight and there's a group of cottages on the way. I think that gardener of Mrs. Gabriel's, the one who saw Miss Fyffe come running down here the other evening, lives in one of them. And I don't know that someone at one of the windows didn't see me go by."

"Was there anyone in the any of the gardens, or did you meet anyone in the road?" I asked.

"No."

"Are you sure?"

"Yes, I'm quite sure about that. I was thinking so hard about getting back here without being seen that if I'd met anyone I'd have been scared out of my wits and wouldn't have forgotten it. But I could have been seen from one of the cottages."

I thought it over, taking a little time about it as I rinsed out the coffeepot and swabbed the sink.

After a moment I said, "I still think it would be an awful mistake to run away all of a sudden. The only thing for you to do now is to stay on as if you don't feel in the least concerned about anything, and when the police ask you where you were yesterday afternoon, as I suppose they will sooner or later, volunteer the information that you went for a walk and passed Basil's house. Then if someone did see you from the cottages, your going past will seem quite innocent."

He did not look convinced. "You've got such an awful conviction that truth will prevail. It often doesn't, you know."

"That wouldn't be exactly the truth."

Recognising that it would not seemed to reassure him a little. It always seemed to Felix safer to put his trust in a lie than in any approximately accurate statement.

"I suppose I could say I saw a dim figure at one of Deering's windows," he said. "Say, someone with a beard and long red hair."

"For heaven's sake, don't say anything of the kind!"

"Well, all right, I'll stay on for the moment," he said. "I wonder how long we've got before the police come round again. I don't look forward to it. I'm not worrying about myself, but your face will give you away. They'll see at once you know more than you ought."

"If that's how you feel, you shouldn't have told me anything about it."

"That's what I've been thinking. But the fact is, I needed someone to talk to. Pure weakness—I shouldn't have done it. It wasn't fair to you really. Now let's go and do this shopping."

We set out with Helen's list and shopping basket.

The morning was much cooler than it had been the day before, with dull grey clouds covering the sky. There was a feeling of damp in the air, as if rain might be coming. It looked as if the spell of fine weather that we had been having could be nearly at an end.

We walked down the lane to the main road, then turned to the left into the village. It was a very picturesque village, all thatch and white walls and dark beams, mostly inhabited by retired people and a few who commuted to Wandlebury. There was one pub, the Hare and Hounds, a small stone church of great charm, an excellent grocer of the modern school, whose shelves were stacked high with everything that the most sophisticated of his customers could desire, a small school in a very ancient building, which it was said had been in use as a school for three hundred years, and one glaring new red brick cottage that housed the village constable.

As Felix and I passed this cottage we saw two police cars drawn up outside it and through one of its windows could see that the room inside was filled with bulky-looking men.

"You see," Felix said in a half-whisper to me, as if they might overhear him, "the body's been found. They're gathering. I shouldn't be surprised if we find them in the house when we get back."

"I don't see why," I said. "There's no reason why they should be specially interested in us. They're probably hunting that intruder Andrew talked about. I thought he was right that that was the most logical explanation of what's happened."

"No," Felix said. "It seemed logical to Andrew because he didn't know yet about the second murder. All he knew about was Mrs. Mansell's, and what he said made sense of that. But that intruder was hardly likely to come back next day to polish off Deering. Of course, you can believe if you want to that the two killings aren't connected, but that seems to me very improbable."

"The two methods of murder were quite different," I reminded him. "One was a shooting and the other was a stabbing. Don't criminals usually stick to the same method in most of their crimes?"

"I'm not sure that this murderer is what you could exactly call a criminal," Felix said. "I mean, I don't think he's a professional. And when you've an amateur at work, he may do the most unexpected things. The thing that's puzzling me most at the moment is the motive. There are plenty of people with a motive for killing a blackmailer like Deering, but why Mrs. Mansell too? I suppose Deering might have told her some of the things he knew about various people, but from what I've heard of her, I can't see her trying to make use of them. Not that people aren't always acting out of character. Who would ever guess, for instance, seeing you walking along with that basket on your arm, that you've known ever since yesterday evening that there's a murdered man lying in Deering's pink house?"

"Only someone who's able to estimate the peculiar effect you have on me," I said. "I'm never myself when you're around. That's why I couldn't stay married to you. Here we are now." We had reached the village shop. "We'd better stop talking about murder while we're in here."

The shop was the kind where you help yourself from the shelves and Felix immediately started choosing things that were not on Helen's list. At the small meat counter he bought some stewing steak, then he bought onions, tomatoes, a green pepper and some sour cream. It was evident that he intended to do the cooking that evening and that what we were going to have would be his version of goulash. This would be an improvement on Helen's cooking, but I felt that we ought to have paid for these extras ourselves instead of having them put on her account. Felix, however, thought this unimportant. We left the shop presently, with Felix carrying the basket, which had grown heavy, and made our way back to the Boscotts' house.

I had an unpleasant feeling that we should find police cars in the drive, but it was empty. I was not sure whether or not this was a relief. They would come, I felt certain, sooner or later, and it might have been best to get it over quickly. We went to the kitchen and unpacked the basket.

"Now remember," Felix said, "when the police turn up we're as surprised as Helen and Andrew to hear about the murder. We needn't try to appear as shocked as they'll be, because we hardly knew the man, but we're just as astonished at what goes on in a quiet little place like Stillbeam. And personally I shan't find that difficult. I'm truly astonished."

"But you knew about the blackmail before you came here," I said, "and doesn't blackmail often lead to violence? I didn't know anything about any of it, so I'm sure I'm much more astonished than you are."

"Yes, well, don't overdo it, that's all. Just be your normal restrained self, covering up your feelings. Anything else will strike the Boscotts as peculiar, even if the police don't notice it."

I was putting Helen's butter and milk into the refrigerator.

"I still think it's possible the two murders may have been done by different people," I said. "Basil could have killed Carleen, either because of that will she made or because she somehow found out about his blackmailing activities—he may even have boasted to her about them after a few glasses of Barbara's champagne—and she may have threatened to give him away, and he may have been staggered and furious at her reaction. Well, if he killed her, mightn't someone else have killed him in revenge?"

"Oh, anything's possible, except that he removed Carleen's body to a place ten miles away and then walked back to chat to the police. It's even possible he normally went about with a gun in his pocket, because a blackmailer might feel he ought to be able to defend himself at any moment. I suppose the person you're thinking about is Miss Fyffe, though she's the one who stood to lose most by Mrs. Mansell's death."

"I wasn't really thinking of anyone in particular—" I broke off as the front doorbell pealed through the house.

"There they are—the police," Felix said. "Now keep calm and above all, don't sit staring at me as if I'd suddenly turned into a monster. You don't seriously think I'm much of a monster, do you, when all I'm trying to do is to keep out of the mess?"

"I think you're an awful fool, but that's another matter," I said and went to open the door.

It was not the police whom I found outside it, it was Barbara Gabriel.

❊ ❊ ❊

Her large, soft face had the blueish tinge of shock. Her white hair looked as if she had forgotten to comb it that morning. She was wearing grey slacks, a dark blue shirt and a bright pink cardigan which she had buttoned wrongly over her full breasts. In fact, she had the appearance of someone who has only just got dressed in a great hurry. As she came into the hall, moving heavily instead of with her usual light, bouncing tread, she seemed to become aware that the buttons on her cardigan had not found the right buttonholes and tore at them with clumsy fingers to undo them.

"Have you heard about this awful thing?" she asked. "Have the police been here?"

I almost said, "Not yet," but that would have implied some knowledge of what she was talking about. I said, "No, what's the trouble?"

"Basil," she said. "They've found him dead—stabbed—murdered!"

"Where?" I asked.

That did not sound quite right to me, but I could not think of the proper sort of thing to say when one is given such a piece of information.

"In his house," she said. "Mrs. Ransom, the woman who does for him, found him when she arrived this morning and phoned the police, and they came round to question me about him almost straight away. I was still in my dressing gown, having breakfast. I always have breakfast late. And they asked me what I was doing yesterday afternoon, because they think that's when he was killed, and they said they were checking the movements of everyone who'd seen him lately. They'd already been to see Olivia, they said. But that wasn't the real reason why they came to me, I know it wasn't. They suspect me, I know it. They've found some dreadful evidence against me."

"I'll fetch Helen and Andrew," I said. "They ought to know about this. Felix, get Barbara a drink. She could do with one."

I left her to him and ran off through the back door and across the lawn to the workshops.

Andrew said, "Damn!" when I told him what had happened, which seemed to me an inadequate reaction to my news, but it seemed that he was in the middle of a delicate operation and that interrupting it now would ruin a morning's work. However, he put his tools down and with Helen, who seemed more shocked than he did, followed me back to the house.

Felix had got Barbara settled in a chair in the living room, with a glass of whisky in her hand. She gave a little moan when she saw Helen and Andrew and started to pour out her story again.

Andrew helped us all to drinks, except for Felix, who refused one. He was evidently anxious to remain extremely sober, because apart from the fact that he never much enjoyed drinking, he had a very poor head. Particularly this was so when he was trying to contain any excitement.

Even Andrew looked concerned now. He looked at Barbara in a puzzled way and said, "But I don't understand, Barbara. Of course it was horrible for you having the police descend on you suddenly, and hearing the news like that, but why should you think they've anything special against you?"

"Because I know they have," she said. She had buttoned her cardigan correctly now, but her hair still stood on end. "They're certain to have found it."

Felix cleared his throat noisily. "I shouldn't jump to conclusions," he said, "and I'd be very careful what you say. Even though we're all friends here, rumours have an extraordinary way of getting started, and once they do they can do an awful lot of damage."

Helen gave him a look of cold surprise. "Of course we're all friends here, and if there's something Barbara wants to tell us, I can't see any harm in it."

"No, no, of course not," Felix said. "It's just that, even among friends, one can say things one regrets later. I'm sure Mrs. Gabriel thinks the police have something against her only because she's so upset at their coming to see her so soon and telling her about the tragedy. Were you much attached to Basil Deering, Mrs. Gabriel?"

"I hated him!" she answered violently.

Felix looked at Helen and Andrew. "You see," he said. "She shouldn't say that sort of thing even here."

He turned and walked away towards the window. He had gone as far as he could, short of telling Barbara that the wedding photograph of herself and Ralph Leggate was safe in his possession and not in the hands of the police, to stop her betraying her secret. But naturally she did not understand him and was determined to pour out her story to Helen and Andrew to enlist their sympathy before they heard it from anyone else. That, at least, was how I interpreted her urge to talk.

"You see, there's something Basil knew about me," she said, "which he's been holding over my head for years. Yes, really, years. And I've been paying him thousands to keep quiet about it. And really it was nothing so very awful. It never did anyone any harm. It was just something fearfully stupid I did, but it was the sort of thing which would have upset poor Nick terribly if he'd ever found out about it, and even now, if it got out—as I know it's going to get out, God help me!—it'll ruin my standing here and it may even lead to my going to prison. I don't know about that. Bigamy's a crime, isn't it, but does it still count if your husband—I mean the man who's never really been your husband because you've been married to someone else all the time—does it count if he's dead? I'm only telling you all this because I know you two are the sort of people who'll understand and won't absolutely despise me for it, as a lot of people in the village are going to. And I thought perhaps you might advise me what I ought to do and even talk to the police for me—tell them, I mean, how young I was and how difficult everything was for me. You could put it all so much better than I could. I've no one else to help me."

"Bigamy—?" Andrew began in a startled voice, then paused and after a moment went on cautiously, "You've committed bigamy and Basil's been blackmailing you for it, is that it?"

"Yes, yes, yes!" Either talking or the whisky had brought a bright flush to Barbara's cheeks. "That's what I'm telling you. It happened years ago. My first marriage, I mean. I was in London, doing my secretarial training and I hardly knew anyone and I was really very lonely. Then one day Ralph came to see me. He'd come to London too, working as a pupil in an architect's office, and he was as lonely as I was. We'd known each other since we were children, of course, both growing up here in Stillbeam. So we started going out together and somehow we convinced ourselves we were in love and we got married. We'd hardly any money. We lived in a bed-sitting room in Fulham, with a cooking stove in a cupboard and a sink out on the landing that was used by several other people, and just one lavatory to the whole house. At first it was wonderful and we were very happy. But then I got my diploma and started looking for a job and I got one with Nick's firm. And you see, I shouldn't have got it if they'd known I was married. That's how the trouble began. It wasn't nearly as easy in those days for married women to get jobs as it is now. They thought, just because you were married, that you'd be having a baby any time and leaving them, so it wouldn't be worth their while to train you. Now they know you can have a baby just as easily if you aren't married, so they don't bother so much. But anyway, when I took the job I said nothing about being married and the money

I earned was a great help. But Ralph wasn't at all happy. He hated having an office job and he hated London and he longed to be a farmer, or something like that, only of course he hadn't any capital to get started in this country. And then we started getting on one another's nerves."

She was talking in the compulsive way of someone who did not know how to stop, but she paused now for a moment, finished her whisky and looking unaware of what she was doing, held out her glass for more. Andrew refilled it, then sat down again with his gaze on her face with a brooding kind of curiosity, hardly believing, it seemed, in the woman whom she was revealing herself to be.

"Yes, we started to quarrel, and cooped up in that bed-sitting room it was terrible," she went on. "We couldn't get away from one another. And it wasn't even as if you could ever have a real quarrel with Ralph. If I annoyed him somehow, he'd just go silent—you know how he does—with a sulky look on his face that I simply couldn't bear, and sometimes that would last for days till I was near to screaming, because I'm the kind of person who flares up quickly, then gets over it. Betweenwhiles we'd talk it over and agree we'd both try harder to make things work, but they only got worse and worse. Then Ralph got an offer of a job from an old friend who'd gone to South Africa. He'd got a fruit farm and he wanted someone to help him manage it. So we agreed that Ralph should go and that I'd follow him as soon as he'd got himself established, but I think we both knew that that was never going to happen. But, of course, what we didn't know was that only a year after I'd become his secretary, Nick Gabriel would ask me to marry him."

She caught her breath in a long sigh, then looked round at us all, searching our faces for what we were making of her story. I think we were all trying to show as little as possible.

"Looking back, I know what I ought to have done," she said. "I should have told Nick the truth about my being married and gone ahead and got a divorce from Ralph for desertion. But by then I didn't even know where he was. Things hadn't worked out with the friend in South Africa and Ralph had moved on. It hadn't surprised me much. You may think he's a very quiet, controlled sort of person, quite easy to get on with, but really he's always taken offence at the slightest thing and gone into one of those awful grim moods of his, and I expect the friend hadn't been able to stand it. Anyway, I didn't know how to get in touch with him, and even if I had, I think I might have been scared of telling Nick I was married. He was a dear, conventional thing and I thought my having to go through a divorce might frighten him off. So I said nothing about Ralph, and Nick and I got married and we were wonderfully happy. As I said, my having been married before and not having had it dissolved never did him the slightest harm. I used to feel quite genuinely that that first marriage had never really happened. Then Basil appeared on the scene."

"But how had he found out about your first marriage?" Andrew asked.

"It was just by chance," she answered. "He'd known Ralph and me slightly in our Fulham days and one day he happened to see our wedding photograph in a photographer's window, and by then he'd heard I'd got married to my boss, and I suppose, even then, though I don't think he can have been more than twenty, he thought it might come in useful sometime. So he got a copy, but he didn't do anything with it till he moved down here and we met in a friend's house and he realised how rich Nick was. When that happened he started to threaten me, only laughingly at first, as if he didn't really mean it, but when I told him Ralph and I had had a divorce he laughed still more and said Somerset House had no record of it. He'd actually been to the trouble, you see, of checking up. And from then on I was at his mercy."

"And you think the police are going to find this photograph now," Andrew said, "and the whole story's going to come out."

"Of course," she said.

"But you seemed on such good terms with Basil the other evening," Helen said wonderingly. "You seemed so pleased about his engagement to Carleen. How could you be, knowing the kind of man he was?"

Barbara smiled.

"Don't you understand, that was how I managed to turn the tables on him?" she said. "Because he really wanted to marry Carleen, you know. I've no idea if it was for the sake of her money, because he wasn't so very well off himself, not nearly as much so as he liked people to think, or if he'd fallen in love with her. I suppose that could happen even to a man like him. But I remember I was very surprised when he first told me about it, because, though I knew he was always going to the bungalow, I thought it was Olivia who attracted him. She's so very much the more beautiful of the two, and much the cleverer. But perhaps she was too clever for him and saw through him, that may have been the trouble. Carleen was a sweet, gentle, romantic sort of person who I'm sure thought the world of him. So at last that gave me power over him. I knew I'd only to tell her she was marrying a common blackmailer for her to break the engagement off. I pointed that out to him. And I said that was what I'd do if he didn't hand me over my photograph and that he needn't trouble to have it copied to use again, because if he ever tried that, I'd tell Carleen the truth. So we came to an agreement that he'd give me the photograph and I'd say nothing to Carleen, and I even said I'd give that little party for them to celebrate the engagement. Can you wonder I felt like celebrating? I felt marvellous that evening, because I'd realised I actually had more power over him than he had over me. And I let him see I knew it. Oh, it felt wonderful!"

I was thinking how fantastically wrong I often was about people. From the little that I had seen of her, I had assumed that Barbara Gabriel was a simple, good-natured, rather muddle-minded woman, probably generous and loyal to her friends. Now, by her own account, she appeared crafty and ruthless, concealing her first marriage so that she could marry her rich employer, perhaps even helping to dispatch her first husband to South Africa to make the second marriage possible, then, when she found herself in the horrible toils of a blackmailer, using her friendship for another woman to escape from him.

But she herself seemed unaware that this was the picture of herself that she had painted. Whether or not she noticed the shocked way that Helen and Andrew, and I, too, were looking at her, I did not know, but I did not think so. She felt sure that the fact of her bigamy would not horrify any of us too deeply, and it did not occur to her that, even if it did not, we might recoil from the conscienceless way in which she had treated Carleen Mansell. My impression of Barbara now was that she was the kind of person who has a kind of innocence because she sees all her own actions as beyond criticism, and if at any time she encounters it, feels for certain that it can only be the result of some cruel misunderstanding.

Felix, strolling back from the window where he had been standing while she was talking, was the only one of us who showed no surprise or disapproval. He expected so little of other people that it was easy for him to readjust his view of them.

"But you haven't told us the worst thing that Deering's been holding over you, have you, Mrs. Gabriel?" he said.

She promptly began to cry. The tears ran down her big face with the pretty little features in the middle of it like tears spilling down the cheeks of a child.

I did not know what Felix was talking about, but someone crying always moves me and I found myself all at once feeling sorry for her. No one had ever tried to blackmail me, so I did not know how I might behave, what desperate action I might take, what friend I might sacrifice, if such a thing should happen to me.

"Someone told me recently, I can't remember just who it was," I said, "that bigamy isn't treated as such a terrible offence nowadays, so even if the police find your photograph, and very likely they won't, they may not make any serious trouble for you. I shouldn't be too worried."

"That may or may not be true," Felix said sternly, just as if he had not been pointing out the advantages of bigamy only the day before, "but it's a very serious offence to defraud the Inland Revenue. You can inherit from a spouse without paying death duties, and that's what you did when Nicholas Gabriel died, isn't it? But since you were never legally married to him, the tax you should have paid must have been considerable. It was to keep that quiet, wasn't it, that you've been paying Basil Deering blackmail?"

# Chapter Six

A fresh cascade of tears was Barbara's answer to Felix.

"I know, I know," she spluttered through them. "But what was I to do? I didn't want to defraud anyone, but how could I pay the taxes I owed without giving it away that Nick and I had never really been married? Sometimes I thought, to be on the safe side, that I'd send the Customs and Excise people a money order anonymously. I believe people sometimes do that when they've fiddled their income tax. They call it conscience money. Then I realised that if they didn't know where it came from I shouldn't be protected. And I couldn't face the truth coming out. But now it's sure to and there's no way I can stop it."

"Did Ralph know you were being blackmailed?" Andrew said.

"Yes, of course," Barbara answered. "I told him about it as soon as he came to live here. It was funny, wasn't it, the way we both came back to where we grew up? He advised me not to pay, because he said Basil had nothing to gain by giving me away and his only real hold on me was my fear of him. I'm sure Ralph was right, but I hadn't the courage to try it."

"Did Basil ever try to blackmail him, because I suppose condoning bigamy is an offence of some sort?" Andrew said.

"I don't think so," she replied. "Ralph never said anything about it, and I think he would have if it had happened. He and I get on pretty well these days. We're not bad friends, everything considered. And he hasn't much money, you know. I don't think Basil could have got much out of him, even if he'd tried."

"Ralph has never put any pressure on you himself?"

"Oh, good heavens, no. He wants to keep things quiet as much as I do."

"If I may offer some advice," Felix said, "I really wouldn't tell the police any of this until they start asking you questions about it. Once they do that, it might be advisable to stick to the truth, but till then I wouldn't give away anything you can avoid. Least said, soonest mended—it's an excellent maxim."

Andrew gave him another of his thoughtful looks. I was sure that he no longer took Felix at face value and that soon he was going to have to give more of an account of himself than he had done so far. But the time for this was put off by the arrival of Superintendent Pryor and Sergeant Waller.

Finding Barbara with us, Mr. Pryor said that he supposed that we had heard from her of Mr. Deering's death and he then went on to ask all the questions that might have been expected—where each of us had been the afternoon before, when we had seen Basil Deering last, had he ever spoken to us about an enemy, or of fearing for his life. Not one of us had an alibi. Helen and Andrew had been in their workshops, I had been alone in the garden after Felix had left me, and then in the living room, reading, and Felix, following my advice, said that he had been for a walk and had actually passed Basil Deering's house at about the time when, according to Mr. Pryor, the murder had probably been committed, but had seen nothing suspicious.

Felix was further still from telling the truth, however, when he was asked for his address and what his occupation was. He gave the address in Little Carbery Street correctly, but said nothing about being a private detective. As he had told me when he first arrived, he said that he had recently left a firm of secondhand-car dealers for whom he had worked for a number of years and was now taking a rest. He added that he had recently written a number of poems and had hoped to be able to discuss them with Basil Deering, whom he very much admired.

Barbara, who had been questioned already, was not questioned again. She had mopped up her tears, but sitting listening as the rest of us were, there was an air of growing tension about her. She seemed to expect that the very next question was bound to be about the wedding photograph which she thought the police must certainly have found by now, and when the question did not come, seemed to be plunged only deeper into fear and bewilderment.

Mr. Pryor gave us some information which I did not find as surprising as the others, though I tried to look as if I did. He and the sergeant were at the door, about to leave when he paused and his sadly sceptical gaze, without settling on any of us in particular, yet seemed to take us all in.

"An odd thing about this crime," he said, "is that the motive may have been robbery. Yet the only thing we're sure was stolen was an object of no great value, or so we've been given to understand. It was a carved ivory frog. Mr. Deering's daily, Mrs. Ransom, who discovered the body and phoned us, noticed that it was missing. The reason that she did so is that apparently she was particularly attached to it. She'd given it a name. She called it Percy. She admits she might be mistaken as to its value and that a knowledgeable thief might have recognised that and thought it was worth taking, but she swears Mr. Deering told her it was only something he'd picked up quite cheaply on a visit to Singapore. So in a house containing a number of valuable things, including some good silver and a wallet with over two hundred pounds in it, just this one item was taken. If the motive was robbery, that was distinctly odd, don't you agree? And you can say the same if the reason for taking the frog was to make the motive for the murder look like robbery, when really it was something else. Why take just the frog? Why not something more obvious?"

"Perhaps the chap collects frogs," Felix said, "as some people collect china cats or those Staffordshire dogs that watch you with that awful stare."

I thought that he would have been much wiser to remain silent, but Mr. Pryor nodded.

"Perhaps," he said. "The explanation is probably something simple like that. There's another interesting fact, however. The murderer appears to have been of a nervous disposition. After forcing an entry to the house by a window, committing the murder and calmly pocketing the frog, he went into the garden and vomited. An alternative, of course, is that there were two people in that house yesterday afternoon. One did the murder and departed, the other stumbled on the body, perhaps while he was prowling about the house, seeing what he could pick up, and promptly threw up his lunch. If that's what happened, we'd very much like to talk to that person."

It might have been only my imagination, but my impression was that as he spoke his gaze lingered for a moment longer on Felix than on any of the rest of us, then he and the sergeant said goodbye and left. Felix crushed the stub of the cigarette that he had been smoking into an ashtray, promptly lit another and strolled away to the window again.

Barbara Gabriel stood up.

"Aren't they cruel?" she exclaimed. "Playing cat and mouse with me! They're keeping me on tenterhooks on purpose. I suppose Felix was right and it was best not to tell them anything, but now there's nothing I can do till they pounce. Oh God, I don't think I've ever felt so terrible in my life! I'll go home now. Thank you for listening to me."

"Stay to lunch," Helen said, automatically hospitable.

"No, thank you. Anyway, I couldn't eat anything." Barbara was suddenly in a hurry to be gone.

Helen saw her to the door, then came back and suggested that Andrew should top up our drinks. He did so in an absent-minded way, pondering something deeply.

After a moment he said, "Felix, why did you really come here? You don't really admire Basil and you haven't the slightest interest in his verse and you haven't been writing verse yourself. Basil was important to you in some way, I realise that, but not for the reasons you've given. What were they? After what's happened you may as well take us into your confidence."

Felix said nothing.

Andrew went on, "You were feeling pretty ill, weren't you, when you came back from your walk yesterday evening? You looked as if you'd just been as sick as a dog. And someone, we've just been told, vomited in Basil's garden. Is that a coincidence?"

"Why not?" Felix said, still with his back to the room. "I must have picked up a bug when I was in Wandlebury, and I expect the murderer did too. These things get around, once they start. They're very infectious."

"They'll probably analyze the vomit," Andrew said. For someone so small and generally unkempt, he was capable of assuming a disconcerting air of authority. "Would it be very surprising if they find bread and cheese in it? Possibly they'll even be able to identify Blue Cheshire."

"What a revolting thing to talk about!" Helen exclaimed. "I was going to suggest getting lunch, but you've put me right off the thought of it. I was feeling queasy enough already, thinking of poor Basil. And there's really nothing in the fridge but some more of that Blue Cheshire. I'm going back to do some work before I eat anything. Help yourselves when you feel like it."

She went out. Andrew stayed where he was for a moment, looking at Felix's back, then shrugged his shoulders and followed her.

When they had gone, Felix turned to face me.

"I'm going into Wandlebury for lunch," he said. "Feel like coming with me?"

"If you like," I said. "But why are you going?"

"I think perhaps cheese disagrees with me. Besides that, there are one or two errands I want to do."

"Such as?"

"I want to telephone the office, for one thing. It may be a long call and I don't think it ought to go on the Boscotts' bill."

"You mean you're afraid one of them may come in in the middle of it. Why didn't you confide in them, Felix? Why didn't you tell Andrew what you're doing here?"

"You don't understand," he said plaintively.

"No, I don't. You could trust them not to give you away."

"I don't feel like trusting anyone at the moment. Anyway, are you coming?"

"All right."

We went to the garage. Felix backed his car out of it, I got in beside him and we started down the drive, then turned into the lane and went on along the main road to Wandlebury.

He was silent for a time and I did not try to make him talk because I felt that if he was not in the mood to do so it was a pointless exercise. Either he would not answer at all, or I should be met with obvious evasions. But after we had left the village behind and were on a long stretch of road with a golden chequerboard of cornfields on either side of it, he spoke abruptly.

"What you don't understand is that it's best for Helen and Andrew not to know what I was doing yesterday, or why I came here. It isn't that I don't trust them. It's just that if I told them the truth I'd be putting them in the position of either having to lie to the police about me, or of giving me away. I'm thinking of Helen mostly. I think Andrew would give me away without any violent qualms, but Helen would be badly upset at having to make the choice. She's very fond of you and she'd be sure that giving me away would distress you far more than I imagine it would. But at the same time, lying to the police isn't within her range. She thinks of them as the guardians of society, with a right she'd never dream of questioning to authority over her. She's glad that they're there, she feels they protect her, and she feels that she owes it to them to tell them everything she knows."

"Well, so do I," I said, "and I don't like the position you've put me in at all."

"But you know me," he said. "You know that if I went in for a little breaking and entering it was in a good cause, even if it wasn't strictly legal, and you aren't suddenly going to start feeling suspicious that I murdered Deering, so you aren't too seriously worried."

He was right that I did not suspect him of the murder. One of the few things about Felix of which I was absolutely sure was that violence frightened and repelled him. Of course, I could not say for certain how he would act if he was cornered and was truly afraid for himself. None of us who have lived comfortably sheltered lives can ever say this for sure. Perhaps he would find the courage to fight back rather than let himself be finished off without a struggle. But it would be strictly a last resort. And Basil Deering, so he had told me, had been stabbed in the back, so it looked as if at the moment he had not been trying to attack his murderer, and I was quite ready to believe Felix that the mere sight of the dead body had been enough to make him rush out into the garden and throw up.

"How much of all this are you going to tell your boss?" I asked.

"I haven't quite made up my mind," he said. "I don't know them very well yet and I'm not sure how far they'll back me if I get into trouble with the police. Not very far, I feel. They'll say I was exceeding my instructions, and among other things I'll find myself out of a job. So I'm going to be a bit careful."

"You know, Felix, I don't think you're going to make a very good detective," I said. "Oughtn't you to be tough and strong and ruthless?"

"Most of the ones I've met so far have been furtive little men with chronic colds, from all the hours they have to spend lurking in dark doorways. And you must remember, I've got imagination, which is the vital thing. You can go a long way on imagination."

"Too far, sometimes."

He shook his head. "We've never agreed about that. Well, never mind. Let's have a good lunch. The food in that pub I stayed in wasn't at all bad."

❧ ❧ ❧

The hotel to which he referred was in the marketplace of Wandlebury. It was market day and the square was full of stalls of vegetables and flowers and cheap cotton dresses on hangers and brightly coloured plastic goods and a slow-moving stream of buyers, looking for bargains which they were most unlikely to find. One side of the square consisted of a not very impressive Victorian Gothic church, flanked by two banks, one side of the usual row of chain stores, Boot's, Woolworth's, Smith's, one of small, cosy, remarkably expensive shops, and one of the hotel to which we made our way once Felix had parked the car, a few more banks, a post office and two or three travel agents.

The hotel was nearly the only Georgian building left of those that surrounded the marketplace. It was a square, pleasant-looking building of weathered red brick, with a handsome portico and a glimpse through sash windows of a spacious dining room, in which tables covered with white tablecloths were set agreeably far apart. It had a look of peaceful comfort and of considerable expense, but luckily I had brought a fair amount of money with me, because I had known that when it came to paying the bill, Felix, although maintaining the fiction that he was host, would reach for my handbag and help himself from it. He always did it when we met for a meal, just as if we were still married.

We had excellent steaks, a carafe of red wine and coffee. I remembered that Felix intended to make a goulash that evening and thought that I should not want much of it. All the same, the good food made me feel better after the distressing morning.

We had arrived at the hotel late for lunch and by the time that we were finished we were the only people left in the dining room.

"What now?" I asked.

"I'm going to make that telephone call to the office," Felix said. "Then I want to go to the post office."

"What for?"

"I want a couple of registered envelopes."

"One to send your client's letters to the office in," I said. "Why d'you want the other one?"

"To send Barbara Gabriel her photograph, of course. You didn't think I was going to keep it, did you?"

"I hadn't really thought about it."

"That's why I wanted to come to Wandlebury. If I'd posted it in Stillbeam she might have guessed who it came from. Naturally I'd have liked to give it to her this morning to put the poor woman out of her agony, only I couldn't do that without giving it away that I'd been in Deering's house. But if I post it to her now, without any covering letter, there's no reason for her to guess who sent it."

"Has it struck you," I said, "that once Carleen was dead, Barbara was back in Basil's power? She'd a hold over him as long as he'd a wife whom she could tell about his unpleasant activities, but with her gone, Barbara was back where she was before."

Felix looked interested. "I hadn't actually thought that out, but you're quite right, of course."

"So, after all, it isn't so very improbable that we've two murderers, is it? One was an ordinary thief who killed Carleen because she caught him in the house, and the other was Barbara, who may have been more than usually in a mood for murder just because for a little while she'd felt so safe. I like that theory."

"It isn't bad. But can you really see Barbara Gabriel as a murderess?"

"After this morning I can. I don't think she's got much of a conscience."

"That's just because you take such a poor view of bigamy, and because you'd never be such a fool as to start paying blackmail yourself. You're the kind of person who'd say, 'Publish and be damned!' "

"I'm not at all sure that I should. I realised this morning that I hadn't the faintest idea how I'd react if someone got hold of something about me that I couldn't bear to have known. The trouble is, I've led such a humdrum life, I don't think I've ever done anything that could be used against me."

"You have, you know."

The elderly waitress was hovering near us, flicking imaginary crumbs from tables that had been stripped of their cutlery and trying to will us to leave.

"What?" I asked.

"You've condoned my breaking and entering, you haven't told the police half of what you know, you know I helped myself to Percy, you failed to report a murder—oh, you've quite a score against you."

"But what I know is all hearsay," I said. "And, anyway, you're my husband. I can't give evidence against you."

"I'm glad you sometimes remember that, and of course your secret is quite safe with me." He stood up. "Now I'll make that telephone call. It may take quite a while. You'd better wait for me in the lounge."

There were some telephone boxes in the lobby and Felix shut himself into one of them while I went on to the lounge. It was a big room full of cretonne-covered easy chairs and little round tables. Seated at one of these tables, with a tiny tray of coffee before them, were Olivia Fyffe and Ralph Leggate.

I did not want to join them. I would have liked to sit down in a corner and commune with myself for a while. I needed some quiet. It seemed to me that ever since Felix had arrived in Stillbeam too many things had been happening, and though they were not his fault, I felt as if his coming had triggered them off. Certainly if he had not appeared I should not have found myself as much involved with them as I was. I could have continued my restful holiday, which I had been enjoying so much until he had intruded upon it, without being too much disturbed by the fact that there had been two murders in the neighbourhood. I could have talked them over with Helen and Andrew, agreeing with them that it was terrible that such things happened so frequently nowadays, but as I had hardly any knowledge of the victims, I need not have felt much more about them than I should have if I had read an account of them in a newspaper.

I did not think that Olivia and Ralph wanted to see me any more than I wanted to see them, but they were mannerly people and made vaguely welcoming noises, so that I had to go over to them and in a minute found myself sitting in one of the chairs at their table. I told them that I was waiting for Felix, who was making a telephone call.

"We came out to escape the press," Olivia said. "They got the news that Carleen had been found almost as soon as I did and descended in force. Ralph rescued me and brought me here. You've heard about Basil, of course."

There was no sign of hysteria about her today. She was composed and spoke almost casually. Yet I had had an impression, as I walked across the room towards them, that she and Ralph had been quarrelling. At least, she had been doing her best to quarrel with him, while he had been sitting very still and, as usual, saying nothing. She had been leaning forward, speaking rapidly and hitting one knee with a clenched fist, trying to ram home some point which he could not or did not want to understand. But as soon as I joined them she had relaxed, giving me a grave, sad, smile.

In a pallid, washed-out way, with an air of great weariness about her, she was looking very lovely. Her smooth golden hair was drawn straight back from her face and pinned up in a roll, which gave her delicate features, with the touch of arrogance about them that I had noticed the first time that I saw her, almost a kind of nakedness that enhanced their beauty. They had a fine-drawn look of strain. She was wearing a dark green linen suit and I remembered that she had been wearing black when I had first seen her, and guessed that she usually wore dark colours to make the most of her fairness.

"I'm sorry you've been drawn into these troubles of ours," she went on. "It doesn't seem fair on you. I suppose the police have been to see you."

"Yes, this morning," I said.

"Asking for alibis?"

"Yes. As it happened, not one of us had one."

"You haven't any motive either. I don't expect they'll bother you again. Does it sound callous if I say I'm glad they've found Carleen? I started wondering quite seriously, you know, if I was going mad. Finding her body missing when I knew she couldn't have got up and walked away was about the worst shock I've ever had in my life. Worse than finding her dead. That was terrible, but in its way it was at least natural. But that empty room frightened me beyond endurance."

"Don't keep on talking about it," Ralph said with a touch of bluster in his tone. "Try not to think about it."

Though he had glanced at me briefly when I had joined them, his gaze had immediately gone back to Olivia and now was fixed steadily on her. Yet there was something hostile in it. It brought back my feeling that my arrival had interrupted a quarrel.

"As if I could!" she said. "I've a feeling it's something I'm never going to be able to stop thinking about. Not for the rest of my life. Of course, I know that isn't so. One can get over the worst imaginable things that can happen to one if one's got the courage. But it doesn't help to try to dodge them at the time. One's got to live through one's grief, not run away from it."

His quiet anger seemed to grow. "But there's no need to wallow in it."

"Ah, you've got that wonderful stiff upper lip that used to be thought of so highly." She turned back to me. "Have you the impression that I have that it's rather gone out? Perhaps it was just the empire that made it a necessity. It seems to me we're all much less afraid than we used to be of showing our emotions."

It seemed to me that of the two of them, Olivia was showing far less emotion than Ralph. But what he was showing was relatively simple. It was the fierce sense of frustration of a man in love who was being firmly kept at a distance. What Olivia's feelings about him were I could not tell. She had been angry with him when I arrived and was concealing that fact now, but whether it had been merely because she found his love for her, particularly at that time, an irritant, or for some more hidden reason, I had no idea.

Felix came in then and saying that he and I must not stay because we had a number of odds and ends to do in Wandlebury, promptly sat down and told Olivia how much he sympathised with her for the loss of her sister and also of her friend, Basil Deering.

"No friend of mine," she answered. "D'you know, Ralph's been trying to persuade me to contest Carleen's will. I don't want to do it. I won't. She'd a right to leave her money as she chose."

"But now that Basil's dead too," Ralph said, "God knows where that money will go to. Probably to someone Carleen never heard of. It ought to come to you. It's yours."

She shrugged her shoulders, then told Felix what she had told me, that it had been a relief to have Carleen's body discovered, because at least it had reassured her of her sanity.

He nodded sympathetically. "I know how you feel. The fear that we could go mad is almost the worst fear there is, isn't it? It happened to me once. I'd been to the South of France and on my way home I stayed for a few days in Marseilles and there I got talking to a friendly stranger who happened to have a parcel that he wanted delivered in London. He didn't trust the post, he said, such a lot of things seemed to get stolen and this parcel was of great sentimental value. Can you believe it, I fell for the story? But I was very young then—just a student—and when you're young enough you have a kind of invulnerable feeling. You don't believe that anything really bad can happen to you."

He smiled reminiscently, apparently picturing to himself that idiotic young man.

"Anyway, I took the parcel," he said, "and tucked it away in my rucksack, hoping that I shouldn't have to open it at the Customs. Then on the train my rucksack was stolen. I couldn't imagine why, because there was nothing in it but a couple of dirty shirts and my swimming trunks and some paperbacks, apart from the stranger's parcel. Well, I got hold of the guard and told him what had happened, but my French wasn't up to much and perhaps because I hadn't the money to tip him he wouldn't do anything, so I decided not to bother. I hadn't got the stranger's address, so I couldn't write to him to tell him what had happened, but I had the telephone number of the person to whom the parcel was to be delivered, so when I got back to London I phoned him and told him about the theft and that night two men with guns came to my bed-sitting room and marched me out into the street and down a dark alley, asking me all the time what I'd really done with the parcel, and when I couldn't tell them, beat me up."

He laughed at himself.

"Of course, by then even I had realised that the parcel contained drugs. But I simply couldn't believe it was all happening. I felt that I'd somehow strayed into one of the thrillers I'd been reading and that at any moment I was going to come to the end of the chapter and that everything would be all right, because in that sort of book the hero always comes off best. But perhaps I wasn't the real hero of that story. Anyway, they beat me unconscious and left me. I came to in hospital and when I asked to see the police they wouldn't believe a word I said. It seems I stank of whisky when they picked me up and they were sure I'd got into a drunken brawl and was trying to cover it up. And after a bit I began to think they must be right. It seemed a lot more probable than what had happened. And then, when I got home, I began to think I was being followed about and I kept expecting to see the two men with guns, come to beat me up again, and that's a sure sign of paranoia, isn't it? So I actually went to see a psychiatrist, and luckily for me he was a very sound chap who managed to persuade me that everything I told him had really happened. It was an enormous relief."

I had heard this story before and not a word of it was true. As a matter of fact, I had been with Felix when he had watched the film from which he had taken it. A minor inaccuracy in it was that he had ever been a student. He had had a moderately good education, either, as he usually claimed, at one of the less-distinguished public schools, or else, as I had heard him let slip, at the local grammar school, but then, as soon as he could, he had left home and begun his career of drifting from job to job. He was a little hazy about it all. The one thing about his youth of which I was sure was that he had hated his father, who I believed, though I was not certain, had been in the army, but whether he had been the colonel that Felix asserted, or at most a sergeant, I could not have said. At all events, he had represented to Felix the authority that he had rejected all his life and against which he was struggling, after his fashion, to that day.

I thought that Olivia did not believe the story either, but it amused her and she was grateful to Felix for telling it. Possibly, for a few minutes, it had taken her mind off the deaths that were so close to her. When she smiled at him, Felix's blue eyes sparkled. I thought that if he stayed on in Stillbeam for a little while and saw some more of Olivia it might make him forget his alcoholic love. But I did not think that Olivia, without her sister's money, was quite rich enough to make a suitable wife for him. Only living in a very high state of luxury would ever keep him straight.

He stood up. "Well, Virginia and I must go. Come along, Virginia."

He made it sound as if it had been I who had been delaying him there.

Olivia looked up at him. "Will you tell me something, are you two married?"

"Nominally," I said, "but separated several years ago."

"You should keep hold of him," she said. "There can't be a dull moment while he's around."

"I like dull moments," I said. "My nervous system requires them."

She seemed sorry that we were leaving. The person who looked glad to see us go was Ralph Leggate. Yet when I glanced back at them from the door it looked to me as if their quarrel had been resumed. He was sitting upright in his chair in stiff-backed silence while Olivia was talking to him in a rapid undertone, once more striking her knee with her fist.

❀ ❀ ❀

We went to the post office where Felix bought two registered envelopes, stuffed some letters into one of them and Barbara Gabriel's wedding photograph into the other, addressed them and posted them. We walked back through the crowded marketplace to where he had parked the car.

As he started it, I said, "I'm sorry for Ralph Leggate. He's in a rather appalling position. I'm sure he'd like to marry Olivia, but he can't because he's married to Barbara, and he can't go ahead and get a divorce without giving away the fact that he's been covering up her bigamy for years. Yet he probably only did that out of good nature, before he thought he might want to get married again himself."

Felix drove for a little way in silence, then asked in a troubled voice, "Do you think he really wants to marry Olivia?"

"He's in love with her," I said, "whatever he means to do about it."

"Is she in love with him?"

"I doubt it. But she's reached an age when getting married may seem a good idea. It may be now or never."

"Well, she can't marry Leggate, that's certain."

"Even if he says nothing about being married to Barbara, who, for her own sake, wouldn't give him away?"

"But she's told the whole story to Helen and Andrew, not to mention you and me."

"Would you give him away? I thought you thought bigamy a trifling matter."

"I certainly don't. You've deliberately misunderstood me," he said stiffly. "Simply because I told you I was thinking of getting married again, but that I hated the thought of going through a divorce, you've acted as if I'd said I was contemplating committing bigamy. You know that isn't true."

"I suppose what you've run into here is enough to have put you off the idea," I said. "You've realised you'd be a sitting duck for blackmail."

"That isn't the point at all. If two people get married, I think they ought to be completely open with one another."

"As you were with me?"

"Didn't I tell you all the important things about myself?"

"Some of them."

"I was young then," he said. "I hadn't thought these things out. And I was so crazily in love with you, d'you know that, that I thought that if you knew the worst about me I'd lose you."

"The funny thing is, you wouldn't have," I said, "because I was just as much in love with you. It was finding things out slowly, one at a time, never getting to the end of it, that was so catastrophic."

He gave an impatient shake of his head. "You took it all too seriously. But I can tell you, if Leggate tries to marry Olivia, I shall interfere."

"I'm surprised," I said. "I really am. It isn't like you. I feel uneasy, somehow, when you start acting out of character. Couldn't you at least leave it to Helen and Andrew to act as they think they ought to?"

"They're too—well, too good-mannered to do anything. They might remonstrate with Leggate on the quiet, but they'd never bring anything into the open. Tell me, d'you think Leggate will still want to marry Olivia if she hasn't got her sister's money?"

"I don't think it'll make the least difference to him," I said. "He's infatuated."

"But he was trying to persuade her to contest Carleen's will."

"Probably for her own sake, rather than his."

"I wonder what sort of person her sister really was," Felix said unexpectedly sombrely.

We were driving through the suburbs of Wandlebury, an area of neat bungalows, built cheek to cheek, standing in small, beautifully manicured gardens. The road was quiet, without much traffic, though a number of children on bicycles swooped dangerously by along the pavements.

"What do you mean?" I asked after I had failed to work out why Felix's interest had suddenly switched to Carleen Mansell.

"Just that it could be an explanation of everything," he said. "We don't know much about her, do we?"

"Just that she was quiet and sweet and romantic."

"That's what Barbara said about her. Didn't Andrew say she was as tough as nails?"

"I think it was just his idea that a successful career woman like Carleen has to have at least a certain kind of toughness. And perhaps in her professional life she had. On the other hand, the tough one of the combination, who managed their affairs, may have been Olivia."

"All the same, I'd like to know the truth about Carleen," Felix said. "D'you know anything about her husband?"

I tried to remember what I had heard about him, but it was not very much. I knew that he had died soon after he and Carleen had come to live in Stillbeam. He had been a good deal older than she was and had just retired. I believed he had been a successful accountant who had acted for the sisters before the marriage. I did not know if anything special had brought them to the neighbourhood, or whether they had simply happened on a house that they liked and had settled there more or less by chance. His death was spoken of as very sad, coming just when he had begun to enjoy his life in the country, and I had always taken for granted, going by the way that people referred to it, that the marriage had been a happy one. But that was all that I could tell Felix, and it was not what he wanted.

"Don't you know anything about what kind of man he was?" he asked.

We were in the open country by now, among the corn-fields. The afternoon was finer than the morning had been and sunshine lay warm and golden on the wheat.

"I don't think I've ever thought about it," I said. "People tend to talk about him as Carleen's husband, not as anyone in himself."

"So in spite of being so sweet and gentle, she was a bit dominant."

"She may have been. I don't know."

"His death was unquestionably natural, was it? There were never any suspicions about it?"

"Of course there weren't. Felix, what *are* you thinking about?"

"I'm just floundering around," he said, "looking at every aspect. I'd very much like to solve this thing. It would put me in good standing with the firm."

"You haven't got a client," I said. "Who's going to pay you?"

"Not necessarily anyone, if I don't take too long about it. The firm would like to be able to hand the police the solution on a plate. It would be good for their prestige. They need that. They're a very small firm."

"I'd leave it to the police, if I were you."

"But, as we both know, you are not me and I am not you, and after all these years we're as far from understanding each other as we ever were."

"I know. It's sad."

The sadness of it silenced me for the rest of the drive. As long as I did not see too much of him, I always enjoyed Felix's company and when I was in the mood to do so, used to catch myself turning over in my mind the possibility that even now we might make a tolerable success of our marriage. Often, living by myself, I felt very lonely and would sometimes long to reach for the telephone just to talk to him for a little and perhaps arrange a meeting. But I knew it would be hopeless if I ever let him move into my life again, apart from the fact that I doubted if he still had any desire to do so. Going our separate ways had been as much of a liberation for him as it had for me.

Reaching the Boscotts' house, he drove into the garage, then as we got out of the car he turned, not towards the house but towards the workshops.

"Where are you going?" I called after him.

"I want to talk to Helen," he said. "I want to ask her what she knows about Mansell."

# Chapter Seven

Felix returned to the house in a short time, but instead of coming to tell me what, if anything, Helen had told him about Carleen's husband, he went to the kitchen and began preparations for his goulash. I left him to it. Felix in the role of detective was something that I found difficult to take seriously. However, he seemed to be taking it very seriously himself, as he did most of his fantasies while they lasted, and he would only be irritated if I interrupted his present daydream.

Soon I smelt frying onions, then other savoury smells. I settled down in the living room with my book and after a little while Helen joined me there. As she dropped limply into a chair she looked tired and troubled.

"Felix seems to have taken over the kitchen," she said. "I'm so thankful. I've been wondering what on earth to cook this evening that wouldn't take any trouble at all. After what's happened I don't seem able to think about food."

"It's his way of showing gratitude for your hospitality," I said. "It'll probably be very good."

"He's been asking me some rather odd questions about Godfrey Mansell," she went on. "I couldn't tell him much.

Virginia, what is he really doing here? Do you know, or has he been as mysterious with you as he has with Andrew and me?"

"He's always been a mystery to me," I replied evasively, as usual doing my best to protect him from other people's probing. That was a habit that I could not shake off. "I do my best not to think too much about it. Did you know Godfrey Mansell?"

"Oh yes, but not very well. He didn't spend much of his time here. He was an accountant who handled Carleen's and Olivia's affairs and his office was in London. He only came here for weekends. I believe they chose Stillbeam because he'd got a sister living in Wandlebury. I only met her once and that was at Godfrey's funeral, but I believe she and Carleen were friends. In fact, I've an idea that it may have been through knowing the sister that Carleen and Olivia went to him to sort out their income tax for them when they first started making a lot of money, but I may be wrong about that."

"What did he die of?"

"Felix asked me that. He seemed to be wondering if it had really been a natural death. He's rather got murder on the brain, hasn't he? I told him he could put that idea out of his head. It was cancer of the throat."

"There's no doubt about that?"

"Absolutely none. He died in Wandlebury Infirmary a day or two after they operated. Virginia, you're being as puzzling as Felix. Do tell me what's on your mind."

"I don't know myself," I said. "I'm just trying to follow his thought processes. Did he seem disappointed that you couldn't tell him more?"

"No, he seemed quite pleased. He wanted to know whether or not Godfrey's sister was married. I told him she wasn't."

I could think of only one reason why Felix had wanted to know that. If Godfrey Mansell's sister was unmarried her name would still be Mansell, and he would be able to find it in the telephone directory, would be able to get in touch with her and perhaps even go to see her. But why he should want to do so, unless out of sheer inquisitiveness, was beyond me.

"Did he want to know anything else?" I asked.

"I don't think so," Helen said. "Oh yes, he did. He asked me if Godfrey had been an attractive man. That seemed to me a very odd question. I said not specially to me, though I supposed he was good-looking, but it was in an awfully obvious sort of way, if you know what I mean, that never appealed to me much."

Coming from Helen, who to the best of my knowledge had never looked at any other man once she had met Andrew, that was not a surprising answer. But I found Felix's question surprising. I could not link it to anything in the present situation. However, it was always possible that there was no link. Felix might have asked it only to conceal where his real interest lay, which I thought was certainly in Miss Mansell.

I found that I was right in this next morning when he brought me my early cup of tea. We had spent a quiet evening, watching television after eating Felix's dish, which he had modestly called stew and which had been excellent, then we had all gone to bed early. Coming into my bedroom, carrying two cups, he gave one to me, then sat down on the edge of my bed and sipped the hot tea from the cup that he had brought for himself.

"I want to go into Wandlebury this morning," he said. "Do you want to come with me?"

"You're visiting Miss Mansell, I suppose," I said.

"That's right—Miss Alice Mansell. I found her address in the phone book." He looked at me curiously. "How did you guess?"

"I've been talking to Helen too."

"Then you think it's a good idea."

"I can't see any point in it at all."

He looked relieved, because that told him that I had not fathomed his reason for wanting to talk to Miss Mansell, of which he wanted to make a little mystery.

"Perhaps there isn't really any point," he said, "but it might be useful. The more we know about the background of the case, the better, don't you think?"

"I've told you I think it would be best if you'd leave the whole thing to the police," I said. "When do we go?"

"I'll ring her up presently and make an appointment. It's too early to do it now. I'll try after breakfast. I'm glad you're coming, because we can talk over what she says and see if we agree about the meaning of it. One's own recollections of a conversation aren't always reliable. One tends to remember what one said oneself so much more clearly than what the other person said."

"Do you think she murdered Carleen and Basil?"

"Now you're trying to be annoying. Of course not."

"Why not?"

He appeared to consider it. "Perhaps one shouldn't rule it out as a possibility. We'll know more about that when we've talked to her."

"I don't think we shall. But if going to see her will stop you doing other crazy things, like breaking into people's houses and stealing their frogs, I'm all for it."

"Good. Well, I'll see you later."

He finished his tea and left me.

He said nothing about Miss Mansell to Helen and Andrew at breakfast and waited until they had gone to their workshops before making his telephone call. I listened while he did it. His tone was quiet and businesslike. Apparently he was not asked his reason for wanting an appointment, the only explanation he gave of why he did being the statement that he and his wife were friends of Mr. and Mrs. Boscott and were staying with them in Stillbeam. But that must have told Miss Mansell, who would have read of the Stillbeam murders by now in her morning newspaper, even if she had not already been visited by the police, that our desire to see her had something to do with her sister-in-law's death. It appeared that she was quite ready to talk about it, for she gave Felix some directions how to find her house, which he noted down on an envelope.

When he put down the telephone he said to me in a satisfied tone, "We're seeing her in half an hour. We needn't tell

Helen and Andrew anything about it. I don't think they ever wonder what other people are doing. They're wonderfully fortunate, aren't they, to have found work that absorbs them so completely?"

"Your new job seems to be absorbing you pretty completely," I said. "One might almost say it obsesses you."

"Do you mind that?" he said. "You used always to be on at me to dedicate myself to something or other."

That was true, though in the long-ago days of which he was speaking I had thought in terms of his somehow turning out to have gifts as an actor, or a barrister, or even a parson, or anything which would provide an outlet for his histrionic abilities. It had never entered my head that he might some day become a detective.

The morning was fine and growing hotter as the sun rose higher. The sky was a glittering blue and without clouds. Passing the Hare and Hounds in the village, I saw several cars parked outside it and thought that the press was increasing in its numbers. Two murders, naturally, have more than double the interest of one. I was glad that the reporters so far had not sought out Helen and Andrew.

We had some difficulty in finding Miss Mansell's house, because Felix found that the jottings that he had made of her directions were illegible. But we had to stop and ask the way only twice before we found the street in which she lived. It was a quiet street of semi-detached Victorian houses, all built of yellowish brick, with robinias shading the pavements and small front gardens, most of them turned into unenterprising rockeries.

In one of them a woman with her back to us was working away with a trowel. Stooping, her hindquarters looked massive. Her legs, streaked with varicose veins, were bare and she was wearing a much-washed cotton dress which was so short that it had to date from several years ago. The number on her gate was the one for which we were looking.

It squeaked as Felix pushed it open and she straightened and turned, rubbing her back where the stooping had stiffened it.

122  *E. X. Ferrars*

"Mr. and Mrs. Freer?" she said. "Good morning. I'm Alice Mansell."

She stripped off one of the gardening gloves that she was wearing and shook hands with both of us. She had a square, plain face with a long, broad nose and a heavy jaw, yet with something pleasing about it that came from friendly grey eyes and a wide, agreeable mouth.

"Terrible, all this," she said cheerfully. Murder did not appear to depress her. "No end to it. Never is."

Felix agreed sadly, "Yes, we live in a violent age. It's very shocking."

"I was talking about the weeds," she said. "I never get really on top of them. And with all this fine weather, the ground's like iron. I can't do a thing with it. Violence—yes, well, that's another matter. Come in and I'll make some coffee."

She climbed the half dozen steps to her front door, which stood open, and led us into the house.

She took us into her living room and left us there, saying that it would take her only a minute to make the coffee. Since it was instant coffee, this was not much of an underestimate. Returning, she set the tray down on a brass Benares table and filled our cups for us. The room was an amazing jumble, its staid Victorian dignity badly at odds with an imitation Jacobean fireplace that someone had once thought picturesque, and was so crammed with furniture that there was hardly room to move about in it. A bay window overlooked a small garden which was very well kept. Miss Mansell's enthusiasm was plainly for her garden, rather than her house, for the room was dusty, the cretonne chair-covers had not been to the cleaner's for a very long time and the dark green velvet curtains were almost black with age.

As she sat down her short cotton skirt rode up, showing an expanse of muscular thigh.

"Now what's this all about?" she said and looking at Felix stated, "You're not a journalist. If you were you'd have said so on the telephone, hoping I'd be excited at being interviewed. And you wouldn't have brought your wife. I don't expect newspapers pay the expenses of wives to accompany their husbands when they're out on a job."

"As a matter of fact—" Felix began, but she interrupted him.

"And you're not a policeman, for the same reasons."

"I was going to explain—" Felix started again.

Once more she stopped him. "No, let me guess. I know— you aren't a journalist, you aren't working for a newspaper, but you *are* a writer. That's why you're interested in me. You're on the spot, staying with your friends in Stillbeam, when these awful things happen, and you think at once there's material here for a book, but what you need is some information on the human side of it all, and you think I can give it to you. Now isn't that right?"

"Extraordinary!" Felix said. "I don't know how you guessed it."

"It's just a gift," she said. "I'm nearly always right. But I'm afraid I haven't come across any of your work, Mr. Freer. What kind of books do you write?"

"True crime mostly," he said without hesitation. "You haven't come across my latest, *Heads, Bodies and Legs*? It's a study of trunk murders—trunks left in left-luggage offices and places like that, you know."

"I'm afraid I haven't seen it."

"It did very well in paperback, and it was translated into a number of languages, Swahili and Japanese among others."

"It sounds very interesting. I must look out for it. Tell me, how did you get started in this line of work? If I may say so, you don't look at all as if crime would interest you."

"It was my wife who steered me in that direction," he said. "She thinks it's important in the society we live in to take an interest in the psychological and sociological aspects of crime. However, this is the first time I've been, as you put it, on the spot when a murder happened. Usually I start my investigations months, years, even centuries after the crime occurred."

"So you want me to tell you what I knew about Carleen," Miss Mansell said, as eager to impart information as Felix could be to obtain it, "because you think the explanation of her murder must lie in her character. The victim brings his own murder about, isn't that the fashionable view nowadays? As a matter of fact, I've been thinking about that myself, but I can't see how it can apply in Carleen's case. I taught history in the school in London that she and her sister went to, you know, and I like to think I may have been the person who stimulated the interest in history that led them later to write their very successful books, but of the two I should have thought Olivia was far the more likely to get herself murdered. She'd got far the more positive character and far the stronger will. She was rather a troublesome child, but a good deal of that was because she was so intelligent. She'd a far better brain than Carleen, and of course she was ever so much the more attractive. Yet Carleen had her own sort of quiet attractiveness. My brother was very deeply in love with her and he could have chosen from any number of women, he was so attractive himself." She nodded at a photograph in a silver frame, standing on the upright piano. "That's Godfrey. You can see how good-looking he was."

I remembered what Helen had said about Godfrey Mansell being attractive in an obvious way that had never appealed to her, and I thought that the photograph bore this out. He had an oval face with tidy, regular features, large dark eyes, smoothly waved dark hair and a small mouth which the camera had caught gravely smiling. But a photograph is not always revealing, and I recognised that it was possible that when this apparently characterless face was animated, it might have had more charm than appeared.

Miss Mansell beamed at the photograph lovingly.

"It was such a tragedy, his early death," she said. "Cancer, you know. He was only in his forties, much younger than me. But he and I were always very close. We lived together until I retired and thought I'd had enough of London. Our idea when I found this house and first moved in was that he should keep on the flat in London and spend his weekends with me. But then he got married, so of course that didn't work out. But he and Carleen bought that bungalow in Stillbeam so that they could be near me. Wasn't that sweet of them? I always had a splendid relationship with Carleen. I brought them together, I suppose you could say. I'd gone on seeing a fair amount of the Fyffe sisters after they left school. That happens sometimes. One manages to form a real friendship with certain children that lasts beyond their school days. And when their books began to sell and they needed an accountant, I introduced them to Godfrey. I knew at once he was extremely interested in them, and naturally I took it for granted that it was Olivia who was the attraction. But perhaps she was too clever for Godfrey, though I know he respected her immensely and thought her very beautiful, but it was Carleen he married. I'll admit I was rather relieved. She was always so easy to get on with, whereas Olivia was oversensitive and very easily offended."

"What did you think of Mrs. Mansell's engagement to Basil Deering?" Felix asked.

She frowned slightly. "I was very surprised when I heard of it. But I hadn't seen her for some time. That wasn't for any special reason, we hadn't quarrelled or anything of that sort, it was just that we'd both been busy. She and Olivia had been working hard on a book and I have all sorts of local commitments. Still, I was surprised. And rather hurt. I'd never thought of her getting married again, though of course she'd a perfect right to do so if she wanted. But that man Deering after Godfrey..." She gave a sad shake of her head.

"You didn't like Deering?" Felix said.

"I hardly knew him. He wasn't the sort of man who'd be interested in an aged spinster like me. But I thought him a coarse type, disagreeably sensual. Yet there must have been another side to him or he couldn't have written such beautiful verse, could he? Such delicacy of feeling, and one can actually understand it, which is such a nice change nowadays. I suppose Carleen knew that side of him."

"When did you hear of the engagement?"

"The evening before she died. She telephoned me and told me about it, and said we must meet sometime soon and she'd tell me all about it. She said she was wonderfully happy. But d'you know, I felt at the time something was wrong. I know that could be hindsight, but honestly I really felt there was something the matter, because I remember quite clearly I thought the trouble was that she was afraid to tell me about the engagement because of Godfrey. I thought she'd some idea I might be angry with her because she wasn't being true to his memory. And in a way I was, but I'm not so sentimental that I really held it against her. If only it hadn't been that man... But now, of course, I'm inclined to think she was afraid of something quite different."

"Afraid?" Felix said. "She really sounded afraid?"

She made an uncertain gesture with one of her big, work-roughened hands. "Oh, I don't know. I may be quite wrong about that. Hindsight, as I said. If she was killed by a burglar, which is what the police seem to think, she can't have been expecting it, can she? So if my impression was right that there was something wrong, it may have been for the reason that I thought at the time."

"The police have been to see you, have they?"

"Yes, only just before you telephoned this morning."

"And do you believe in that burglar?" I asked.

She gave a start, as if she had forgotten my existence, and turned to me. "You mean because of Basil Deering's murder next day, Mrs. Freer? You think the two things must be connected and that rather bars out a burglar. But I'm not sure about that. Perhaps I shouldn't offer an opinion, talking to an expert like your husband, but don't you think it's possible that the burglar was someone Basil Deering knew, and who had to come back to Stillbeam to silence him?" She hesitated, pushing back a strand of her hair. "Is that clear, or is it too complicated? It's the theory that makes the most sense to me."

"Admirable," Felix said. "Most suggestive. If I make use of it in my book, which I hope you'll allow me to do, I'll attribute it to you, Miss Mansell."

"Oh no, please don't do that," she said, though she looked pleased. "Now have some more coffee."

We both declined and a few minutes later we left, Felix promising as we went down the steep steps to the street to send Miss Mansell a copy of his last book, which she begged him to autograph for her and perhaps also to inscribe with some suitable sentiment.

❀ ❀ ❀

As we got into the car, I said, "What a pity it is that that book doesn't exist. Actually, writing it would have been so good for you."

"I'll get around to it when I have the time," he said.

I had heard this so often that I did not pursue the matter.

"What are you going to do about sending her a copy?" I asked.

He started the car. "I don't suppose it'll surprise her if a writer's forgetful. But I'll be sorry to disappoint her. She was very nice, wasn't she?"

"What did you really want from her?"

"What I got. Some background to the case."

"I'd a feeling you were after something special."

He did not answer, but gazed ahead of him as we cruised along the street with a sombre expression on his face which made me wonder which noted detective of fiction he was identifying himself with at the moment. We emerged into the marketplace, which the day before, having been market day, had been full of stalls and noise and colour, but today was quiet and almost empty. He stopped the car in front of a fruit and flower shop.

"Let's buy something for Helen," he said. "I'd like to take her back a present."

"That's a nice idea—go ahead," I said, but stayed where I was, thinking that since the idea was his, he ought at least to pay for whatever he bought.

Getting out of the car, he went into the shop and after a few minutes emerged with a basket of peaches. I nursed it for him on the drive home, but when we arrived at the house I gave it back to him so that he could present it to Helen himself, and no doubt he would have enjoyed doing so, because he loved giving presents, if a moment after he had driven into the garage another car had not drawn up behind us and Superintendent Pryor and Sergeant Waller got out of it.

As it was, the basket of peaches was put down on a table in the hall and was forgotten until later in the day, and while I took the two policemen into the living room, Felix went off to the workshops to fetch Helen and Andrew.

I tried to talk to the two detectives while we waited, but received only monosyllabic answers. Their faces were grave and their manner had altered in some way since I had seen them last. It seemed to me that there was an air of tension about them both which had not been there before. I did not understand it at all, but I found it alarming. They would not sit down, but stood waiting with obvious impatience for Helen and Andrew to come in.

When they did the Superintendent said abruptly that a matter of some importance had come up about which Andrew might be able to give him some information. Andrew replied that he would be glad to help in any way he could and at that point we all sat down. The sergeant stared straight in front of him with his bold, hard stare in a way that I found singularly disturbing. He did not look at anybody, indeed, there might have been no one else in the room with him, but I had the feeling that by some strange trick of his he was really looking at us all at the same time. Yet the melancholy, sceptical gaze of Mr. Pryor, dwelling with a kind of intimacy on Andrew's face, was far the more intimidating.

"Am I right, Mr. Boscott," he said, "that you were related to Mr. Deering?"

"Distantly," Andrew answered.

"May I ask what the actual relationship was?" Mr. Pryor said.

"He was my second cousin. That means his mother and my father were first cousins, and his grandfather and mine were brothers, and we had the same great-grandfather. Does that answer your question?" Andrew spoke irritably, as if he had found the question ridiculous and irrelevant.

"Had he any other living relations that you know of?" Mr. Pryor asked.

"I don't think so," Andrew answered. "My family wasn't very prolific."

"Are you sure about that?"

"Yes, quite sure. Why?"

Helen began to look worried. She moved closer to Andrew on the sofa on which they were both sitting.

"It may turn out, you see," Mr. Pryor said, "that you're Mr. Deering's heir. So far as we've been able to discover, he died intestate, and if you're his nearest relative, you would inherit his estate."

"Oh no!" Helen exclaimed, as if the thought were shocking.

Andrew pushed a hand through his untidy hair, frowned and muttered, "That's absurd."

"You didn't know of it?" Mr. Pryor said.

"Of course not," Andrew answered. "He couldn't have meant me to inherit anything from him. We weren't even on good terms."

"Yet he came to live near you. How did that come about?"

"Well, we used to meet occasionally. As a matter of fact, I did some work for him. He'd a rather nice set of Regency chairs that he wanted restored and he knew I did that sort of thing and he thought, being family, that I might do it on the cheap. I didn't. I charged him the normal price. That's always a lot more than people expect, though I simply charge by the hour as a skilled craftsman. But that can sometimes come to a lot more than they paid for the thing in the first place, if they bought it, say, ten years ago and it was in a damaged state. I'm often accused of overcharging, though in fact my prices are strictly fair."

"Did Mr. Deering accuse you of overcharging?"

"Good Lord, yes. He was as mean as hell."

"All the same, he did come to live near you."

"That was more or less accidental," Andrew said. "That house he lived in came on the market just about the time I was doing that job of work for him, and he'd come to see how it was coming along—thinking I could do it in half the time it took me. And he happened to mention that he was looking for a house in the country and I said there was a nice house going near here, without for a minute thinking he'd be interested. If I'd thought he might be, I might not have said anything about it. As it was, I was just talking. But he went straight off and bought it, and the first thing I knew of it was when he rang me up and told me to deliver the chairs to him there. But we never saw much of each other. For a time we both made efforts to be good neighbours, but we never liked one another. I'm sure you're making a mistake if you think I inherited anything from him."

"It may not have been his intention that you should," Mr. Pryor said. "From what his solicitor told us, it seems he was intending to make a will, leaving all he had to his future wife, Mrs. Mansell. But he appears to have been the kind of man who procrastinates. He talked of making the will, but did nothing definite about it. And he never said anything about having made a prior will, which he was cancelling, and the implication of that is that no such will ever existed."

"But—but then—" Helen began, then clapped a hand over her mouth, staring at the Superintendent incredulously.

"I think I know what you were going to say, Mrs. Boscott," he said. "You're quite right. Mrs. Mansell did make a will, leaving all she had to Mr. Deering, and since she predeceased him, that's part of his estate, and if it turns out to be correct that he died intestate, it will all be inherited by your husband."

"That can't be true," she said in a half-whisper. "Not if neither of them intended it. It's monstrous."

"I suppose it's possible Miss Fyffe may contest her sister's will," he said, "and if you feel that you shouldn't oppose her, no doubt that could be sorted out. But as things stand at present, it looks as if your husband is Mrs. Mansell's heir as well as Mr. Deering's."

"And just what is the importance of all this?" Andrew asked in a voice that had suddenly become icy. "Am I supposed to have murdered them both to get their money?"

I saw Helen give him an apprehensive look. I did not understand it. His suggestion seemed to me wholly preposterous. In all the years that I had known him, I had never seen Andrew in a rage. I had seen him irritable, withdrawn, bored, walking abruptly out of the room sooner than become involved in an argument, but I had never seen him furiously angry. So I did not know the warning signs, as Helen did. Putting out a hand, she took hold of one of his, drew it towards her and clung to it, as if she were trying to hold him back from what he was about to do.

For the moment he did nothing. His face was whiter than usual, and the corners of his mouth were dragged down in a kind of inverted smile.

Mr. Pryor, giving a slight shake of his head, looked more resigned even than usual, as if he were only too accustomed to being misunderstood. "That's going too fast for me, Mr. Boscott. I only wanted to know if by any chance you knew anything of your cousin's having made a will. I thought he might have spoken to you about it, possibly even asked you to act as an executor. I didn't realise you saw as little of each other as appears to have been the case."

"Didn't you?" Andrew said softly.

"No, I assumed that as cousins, living so near one another, you must be fairly intimate."

"Do you mean to say that among all the people you've been questioning since you discovered my cousin's death, not a single one has told you that he and I were well known to detest one another? We never made any secret of it." Andrew's tone was still very quiet. "Have they all been too good-natured to tell you the simple truth?"

I thought Mr. Pryor looked embarrassed, as if Andrew had caught him out.

"When people tell us that kind of thing," he said, "we don't always take too much notice of it. However, you yourself seem to have confirmed it. But luckily, a lot of us can detest people heartily without feeling moved to murder them."

"Even when there's a splendid motive, like a lot of money coming to us if we can get the murder in before the victim makes a will? And when there was plenty of time to commit the murder—both murders. I'm supposed to have been in my workshop when Carleen Mansell was killed, but who knows if I really was? And I was in that convenient workshop again when I understand my cousin was stabbed. By the way, what sort of weapon did I use? I can't seem to remember."

"Oh, Andrew, please," Helen said with a tremor in her voice. "No one's accusing you of anything."

"Aren't they, by God!" He leapt to his feet, throwing off her hand. His eyes blazed with fury. "I'd like to know why you haven't given me the usual warning yet. Shouldn't you have told me that anything I say may be written down and used in evidence? In any case, I'm not saying any more. You can get out of this house. I was willing to give you any help I could, but I'm not going to let you stick around, waiting for me to convict myself."

"But it seems to me that's just what you're trying to do, Mr. Boscott," Mr. Pryor said disconsolately. "You're going much too fast for me."

"You tricked me into it," Andrew retorted violently. "You asked me harmless questions about my cousin, then threw this bomb at me about his will. D'you think I don't know why you did that? D'you think I don't know what's in your mind? So I'm saying nothing more now, except to tell you to leave this house immediately. You have no right to be here except by my invitation."

The two detectives stood up. They were both big men and Andrew was small, but it was astonishing how dominating he was made by his anger.

"Incidentally," Felix said, "what kind of weapon was Deering stabbed with? It would be interesting to know that."

Since he had seen the weapon himself when he had stumbled over Basil Deering's body, I assumed that he was asking the question only to bring a little calm back into the atmosphere.

"A common kitchen knife," Mr. Pryor answered. "Extremely sharp and normally in use for chopping meat and vegetables. Mrs. Ransom, Mr. Deering's daily, identified it for us as one that was always kept in a drawer in the kitchen, but is missing from it now."

"I suppose that means the murderer knew where to look for it," Felix said. "In other words, it was someone who knew his way about the house fairly well."

That gave Andrew another opportunity to vent his rage. "I knew my way about that bloody house very well, Superintendent. Every time that Basil thought I could do some little job for him, even if it was just sticking in a rawl-plug, he'd remember we were cousins and invite me over. And because I don't like quarrelling with people, I'd go and do it, instead of telling him to get in the village joiner. I don't know what murderous tools he kept in his kitchen, but there's no reason why you should believe that. Mrs. Ransom will tell you, if she hasn't done so already, that I was alone in that kitchen more than once, putting up some shelves for him. Most people keep knives somewhere in their kitchen, and I had a perfect opportunity to find out where Basil kept his. Do you want any more evidence? So either give me that warning and charge me, or get out."

The two policemen decided to get out, but they looked put out about it, as if the interview had not gone at all as they had intended.

As soon as they had gone, Andrew, muttering to himself, strode off to his workshop, and Helen, beginning to cry, followed him. Felix lit a cigarette, dropped on to the sofa and lay back comfortably. I sat down, then thought that I would like a drink, got up and helped myself to a whisky and soda and sat down again. I was suddenly aware of feeling appallingly tired. Conflict, even the conflict of other people, always wears me out.

"You know, Andrew was really quite clever," Felix remarked, puffing smoke towards the ceiling. "Everything he said was true, yet he managed to make it sound absurd. A very neat job."

"D'you mean you think the police really suspect him of the murders?" I asked.

"Of course they do. But they came here expecting evasions from him, and lies about what good friends he and Deering were, when they'd certainly already been told what bad terms the two of them were on, and so on. What they weren't prepared for was for Andrew to take the whole thing into his own hands and prove the case against himself. They'll think a bit before they make another move. But d'you still think I ought to keep out of things and leave the case to the police?"

I was less sure of this than I had been, but I was not convinced that Felix was capable of doing anything helpful.

After a moment he went on, "You know, I was just wondering if Deering ever tried to blackmail Andrew."

"Blackmail *Andrew*?" I said incredulously. "Whatever for?"

"Oh, it was just a passing thought," he said. "Probably nothing in it. But the distinction between restoring furniture and faking is pretty subtle, isn't it? And suppose Andrew's overstepped the line from time to time and Deering knew of it. He could have threatened to blast Andrew's reputation as an honest craftsman. And that could be why Helen got frightened by the scene just now, because she was, you know. I wonder if the police have thought of that yet."

I told him not to be a fool.

# Chapter Eight

He grinned and said, "I wasn't wholly serious."

"This isn't a time for flippancy," I said.

"But I wasn't being wholly flippant either. To you Andrew seems a model of all the virtues, but I ask myself, what's on the other side of the coin? Often, if you want to know the truth about somebody, you've got to look at the opposite of how they normally appear to other people. We all wear masks, don't we? I'm prepared to swear Andrew has done a bit of faking in his time."

"I don't believe you," I said. "He's told me he's seen some of his work on sale guaranteed as absolutely genuine eighteenth century, but that happened after he'd parted with it. He says he takes absolutely no responsibility for what a dealer he's been working for may do with a thing once it's been handed over to him."

"There you are," Felix said. "He knows the dealer's a crook, but he doesn't mind working for him. Is that completely honest?"

"It's honest enough for me."

"Then take Helen," he went on. "A loyal and devoted wife, very hardworking, quite indifferent to money. But suppose she isn't any of those things."

"She *is* all of those things."

"How can you be sure. Suppose she's dead tired of having to work so hard to keep a roof over her head. Suppose she'd like a bit of luxury and idleness for a change, some foreign travel perhaps, and not having to make her own clothes, even though she's so clever at it. Suppose she thinks Andrew might get down to the job without her help for once of earning them a decent income. And suppose she somehow found out he was Deering's heir, because it's even possible, you know, that she and Deering were more intimate than anyone realised. We've kept hearing about how much Andrew disliked him, but have we heard the real reason? Suppose Helen was the real reason why Deering came to live here, and that's what Andrew had against him. She might even have known where the kitchen knife was kept."

The game that he was playing began to have a horrid fascination for me. As if I were taking it seriously, I said, "She's got a perfect alibi for the time of Carleen's murder. She was with you and me at the time."

"Yes, well, I wasn't really thinking about the murders," he said. "I was just suggesting that there might be a hidden side to her nature that you don't know anything about, just as her marriage may not be quite as perfect as it appears. There may be a hidden side to that."

"And that's the real side?"

"Only if you add it to the side you see. But it may at least be as real as that side."

"I don't believe it. However, let's take everyone else to pieces. What about Barbara Gabriel?"

"On the surface fluffy, incompetent, a bit stupid. Under the surface, and not so very far under, shrewd, hard, acquisitive."

"And Olivia Fyffe?"

"Ah, Olivia." He brought the tips of his fingers together and looked profound. "A very calm, well-balanced woman, capable, detached, a bit ironic. Yet when she finds her sister's body isn't where she left it, she gets a fit of screaming hysterics. That was the reverse side of her personality showing itself with a vengeance, wasn't it?"

"I think anyone might have had hysterics in the circumstances," I said. "Corpses don't get up and walk. And we know now what we weren't sure about at the time, that she was telling the truth about Carleen having been murdered."

"Well, why did she come rushing over here when she found Carleen, instead of waiting quietly for the police to arrive? That's what the woman she seems to be would have done."

"Because it dawned on her suddenly the murderer might still be in the house, as he very likely was, and she panicked."

"So the calm, intelligent woman whom one would expect to be able to keep her head in a crisis turns out to be frightened, muddled, extremely emotional."

"And what about Ralph Leggate?"

Felix was silent for a moment, considering. "He works very hard at presenting himself as the strong, silent type. And that suggests to me he isn't really very strong and is afraid that if he opens his mouth he'll talk too much. I never trust that type. But all of this is just guesswork, you understand. I'm just letting my imagination range."

"What else do you ever do with it?"

"There you are," he said once more. "Taking things for granted again. Because I'm imaginative and don't mind showing it, you think I'm not reliable. But the reverse side of my character, if only you'd take the trouble to look for it, is a very thoughtful, sober individual."

"Who's just as much of a liar as the side that shows, even if he's more sober about it."

He shook his head. "You've never understood me. I'm not in the least a liar. I may exaggerate a bit sometimes. I get carried away. But would you seriously claim that I'm ever at all untrustworthy when it matters?"

The trouble was that he believed what he said. He forgot his own lies so quickly that they never weighed on his conscience.

"And what about my hidden side?" I asked.

He laughed. "We both know all about that, don't we? You think people see you as a very upright character, conscientious, truthful and all that sort of thing. Yet you're attracted to villainy, aren't you, or why should you tolerate me—why, that's to say, should you tolerate the person you think I am, even if you're really quite wrong?"

"But I don't," I said. "I found life with you absolutely unendurable."

"Yet we get on excellently when we meet."

"For very brief periods. I think we're getting near our time-limit now."

"Because I suggested your friends Helen and Andrew might not be all they seem?"

"That's one reason."

"Well, perhaps that was going a bit far. Even if Andrew's done some faking in his time, I don't suppose it matters enough for him to let anyone blackmail him about it. As a matter of fact, I don't think blackmail's important in these crimes, except that it's what brought me into it. That's its real importance. If I hadn't gone to Deering's house, looking for those letters he was using against my client, I shouldn't have found Percy the frog and I might never have discovered who was the murderer."

I gave him a startled stare. "You mean you think you know?"

"Of course I do."

"Who is it?"

"Oh, I've no proof," he said casually, as if that were a minor matter. "And you're the kind of person who wants ironclad proof before they'll listen to anything. All the same, I know who and I know why."

"What has that frog got to do with it?"

"Frogs can talk, didn't you know that? *'Brekeke-kesh, koash, koash.'*"

"What on earth are you talking about?"

"Aristophanes. The chorus of frogs. I'd have thought you'd know that. You're much better educated than I am."

I had recognised that he had got into one of his more infuriating moods and that if I pressed him to tell me what he was really talking about, he would only tease me. On the whole it was lucky that Helen and Andrew appeared just then.

They both looked subdued and rather pale, but had an air of being even more deeply united than usual. It made me wonder perversely if they had had a quarrel. I had never known them to quarrel, or even to speak harshly to one another, but I was sure that if they ever did their first thought would be to hide it from other people. Felix had sowed a seed of distrust in my mind. The long years of my friendship with the Boscotts seemed suddenly to be resting on shaky foundations.

Andrew poured out drinks for Helen and himself.

"I want to apologise," he said. "I shouldn't have made the sort of scene I did. It must have been very embarrassing for you."

"Quite understandable," Felix said. "In your place I'd have been a bit annoyed myself."

"I don't often lose my temper," Andrew said, "but when I do, I do it very thoroughly. It was extraordinarily stupid of me to talk to those two coppers like that. Helen's been telling me I was grossly discourteous. That won't have helped them to take a favourable view of me. But I get sickened by the way people take for granted that money's the only thing that can be important to one. If ever I commit a murder, it's going to be out of simple hatred, or jealousy, or fear, or sheer dislike of the other devil's face, not for the sake of money I don't need."

I began to wonder if Andrew was protesting too much. I would never have asked myself this before the talk that I had just had with Felix. The love of money, I thought, is quite as fundamental in the human makeup as hatred, jealousy and fear.

"I'll get some lunch," Helen said. "What shall we have? We could have bread and cheese again, if you don't mind, but the only cheese I've got left is mousetrap. Could you face that?"

Felix and I both said that in the circumstances mousetrap would be fine.

He went on, "You know, I've a feeling that money hasn't got much to do with these murders. Naturally, the first thing the police have to ask themselves is who benefits, but I think our Mr. Pryor will look a bit further than that. He isn't a fool."

"But I treated him as if he were," Andrew said, "which, as I said, was bloody stupid of me. He's not likely to forget it."

Helen finished her drink quickly and put her glass down. "I'll get that bread and cheese. I don't know what we're going to eat this evening. I don't seem able to think about food."

"I was forgetting," Felix said, "Virginia and I went into Wandlebury this morning and got you a little present, Helen. We left it in the hall."

He went out with her to give her the basket of peaches.

We had bread and cheese and peaches and coffee, then Helen and I did the washing-up together. She had gone on worrying about what we were to eat in the evening, since the refrigerator was even emptier than usual, and as she put away the dishes she said that she was going to the village shop to see what she could find there and suggested that I might go with her.

By the time that we set out Andrew had returned to his workshop and Felix was once more lying on the sofa in the living room with a cigarette dangling from his fingers and his dreamy gaze on the ceiling. I guessed that when we returned we should find him just where we had left him. I had never known anyone who could spend as much time as he could contentedly doing nothing.

Helen looked abstracted as we walked along, and although she had wanted my company, she did not seem inclined to talk. We were half way to the village before she said, "Virginia, you and I have known each other for a very long time. We can speak honestly to one another, can't we?"

"I hope so," I said, though I believe that knowing when not to speak honestly is an essential ingredient of any lasting friendship.

"Then tell me, do you think Andrew's happy?"

I was not sure what question I had expected from her, but certainly it had not been that.

"He seems so to me," I said. "Rather happier than most people, as a matter of fact."

"You really think so?"

"What makes you think he isn't?"

"Oh, I don't exactly think he isn't."

"Then what's the trouble? Are you worrying about that outburst of his this morning?"

"A bit. The fact is, you see, there've been rather a lot of those outbursts recently, and he's talked of selling the house and moving to London. But I love our house and I love our life here."

I was astonished. "I can't imagine the two of you living anywhere else. Would he have better opportunities in his work if you moved?"

"I don't think so. He's quite well known in his way. He's got as much work as he can cope with. All the same, if he really wants it…only I'm not sure he does. It could just be a mood he'll forget, and then if we'd moved we'd feel the most awful regrets. But there are times when I get the feeling there's something here he wants to get away from. Altogether, he's been behaving oddly. Look at the way he's been shutting himself away day after day in his workshop."

"I thought he always did that," I said.

"Not as he's been doing it lately. I know he always works very hard, but recently it's been as if he wanted to hide away from the world. And when I went into his workshop the morning after Carleen was killed, I found him just sitting there, doing nothing, then he suddenly grabbed my hand and held on to it and looked as if he was going to burst into tears." She hesitated, then with her face suddenly flaming, burst out, "I'm just a damned silly jealous woman, Virginia, but I've even wondered if he'd fallen in love with Carleen!"

I could think of nothing to say, and for a little while we walked on in silence.

At last I said, "Does he know what you think?"

"Oh, I expect so," she answered. "I've never said anything about it, but he's very shrewd. He nearly always knows what's going on in my mind."

"Then for heaven's sake don't say anything about it to anyone else," I said. "Killing Carleen and Basil for the sake of the money he may or may not be going to inherit may not be much of a motive, but if he was in love with Carleen and had just heard that she was going to marry Basil, he'd have a motive for killing them both. A real case of the traditional *crime passionel.*"

"But that simply isn't possible!" Helen exclaimed. "He'd never hurt anyone."

"But isn't that fear at the back of your mind?"

"No, certainly not." She looked quite angry. "What an awful thought! For one thing, we've never owned a gun, and if he could have got hold of one somehow, he wouldn't have known how to use it. And for another, even if the police think he'd time to shoot Carleen, he couldn't have got rid of her body and the car, could he?"

"No, but all the same, I wouldn't talk about these fears of yours to anyone else at all." Then I wondered if I were sounding too cold-blooded. As comfortingly as I could, I said, "Anyway, I'm sure there's nothing in them, Helen. I don't think Andrew even liked Carleen much. I remember he called her as tough as nails. He's never cared for anyone but you. Anyone can see that."

She smiled unhappily. "Of course, you've been through it all yourself, haven't you, breaking up with Felix? I suppose that's why I wanted to talk to you. You know what it's like."

"Only in our case there wasn't any other woman, at least no one in particular," I said. "It was sheer incompatibility."

We reached the village shop.

"Perhaps you should give it another try," Helen said as she pushed the door open. "You might find it worked better the second time around. Now what shall I get us to eat? Something frozen, I think, that I've only got to warm up. I hope Felix won't mind. When someone's as good a cook as he is, it must be pretty terrible having to put up with my sort of efforts."

"Oh, he isn't one of those awful food-snobs," I said. "Luckily, he'll eat anything you put in front of him without showing any signs of scorning it."

"That's a good thing."

She picked up a wire basket and made her way slowly round the shop.

We emerged presently with some frozen chicken pies and peas, a tin of Scotch broth and some fruit. On the way home Helen relapsed into silence. I thought that she had begun to feel sorry that she had spoken to me as she had, because there are times when talking of a thing to another person gives it a kind of reality which it lacks so long as it is only a fear secretly nursed at the back of one's mind. Of course, it can work the other way about. Bringing a fear into the open can exorcise it. But I did not think that that had happened to Helen, perhaps through my fault. I had not been very reassuring, mainly because I had been so amazed at what she had told me.

We were just turning in at the gate of the Boscotts' house when we heard someone call out, "Helen!"

It was Barbara Gabriel who came plodding breathlessly along the lane behind us. I realised that she had seen us ahead of her for some minutes and had been trying to catch up with us.

"May I come in?" she panted. "A perfectly extraordinary thing has happened and I want to tell you about it. I simply don't know what to do."

Helen held the gate open for her. "Yes, of course, come in."

Passing through the gate, Barbara pressed a hand over her heart as if to stop it racing.

"Oh dear, I know I ought to lose some weight," she said. "I'm just not made for hurrying. I called out to you several times, but you didn't hear. Not that it mattered, because I knew you were going home, but all the same I did so want to speak to you and I was a bit afraid there might be someone in the house besides yourselves. There won't be, will there? No police or anyone?"

"We had the police before lunch," Helen said, "so I shouldn't think they'll interrupt us again just yet. There'll just be Andrew and Felix."

"Oh, I don't mind them," Barbara said. "In fact, I want Andrew's advice. He's got such a lot of common sense."

"I'll go and fetch him then," Helen said and while I took Barbara into the house, set off round it to the stable block.

As I had expected, we found Felix where we had left him, lying on the sofa in the living room, placidly smoking. An ashtray on the floor beside him, full of stubs, showed how many cigarettes he had consumed while Helen and I had been gone. There had been a time when I had tried to cure him of smoking, but he was one of the people who are convinced that cancer is a thing that only happens to others.

He scrambled to his feet when he saw Barbara.

She sank into a chair and said, still gaspingly, "I feel terrible. Perfectly terrible. A simply terrifying thing has happened. Ever since this morning I've been sitting alone in my house, trying to tell myself that it isn't really so awful and that I've nothing to worry about, but the more I think about it, the worse it seems to get. I think if I'm not very careful I may get murdered."

"Murdered—you?" I exclaimed incredulously. It was not a very intelligent remark.

Barbara gave a deep sigh, after which, relaxing in her chair, her breathing seemed to become easier. "I'm afraid I'm really a very cowardly person. I always imagine the worst. And the house felt so empty and quiet. I thought anything could happen to me there and no one would know. My daily comes in for two hours, but after that I'm quite alone. I felt so scared I came over this morning, but I saw the police cars here, so I went away again. I don't want them to know anything about it."

"But aren't they just the people who ought to know," I said, "if you've been threatened?"

"I haven't been threatened. Not exactly. Just warned. That's rather different." She looked towards the door as Helen and Andrew came in. "Here I am, bringing my troubles to you again," she said. "Please be patient with me."

Helen sat down beside her. Andrew stood on the hearth-rug with one elbow resting on the old beam across the fireplace.

"Well, tell us about it," he said.

"I'm so frightened," she answered. "A fantastic thing happened this morning. I got a registered letter and when I opened it there was the photograph of Ralph and me inside it— our wedding photograph that I told you about. And that was all. No letter, nothing to explain it, just the photograph."

"I should have thought you'd be glad to get it," Andrew said. "Why were you frightened?"

"Don't you understand?" she said. "There's only one person who could have sent it and only one reason why he did. I've been thinking and thinking about it all the morning and that's the conclusion I've come to. The murderer sent it."

Felix had a fit of coughing. His face turned quite red before he managed to stop it.

"A very good-natured murderer," Andrew said, "if he took the trouble to see the photograph didn't get into the hands of the police."

"But that's just what's worrying me." She wove the fingers of both hands together in a gesture of desperation. "He wouldn't have done it just out of good nature, would he? Don't you see, it was just to get the photograph that he went to the house? It was because Basil had the photograph that he was murdered. It was to silence him about my marriage to Ralph. And then it was sent to me to warn me that if I didn't keep quiet about it, I'd be next on his list. And I can't go to the police for protection without telling them about that wretched marriage. I'm help-less, I'm absolutely helpless. I'm at his mercy."

"Oh come," Felix said with a rather offended look on his face. "It's quite possible that the person who sent you the photo-graph isn't the murderer at all. It may have been sent by someone who just wanted to set your mind at rest."

"That's very unlikely," she said.

"The most unlikely things do happen," he asserted. "I shouldn't worry about it too much."

"How can I help worrying about it?" she wailed. "Because of course I know who it is. There's only one person who'd care about the photograph and that marriage, and it's obvious now how ruthless he can be if he thinks he isn't going to get what he wants."

"You're thinking about Ralph," Andrew said.

"Of course, of course. He's desperately in love with Olivia and wants to marry her and he sent me the photograph to warn me what might happen if I tried to interfere with the marriage. I never dreamt he had it in him to do a wicked thing like that, but as a matter of fact, I know it was Ralph who sent it."

"You *know?*" Felix said.

"Yes, you see, the postmark on the envelope was Wandlebury, and it happens I went into Wandlebury myself yesterday afternoon to do some shopping, and I saw Ralph and Olivia there together. I'm certain he posted the letter while he was there."

"A lot of other people were in Wandlebury yesterday afternoon," Felix said. "As a matter of fact, I was there myself. So was Virginia."

"But there's only one person with any reason to worry about my marriage to Ralph and that's Ralph himself," Barbara said. "Of course, he doesn't know I've already told you all about it. And to be honest..." She paused and gave an embarrassed little smile. "Well, if I'd known he'd got the photograph I might not have said anything about it to you. But I thought the police had it and were just deliberately torturing me when they said nothing about it when they were questioning me, and I wanted you to hear the story from me before it got all round the village. I felt sure you'd sympathise with me if you heard how it really happened. But now I wish I hadn't burdened you with it, and I want to ask you if you'd be very careful not to let Ralph know you know it, because I simply don't know what he might do if he found his secret was out and he couldn't marry Olivia. I think he must be out of his mind by now. I think he's mad."

"But surely if he knows we know all about it," Andrew said, "he's less likely to risk harming you."

"But just think of him sending me the photograph in that strange, secretive way," she said. "He can't be rational any more."

"And you mean you want us to let him go ahead and marry Olivia although we know it'd be bigamy and you think he's a murderer?" Andrew said. "Isn't that a bit much?"

"Well, if you put it like that…" She stirred uneasily in her chair. "Perhaps if we could find some proof against him, that would solve things."

"You could solve the problem of your bigamy easily enough," Felix said, "by getting married again, then having a divorce. That would be quite simple."

"He'd never do it," she said. "For one thing, a divorce takes ages and Olivia might marry someone else in the interval, apart from not understanding why he suddenly wanted to marry me instead of her."

"And ingenious as some of your ideas are, Felix," Andrew said, "there's still that matter of murder."

"Oh, of course," Felix agreed. "I don't think we could allow that marriage to proceed."

"Then you won't help me!" Barbara cried. "Oh, what am I going to do? You don't know how frightened I am!"

"I'd advise you most strongly to do nothing at all for the present," Felix said.

"What I don't understand," Helen said tentatively, speaking apparently to Andrew, as if she felt he were the only person in the room who would listen to her, "is what possible reason Ralph could have had for murdering Carleen. She was no danger to him. He'd nothing to gain by her death. I can just manage to believe he might want to kill Basil because of the photograph, but why Carleen?"

"I don't think that's as puzzling as it seems," Andrew said. "We've been talking as if there could have been only one murderer, but actually there's no reason why there shouldn't have been two. Carleen's murder could have been just what I believe the police think it was, the work of a burglar. He came to the house, was caught by her, killed her, then hid when he heard Olivia come in and as soon as she ran out to come to us, bundled Carleen's body into her car and drove away. And that gave the second murderer, the one who wanted to get rid of Basil—whether it was Ralph or not—his opportunity. He realised that if he acted quickly, the murders were sure to be taken for the work of one person, and that person would have to be someone with a motive for killing Carleen. And that's what no one's been able to find. How could anyone have wanted her dead?" His voice grated slightly and I could not stop myself glancing at Helen, but her face was expressionless. Andrew added tonelessly, "She was quite harmless."

❀ ❀ ❀

"That's a very interesting theory," Felix said. "I like it. The implication of it is that it wasn't a coincidence that there were two murderers, but simply that the second one was an opportunist. He could have been waiting for the right chance for years."

"Exactly," Andrew said.

"And the second one was Ralph—don't you see, it has to have been Ralph?" Barbara came quickly to her feet. "But you won't help me by keeping what I told you to yourselves. And I thought you were my friends!"

"We'll think about it," Andrew said. "The police may find that proof you're looking for, then there may be no need for anyone to say anything about your trouble. In any case, I don't think any of us wants to rush straight off and tell them about it."

"I suppose that's something." She gave a dazed look round the room. "Perhaps I've been asking rather a lot of you. And perhaps I'm not in any real danger. All the same, I'm frightened, I really am, and that great empty house scares me. Would you think it terribly silly of me if I asked one of you to come back with me and just look round and make sure—I know it does sound silly—that there's no one in it?"

Felix responded at once, almost too quickly, as if he wanted to get his answer in before Andrew could speak. "I'll come with pleasure." He turned to me. "And you'll come too, won't you, Virginia? A breath of fresh air is just what you need."

Having already walked to the village and back that afternoon, I did not feel in the least in the need of a breath of fresh air, but I got to my feet and together with Felix and Barbara, set off down the lane towards her house.

I let the two of them walk ahead of me. Dragging behind, I began to wonder if I could find an excuse for returning to my own home within the next day or two. I did not see why I should be needed at either of the inquests. The real question was whether Helen and Andrew would sooner that I stayed on or not. In their place, I felt, I should be glad not to have even the oldest of my friends under my feet.

But if they were going to feel that my leaving them was a kind of treachery, that I would be abandoning them just when they needed support, I should have to stay on. Not that I saw what help I could give them. The presence of Felix was a complication. If he could be persuaded to leave, then I should feel more ready to stay. We had seen enough of one another for the present. If we saw much more we were liable to start the kind of quarrelling that had wrecked our marriage, which had arisen out of Felix's bitterness that I had so little faith in him, and out of mine that in my view he was not to be trusted an inch. When we saw each other only occasionally this did not seem to matter, but after only a short while of one another's company the old disillusionments always rose to the surface and we began to look for ways of hurting one another.

I do not think that this was intentional in either of us, it was simply that we should have been two much happier people if we had never met. It was sad really, because a kind of affection lingered on, but I, at least, found that far more exhausting than pleasant because it set up such a conflict in my feelings. Even my dawdling behind at the moment in the quiet of the early evening with the honey scents of the hedgerows in the air was a sign that I had had about as much of him as I could stand.

We reached the main road, turned to the right, turned to the right again, crossed the humpbacked bridge over the Wandle and reached Barbara Gabriel's house. The sound of a lawn mower greeted us as we approached it. A man was driving a motor mower over the wide lawns that surrounded the attractive old Georgian house.

Felix and Barbara waited at the gate for me to catch up with them.

Felix was saying, "Doesn't that man happen to be Vincent Hall?"

"Yes," Barbara said. "Why? Do you know him?"

"No, but if you don't mind, I'd like to speak to him for a moment," Felix answered. "He was the cyclist who saw Olivia Fyffe in the lane, wasn't he?"

"I believe so," she said. "Go ahead, if you want to. I can assure you, he's absolutely reliable. He's worked for me for years."

The man with the mower was approaching us along the edge of the lawn. As he came near, he switched off the motor and stood still. He was a middle-aged man, tall, thin and stooping.

"Evening, Mrs. Gabriel," he said. "I thought I'd look in for an hour or two. I've been letting the grass get out of hand."

"Thank you, Vince," she said. "It does need a bit of attention. This is Mr. Freer. He'd like a word with you."

"Evening," the man said pleasantly to Felix.

"There is just a question or two I'd like to ask," Felix said. "When you saw Miss Fyffe the evening her sister was killed, it was dark, wasn't it?"

"That's right," the man said.

"But you're absolutely sure it was Miss Fyffe you saw, are you? It couldn't possibly have been anyone else?"

The man shook his head. "It wasn't as dark as all that. It was Miss Fyffe. I saw her near the bridge in the light from my bicycle lamp. I called out, 'Good evening,' but she didn't answer. She was running. I did wonder if something was wrong, but she could have stopped me if she'd wanted to. I didn't know about her poor sister, of course. I suppose the truth is she hardly knew what she was doing. I'd have stopped if I'd known."

"But she saw you, did she, even though she didn't answer?" Felix asked. "You're sure of that?"

"Must've done," the man said. "She couldn't have helped seeing the light of my bike, even if she didn't hear my 'good evening.' "

"Thank you," Felix said. "That's all I wanted to know."

Vincent Hall started the lawn mower again and Felix, Barbara and I went on towards the house.

"What was the point of that?" I asked. "We know it was Olivia he saw running along the lane. She came straight to the Boscotts', didn't she?"

"It isn't important that he saw her," Felix said. "What's important is that she saw him."

"I don't understand you."

"You don't think Vince could possibly have been the burglar who got into the house and killed Carleen!" Barbara exclaimed. "I told you, I've known him for years. He's dead honest."

"I'm sure he is," Felix said. "No, I'd be very surprised if he turned out to be the burglar."

She took a key out of her handbag and unlocked the front door.

"But you believe there was a burglar, don't you?" she said. "You told Andrew you liked his theory."

"So I do," Felix said. "I like it very much. It's admirable. I'd like it even more if it was correct."

She looked at him with a perplexed frown. "What do you mean?"

"I mean it's intelligent and plausible, but happens not to be right," he said. "Now would you like me to go over the house to make sure Ralph Leggate or anyone else isn't hiding in it?"

"I feel rather foolish about that now." She led us into the house and into the high, white-panelled drawing-room. "I'm sure there's no one here. For one thing, if Vince has been here for some time, he'd have seen Ralph or anyone else arrive and he'd have mentioned it just now. The fact is, I know I lost my head. It was kind of you to come—it made me feel a lot better— but I'm afraid it was imposing on you dreadfully."

"You're sure you wouldn't like me just to take a look round?" Felix was longing to have a look over the house, not because he was expecting to find anything significant, but out of sheer curiosity.

I had gone to the window and was standing, looking out. It overlooked the terrace and the rose garden beyond it with its encircling wall and the gate that opened onto the meadow with the footpath that led to the Fyffe bungalow.

As I looked, the gate opened.

"You've got a visitor," I said.

Hurrying, Olivia Fyffe came through the gate. She came rapidly up the steps to the terrace and to the French window and rapped sharply upon it. Before Barbara reached it and opened it, I saw Olivia's face. It was white with anger.

The moment Barbara opened the door, Olivia asked fiercely, "Where is he?"

"Where is who?" Barbara asked. "Come in, Olivia."

Olivia remained where she was. "Where's Ralph? He's here, isn't he?"

"Not that I know of," Barbara said. "Why should he be?"

"Because he's gone missing," Olivia answered. "I've been trying to get in touch with him all day. I've been to his house and I've kept telephoning, and he's just vanished. But if he'd wanted to go away, he'd have told me, now of all times. So I believe he must have come here."

"But why?" Barbara seemed to have forgotten that only a short time ago she herself had been afraid that that might have happened.

"Because you're his wife, aren't you?" Olivia said. "You don't suppose I don't know that. And whatever trouble he's got himself into, he knows you can't give evidence against him."

# Chapter Nine

Barbara went almost as white as Olivia.

"So you know that! When did he tell you?"

"Yesterday at lunch," Olivia replied. "He explained why he couldn't ask me to marry him and wanted me to go away with him. It didn't make any difference to me. I shouldn't have married him in any case."

I remembered the impression that I had had when I joined Ralph and Olivia after lunch the day before that they had been quarrelling. It looked as if I might have interrupted an even more emotional scene than I had realised.

"You understand, Mrs. Gabriel," Felix said, "that if Leggate told Miss Fyffe about his marriage, it means he hadn't much of a motive for murdering Deering. Getting hold of the photograph wouldn't have been so very important to him."

"But what was he doing in Basil's house if he wasn't the murderer?" Barbara asked. "Because he must have been there to get hold of the photograph."

"Aren't you a little confused?" Felix said. "You thought he must have sent you the photograph, so he must have been in Deering's house, so he must be the murderer. But if he wasn't the murderer, he may not have been in Deering's house and perhaps didn't send you the photograph. That was somebody else." He turned to Olivia. "Is it important to you to find Leggate?"

"Very," she answered.

"Yes, I can see that," he said. "Well, I think I can tell you where he probably is. I think he's in the police station in Wandlebury, helping the police with their inquiries."

"No!" she said sharply. "I don't believe that."

"I thought you were sure he wasn't guilty, Mr. Freer," Barbara said. "So why should he do that?"

"It isn't only the guilty who help the police," Felix said.

"I don't believe you," Olivia repeated.

"Even when you rejected him after what he'd done for you?" Felix said in the gentle tone which meant that he was in a dangerous mood. "He isn't a man I'd trust very far myself."

She stared at him for a moment, then turned and walked rapidly away across the terrace and down the steps to the rose garden.

"I think Virginia and I will go with Miss Fyffe, if you don't mind, Mrs. Gabriel," Felix said. "I'd like to have a word with her. You aren't afraid of being alone in the house any more, are you?"

She was saying that of course she was not and thanking him for having come to it with her when Felix took me firmly by an elbow and steered me out into the garden after Olivia.

But he did not try to catch up with her. She was almost running and the gate in the garden wall had slammed shut behind her before we reached it. Felix pushed it open and we walked along the path across the meadow towards the Fyffes' bungalow.

I did not try to talk to him. The almost eager expression that he had had on his face when we started out had disappeared and he looked extraordinarily troubled. I suppose I had guessed by then what was coming, though I did not understand it, and I had no idea how Felix intended to handle the scene ahead of him.

I did not think that he had either. We reached the gate in the fence that encircled the Fyffes' garden, went through it and through the trees that surrounded the bungalow and up to the front door. At that point I suddenly thought that Felix was going to turn tail and hurry away, but after an instant's hesitation, he pressed the bell.

No one answered it and he rang a second time, keeping his finger on it until we heard footsteps inside. Olivia opened the door.

"Go away," she said. "I don't want to see anyone."

"Don't you think it would be a good idea if we had a talk?" Felix said mildly. "Quite a short one."

"No," she said and started to shut the door in our faces.

Felix had his foot in at the door. He thrust against it and she stepped back, letting it swing open.

"I just want to tell you what I know," he said, "then you can do what you think best. You might even be able to tell me what you think I ought to do myself. I'm not used to these situations."

She turned and walked into the big sitting room, leaving us to close the front door behind us. In the sitting room she spun round and confronted us.

"Well, go on," she said.

Felix looked embarrassed. "It's so difficult to know how to open a conversation with a murderess," he said. "Can we sit down? It might make it easier."

She remained standing. "I thought you wanted only a short talk."

"I'll make it as short as I can," he said, "but I don't really know where to begin. Mind if I smoke?" He groped for a cigarette and lit it without waiting for her answer. He was trying to look relaxed, but really he was very tense. "Perhaps it would be best to start with the first question I asked myself about you. I asked myself why you really came rushing to the Boscotts' after you found your sister killed. You said it was because you had a fit of panic after finding her, and you certainly seemed to be in a state bordering on hysteria. Yet you didn't seem to me the sort of person who'd normally panic in a crisis and get hysterical. And according to your own story, it didn't happen to you at once. You began by behaving very rationally, calling the police and telling them quite coherently what had happened. But then you carne rushing out of the house, leaving the door open behind you—we know you did that, because you'd no key when you wanted to get back into the house—and then you went to the Boscotts'. And something about that whole story worried me. I was sure you were lying about something, though I didn't know what. Then a little later—next day, as a matter of fact—I suddenly realised why you'd really run out of the house and gone to the Boscotts'."

Felix was speaking slowly and quietly and what he was saying seemed to have begun to fascinate Olivia. As if she were unaware of what she was doing, she sank into a chair.

"Well?" she said.

I sat down too and after a moment Felix looked round for a chair and sat down on the edge of it with his elbows on his knees. He was smoking in short, nervous puffs.

He went on, "You had to get rid of the gun, of course, before the police came. I don't know where you'd got hold of it in the first place. Perhaps you'd had it for years. Was your father in the war and did he bring it back as a souvenir? It isn't important. You had it, that's all that matters, and when you'd killed your sister you had to get rid of it quickly. And what could be a better place for it than the Wandle? It would take you only a moment to run down to it and throw the gun in and run home again. So you went out, leaving the door open, because you thought you'd be back immediately, though you remembered to turn out the light in case anyone was passing and you showed up against it. And then by bad luck, near the bridge, you ran into Vincent Hall on his bicycle. And as soon as you saw him you realised it would look very strange to him and he'd remember it afterwards if you simply went on as far as the bridge, then doubled back into the house. So instead of doing that, you ran on. The gun went into the river, and you went on to the

Boscotts' with your story of having been afraid to wait alone in the house for the police."

Olivia smiled. It was a grimace of a smile which for the first time since I had seen her made her look ugly.

"Do you imagine you've an atom of proof of any of this?" she asked.

"The proof's in the river," Felix answered. "The police will soon find it when they know where to look."

Percy the frog was in the river too. I thought that I was beginning to understand how Felix's mind had worked.

"Then, while I was at the Boscotts', Carleen got up and walked away," Olivia said, "and with a bullet in her brain she drove her car ten miles to the edge of a cliff and in case the bullet hadn't done its job, committed suicide. That's a very convincing story."

"Oh no, because of course it was Ralph Leggate who removed the body," Felix said. "You didn't know he was going to. You didn't even know he was still about when you shot your sister. Your screams when you found her body was missing were of absolutely genuine terror. They've been the one quite genuine thing about the way you've acted since the whole horrible business began."

"But Ralph wasn't there," she said. "We'd said goodbye at the door and he'd gone off home down the lane before I'd even gone into the house. That's the truth. If he'd been in the house at the time you think I killed Carleen, would I have been so terrified when I founded the body had been moved?"

"I don't think you would, but he wasn't in the house when you killed Carleen," Felix said. "But he hadn't gone far down the lane either. He was still near enough to hear the shot. And he turned back to find out what had happened. Perhaps he was afraid you'd run into that mythical burglar we've all been talking about. And he went cautiously round the house instead of going to the front door, because he wasn't too keen on running into him himself, and he looked in at this window and saw Carleen's body and you perhaps still with the gun in your hand, and he was probably too scared to do anything but stand out there among the trees and stare at you. Then he'd have seen you telephone the police and soon after that go running out of the room. He couldn't have known what you were going to do, but he went round to the front of the house and found the door open and went in, then took it into his head to try to help you by removing the body."

"And why did I kill Carleen?" Olivia asked, sounding as if at last she had become genuinely interested in what he had to say. "Had I a reason, or was it just an ungovernable impulse to kill somebody?"

"A bit of each, I'd say," Felix replied, "just as it was when you killed Deering. I've talked to Miss Mansell and I think I understand the reason. Your sister had spoken to her on the telephone, you know, and Miss Mansell had had the impression that there was something wrong. Well, there was. Your sister had become afraid of you. She'd twice taken your lover away from you, hadn't she? First Godfrey Mansell, then Deering. When each of them first got to know the two of you, you were the one they fell in love with. You were more beautiful than your sister and more intelligent and more interesting, and I dare say Carleen had been jealous of you because of those things since early days. She must have heard herself compared with you quite often to her disadvantage. But she'd discovered that she'd got something that you hadn't, and when she spoke to Miss Mansell she'd only just realised there could be danger in using it."

I thought of Helen, who had been jealous of Carleen, not of Olivia.

Felix continued, "I didn't know her, so I can't tell what it was, but I think she may have set herself deliberately to take your men away from you. They seem to have been two very different kinds of man, so she may have meant quite different things to them. To Mansell I think she was probably the gentle, romantic creature, which was the personality she cultivated outwardly. To Deering I suspect she was the successful money-maker, a shrewd business woman, not very emotional and quite hard. She must have been pretty hard to try to humiliate you by having you to live with Deering and herself. Under the surface I'm sure you were far too emotional for him and, of course, too violent. Didn't he want to be the violent one in your relationship? The only time I saw you together he did his best to tear you to pieces. He called you a pathological liar among other things, didn't he? I think he was wrong. I think you only lie cold-bloodedly and deliberately, when you need to, for your own ends. However, he ought to have remembered your violent side when he let you into his house the day after you'd shot Carleen. I don't know if he believed you'd done it or not, but he never guessed he was in danger himself and he let you come into his house, where you knew your way about because of the time when you'd still been lovers, and you knew where to find the knife you used to stab him. Revenge is sweet— or isn't it? Is it rather a disappointment? Perhaps you can tell me."

Olivia had a sardonic look on her face.

"Why didn't we meet long ago?" she said. "We'd have had some interesting times together."

"We might," he agreed. "Until we began to find each other out. Violence terrified me and you'd soon have been disappointed in me. I'm very limited. Ask my wife."

She did not glance towards me. "But how you'd love to have some proof of all this, wouldn't you?"

"As a matter of fact, I shouldn't," Felix said. "It would place a heavy responsibility on me, and as Virginia will tell you, I've never been much of a one for taking responsibility. As it is, I don't have to decide what steps to take."

"You mean you aren't going to the police with all this?" For the first time she seemed to be taken by surprise.

"Well, if I did, the only thing I could do is urge them to hunt for the gun in the river," he said, "and I'm not the kind of person the police pay much attention to. I don't see why I shouldn't be, but I'm not. So for the moment I'd like to do a little thinking before I act, if I ever do."

"Then why did you come here to tell me all this? Do you want me to do a bolt? Flight's generally taken as a sign of guilt. Is that it?"

"Mostly I wanted to see if you could answer any of the things I said, but you haven't even tried to."

"You haven't said anything that needed answering."

"I have, you know. The whole lot. I'm completely convinced by my own case. But perhaps I should add something by way of warning. That man, Superintendent Pryor, isn't a fool, and if I'm right that he's taken Leggate in for questioning, you can be sure he's got hold of some more solid sort of proof than I've got. Something that links him with the way he tried to dispose of Carleen's body, perhaps. Not merely a brilliant flight of the imagination, like mine, but something prosaic, like the white Rover having been seen by someone that evening and the number noted and the driver described. Then perhaps Leggate had earth on his shoes that matched the earth up on those cliffs—things like that. I'm only guessing. But when the police lean on him, I think he'll talk. He was desperately in love with you, enough to tolerate your murders and to try to help you with one of them, but that could easily enough have turned to hate when you rejected him. You took a big risk when you did that."

"What else could I do?" she asked contemptuously. "He's a fool. He's nothing."

"A danger to you, however."

It may have been because she suddenly felt afraid that she lost her temper. She sprang to her feet.

"I've had enough of this! I listened out of curiosity, but I've had enough now. Leave my house!" Her face was dead white again.

Felix stood up. He did not seem put out by her outburst.

"Yes, well, thank you for listening. It's been an interesting experience for me, putting all my thoughts together. Don't bother to see us out. Come, Virginia." He took me by the arm and thrust me towards the door.

❋ ❋ ❋

Olivia did not move, though I heard her give a choking sort of sob. We let ourselves out of the front door and started down the drive to the gate. I glanced at Felix. The predominant expression on his face was embarrassment.

Neither of us spoke until we were in the lane, then he said in a diffident tone, "Well, what do you think of my case?"

It sounded as if he were asking my opinion of some attempt of his at a work of art, some painting, perhaps, or a first novel.

"Oh, you sold it to me," I said. "But are you really going to do nothing more about it?"

"What can I do?"

"You want her to get away, do you? You want her to escape after committing two cold-blooded murders?"

He wriggled his shoulders uneasily. "I said, didn't I, I hate taking responsibility? The police will catch her anyway by their own methods. I'd sooner have nothing to do with it. I'd never have got involved in the thing at all if I hadn't happened to be an imaginative sort of character, and that's hardly my fault, is it?"

We reached the bridge over the Wandle and as if by agreement, paused there, leaning on the stone parapet. Below us the murky, greenish water glided slowly by.

"Will the police ever find the gun down there if you say nothing about it?" I asked.

"I shouldn't think so," he said.

"Then oughtn't you tell them?"

"I told you, I don't want to be dragged any further into this. I've had enough of it. Anyway, they wouldn't listen to me."

"And Percy the frog?" I said. "He's lost down there forever. I think I understand why he seemed so important to you. It was when you threw him in here that you realised that that was what Olivia had done with the gun, why she'd come out of the house and so on. I remember you suddenly looked very odd when you'd just done it."

A little plop in the water made me feel as if Percy had chosen that moment to reemerge, but it was only a fish of some sort rising to snap at the midges that made a faint haze above the surface.

"Yes, and then everything began to fit together," Felix said. "I even remembered, when I realised that Leggate had to be involved in it somehow, how pleased he'd been at Barbara Gabriel's party to hear that Deering was going to marry Carleen. I suppose Leggate knew that Deering had been Olivia's lover and he thought that with him safely married and out of the way, he'd have more of a chance with her himself. I didn't think he'd actually been in on the murder, not only because he'd no motive, but because if he had been he'd have removed the gun with the body and Olivia would never have needed to come out of the house. Of course, I couldn't have allowed him to marry her, not because of the bigamy, but because I knew she was a murderess."

"Well, so did he. He'd have known what he was letting himself in for. But I still think you ought to tell all this to the police."

He shook his head. There was a stubborn look that I knew on his face. "They'll get all they want out of Leggate. I don't want them guessing that I was in Deering's house and found his body and never told them anything about it. It could get me into trouble. I want to go home."

"To marry your alcoholic?"

He looked at me blankly for a moment, as if he did not know what I was talking about. Then he said, "Oh, yes—that."

"You hadn't forgotten about it?"

"No, no, of course not. But I haven't been able to give the matter the serious thought I intended when I came away. I've had so much else on my mind."

"It might work, you know," I said. "After your fashion, you like helping people and you stick to them too, once you've got fond of them, even if you never stick to anything else."

"You don't think I'll stick to this detective job?"

"Will it stick to you if you keep all your discoveries to yourself?"

"Naturally I don't normally do that. This case was exceptional."

"I think you'll always be tempted to do it. You've such an aversion to the authorities."

He gave a melancholy smile. "What a pity it is, if you think I'm some good sometimes at helping people, that you've never needed help yourself, Virginia, though there was a time, you know, when I thought you could help me. I thought you might be able to straighten me out. But it didn't work out, did it?"

I had needed help, as who doesn't, as much as he ever had, but perhaps it had not shown so obviously.

"I haven't got your gift of accepting almost everybody just as they are and never being surprised at anything they do," I said. "I keep trying to reconstruct them to some pattern I make up for them. I know that's a bad mistake."

"Yes, and I suppose you'd go to work on me again if we started—well, if we began to see rather more of one another." There was a faint question in his voice.

I remembered Helen saying that things might work out better between Felix and me a second time around. I felt a weary sense of sadness. We had been over this ground so often before.

"If I were you, I'd stick to your alcoholic," I said. "You might be just the person she needs."

"But I'm not sure she cares for me in the least."

"Well, let me know how it goes and whether or not you want me to take any steps about a divorce."

"I've told you, I hate lawyers."

"They have their uses."

He gave an irritated shake of his head. "You're terribly inflexible. But all right, I'll let you know. I suppose we may as well go on now, or Helen and Andrew will be wondering what's happened to us."

He put his arm through mine and we strolled on through the first soft dimness of the twilight to the Boscotts' house.

We surprised Helen and Andrew in the living room, locked in each other's arms.

They drew apart when they saw us, but Andrew kept Helen's hand in his, holding it as if he were afraid of what might happen to him if he let go of it. There was a flush on Helen's cheeks. She met my eyes, then quickly looked away, a warning,

I supposed, not to reveal in any way that she had ever let me into her confidence.

It was not needed. In whatever way she and Andrew had gone about solving the problem that had lurked under the calm surface of their marriage, whatever pain might even now be distressing them, it was for them by themselves to reach peace of mind again. I did not want to know how they set about it. Other people's secrets can be a heavy load.

"Barbara kept you a long time," Andrew said. "I hope she gave you drinks."

"We didn't actually stay long," Felix answered. "We went for a walk. It's a beautiful evening."

"Let's have some drinks now then."

Andrew sounded quite excited, as if he felt that there was something to celebrate, and when he had poured out the drinks, he and Helen looked at one another as they raised their glasses as if it were a toast. They had just become rich, and sooner or later, for better or worse, that was bound to affect them, but I did not think that that was what was on their minds. Then Helen went out to the kitchen to heat up the frozen chicken pies that she had bought in the afternoon. But we had a bottle of wine with them, as if there were some reason for being festive. She and Andrew went up to bed very early.

Felix and I stayed downstairs, watching television, like the old married couple that, in fact, we still were, however nominally. It was international show jumping, which I do not think interested either of us very much, but it spared us the effort of trying to talk any more.

I knew that he would be gone in the morning. If he could, he always avoided saying goodbye, so when I went up to bed I did not expect to see him again. It surprised me when he appeared in my room in the morning with the usual cup of tea. But he did not linger, and I did not ask him if he was going or staying. In the doorway, as he was leaving, he turned and we smiled at each other across the room. It was the kind of smile of farewell that can hurt dreadfully for a moment, but then leaves a kind of peace behind it. I heard him take tea to Helen and Andrew, then go downstairs. That was the last I saw of him. When I went downstairs presently myself, I found Helen in the kitchen, reading a letter.

She held it out to me. "It's just a note from Felix, saying thank you for letting him stay here."

That was all it was. It was nice, courteous and grateful. There was not a word in it about the murders, or about his efforts at detection. So far as he was concerned, the incident was closed.

❁ ❁ ❁

Later in the day it was also closed for the police. As Felix had guessed, they had spent most of the day before questioning Ralph Leggate, who had later been arrested as accessory after the fact, or whatever the term is. They had picked him up because a witness had come forward who had seen the white Rover being driven in the direction of the Lynechurch cliffs by a man whose description fitted Ralph Leggate. Then another witness claimed to have met him late in the evening walking on the Lynechurch road towards Stillbeam and to have exchanged a few words with him about the remarkable spell of fine weather. His manner had been thought by the witness to be strange. According to him there had been something wild about it and almost savage, which had rather alarmed him and made him wish he had not stopped to chat, and when he heard of the car with the body in it being found at the bottom of the Lynechurch cliffs he had thought it his duty to come forward and report his encounter with the unknown man in the darkness.

Felix had also been right that under questioning Ralph Leggate had quickly broken down. Superintendent Pryor, who called in to see the Boscotts later in the morning, partly, I think, to apologise for his suspicions of Andrew, told us that after a token show of resistance, Ralph Leggate had talked freely, as if he were indifferent to the consequences of what he said to

himself or to Olivia Fyffe. So solid police work had arrived at
the truth almost as quickly as Felix's flight of the imagination,
just as he had said that it would.

But before the police got to her, Olivia had found her own
way out. When they reached the bungalow and broke into it,
because no one came to the door, they found her lying on her
bed with an empty bottle of barbiturates beside her. She died in
the ambulance on the way to the hospital.

I thought of telephoning Felix to tell him this and to ask
him what he thought about responsibility now. But what would
have been the point of it? He would only have claimed that
Olivia's death had had nothing to do with anything that he had
said to her, that she had certainly decided to kill herself before
he and I had arrived at the bungalow, because, once her lust for
revenge was satisfied, she could not live with her guilt. And he
might even have been right.

"There's just one thing I still don't understand," Mr. Pryor
said as he and Sergeant Waller were leaving. "It's why she took
that damned frog from Deering's house. I suppose it meant
something special to her, but if so, what did she do with it?
We've searched the house, but there isn't a sign of it. It isn't
important, but it's a loose end, and loose ends irritate me."

Almost for the first time since we had met him, Sergeant
Waller spoke. "Seems to me someone must have a frog in the
throat," he said and chuckled at his own joke.

I believe a frog in the throat means a temporary loss of
speech. Thinking of Felix and his obstinate silence about his
own activities, I reflected that the sergeant had come closer to
the truth than he himself realised.

I saw Andrew looking at me in the thoughtful way that
I had once or twice seen him looking at Felix. I think by then
he had come close to guessing what Felix had been doing in
Stillbeam. But I also suffered a loss of speech, leaving Percy to
long years of peace in the quiet depths of the Wandle.

We hope you loved *Frog in the Throat.*

We love it, too, and in fact are big fans of the kind of amateur sleuthing that comes with a generous side order of wit. With that in mind, we thought you might enjoy *The Weird World of Wes Beattie*, by John Norman Harris. *Weird World* is set in Toronto, and it follows a charmingly nerdy young lawyer as he does his level and surprisingly funny best to disentangle the titular Beattie—a world-class bumbler—from a fantastical frame-up.

We've attached the first few chapters. If you'd like to read further, you can order *The Weird World of Wes Beattie* wherever fine books are sold. You can also visit our website for a tasty selection of sample chapters from even more titles—try before you buy, at felonyandmayhem.com/collections/book-excerpts!

# The Weird World
# of Wes Beattie

# Chapter One

It was a small seminar, attended by doctors, lawyers and social workers, for the discussion of medicolegal problems.

The discussion leader for the evening was Dr. Milton Heber, an eminent psychiatrist.

"I hope you will excuse the pulp-magazine title I have chosen for my little discourse," he said, "but I have been living in the weird world of Wes Beattie lately, and it is affecting my vocabulary. For the benefit of our distinguished visitors from the U.S.A., I will explain that Wes Beattie is a young man, age twenty-one, who is facing trial for murder in this city. The case is *sub judice,* so I must ask you to keep this information private. I am using it simply because it is live and topical and illustrates the need for greater cooperation among our various professions.

"Now this weird world that Wes lives in is peopled by strange, sinister criminals, grown men and women who seem to have spent a lot of time conspiring against an obscure bank clerk. They are very real people to Wes, and their influence is everywhere. They are out to get him. If you play along with Wes, he will discuss this Mystery Gang quite rationally. If you express doubts or laugh at him, he gets shrill and hysterical; then he withdraws, and won't speak to anyone for days.

"A lot of people have been wondering what made Wes Beattie kill. A timid, shy, immature boy, not strong, commits a brutal murder. The Crown Attorney will present a credible motive. For our American friends, the Crown Attorney is your old friend the D.A. under a different name. Mr. Massingham, our genial Crown Attorney, will claim that Wes killed for money. He was due to inherit a substantial sum from his uncle, Edgar Beattie. Edgar was about to change his will and cut Wes out. So Wes killed him. All very simple. And all, in my opinion, completely false.

"Wes Beattie wouldn't have had the guts to kill for money. He wouldn't have killed for a free pass to Fort Knox. Then what was the motive?"

He smiled and looked at the small audience seated round the hotel salon.

"I will tell you, very briefly, why Wes Beattie killed. First of all, I will touch on the significant factors in his background. Wes's father came from what is called a fine old family, living in a stately home in Rosedale, one of the pleasantest residential districts in Toronto. His father, Rupert Beattie, married a girl his mother didn't approve of, and was kicked out of the home. There were two children—an older sister and Wes. The father went overseas and was killed in Italy. The mother neglected the children. So old Mrs. Beattie, full of contrition, took them away from the mother and raised them in Rosedale. The mother, I may say, had no objections that a little money wouldn't overcome.

"Family pride, more than love of the children, prompted the move. Young Wes was spoiled in a way, but he was, I feel, starved of real affection. The one relation he really loved and admired was his Uncle Edgar, a big, rather earthy man with what old Mrs. Beattie would call 'low tastes.' Uncle Edgar took Wes to ball games and circuses and gave him good birthday presents. I think he made Wes a little ashamed of liking flowers and music and paintings. Wes put on a lowbrow front to win Uncle Edgar's approval, but secretly he had less rugged tastes.

"Well, it all came out in the post-adolescent wash. Wes grew up a dreamer, a lazy boy, a chronic liar who would tell tall tales about having explored the Upper Amazon during his summer holidays and all that sort of thing. His school grades weren't good enough to get him into university, so they got him a job in a bank. He was careless and didn't progress very fast. He had a girl who encouraged him to spend a lot of money. He got into debt. He cadged and borrowed until his family was fed up with him. And at last he reached the fatal day when he couldn't beg or borrow a dollar from anyone at home or at the office, and that day came at a time when he desperately needed thirty bucks or so to take his girl to the Art Gallery Ball—she was on the junior committee.

"If Wes had been a teller, he probably would have borrowed the money from the till. But he wasn't, so what he did was the stupidest thing you could think of. He sneaked away early from the office one Thursday last May, and went to the car park behind a place called the Midtown Motel, over Spadina way, which is really just a hotel and restaurant with some motel units behind it as a gimmick. It is sometimes jocularly referred to as the Mothel, short for motor brothel.

"Wes went to the car park, looked through the cars, saw a woman's handbag in one and stole it. He stuffed the bag under his raincoat and was making off when the car park attendant caught him. He tried to lie out of it. He said the car was his girlfriend's car and the purse was hers too. She was in the bar, and he had come back to get her purse for her. But then the real owner of the handbag came along and claimed it. Wes tried to break away and run. But they took him to the police station, where he told more lies. He gave a false name and address. He said that the girl he had been with was a nice girl, who had obviously run away when the trouble started, because her parents would have been horrified to learn that she had been drinking at a motel; then he decided he had been with a married woman who had a jealous husband, and that *she* had been forced to run away.

"The upshot of all this was that Wes was dragged into police court next day, convicted and sentenced to two months for theft."

"Next day?" a voice said. "And he got two months for a first offense?"

Everyone turned to look at the questioner. He was a short, slender man whose enormous head was surmounted by a mop of wiry black hair. He wore outsize horn-rim specs, behind which he frowned in ferocious concentration.

"Shut up, Gargoyle," somebody said. "Don't interrupt."

Dr. Heber laughed. "Discussion is most important in our little project," he said. "Please don't hesitate to interrupt. Yes sir, Wes *did* get two months for a first offense, and he *was* tried the next day. Perhaps we could go back to that aspect later."

"I certainly think we should," the little man with the large head said.

"Very well. Now everything that Wes said and did at that time indicated an emotional disturbance requiring skilled therapy. What he got was two months in Guelph, where he was a bad prisoner, and when he came home he was moody, surly and withdrawn. He had already made up a story of having been framed by a mystery gang of crooks, and he plagued all his relations with the story until they were sick of it.

"Nevertheless, they handled Wes with considerable intelligence and sympathy. They humored him. An uncle got him a job with an ad agency. They tried to rehabilitate him. But another uncle—Uncle Edgar—behaved with a notable lack of sympathy. He took the attitude that Wes was a rotten little sneak thief who had turned to crime the moment he couldn't get what he wanted honestly. He wanted no part of him.

"Now Uncle Edgar's approval was all-important to Wes. He bugged the man. He phoned him and wrote letters. He said that the theft charge was a frame-up. He went to the police and demanded the address of the woman witness whose handbag had been stolen. They naturally wouldn't give it to him. They don't want released convicts to go persecuting witnesses. This was fuel for Wes's imagination. The woman was a member of the gang, he said. But Uncle Edgar was obdurate, and he had a new will drafted, cutting Wes out. I honestly do not believe that the will had anything to do with what happened.

"For the benefit of our international guests, I will quickly run through the details of the actual murder. Edgar Beattie lived in an old-fashioned apartment where he was looked after by an elderly housekeeper, who was also a distant relative.

"The old lady is arthritic and goes to bed very early. One Friday evening she had gone to bed, leaving Edgar sitting on a sofa watching the television and drinking a few bottles of beer. At about ten-thirty something woke her up and she lay awake listening. All she could hear was the television, but after several minutes she heard the sound of a telephone being dialed—her hearing is quite acute. She called out 'Ed-gar!' but, getting no reply, she shuffled into the living room and found Edgar lying dead on the sofa. Beside him was a heavy blackthorn stick, which normally resided in an umbrella stand in the vestibule. It had been used to crush Edgar's skull with a single blow, delivered with maniacal force.

"The police conducted the normal routine investigations, in the course of which they found some fingerprints on the telephone which were neither the housekeeper's nor Edgar's. They checked them against the prints of known criminals in the files and found they belonged to one Wesley M. Beattie, who had served two months for theft.

"At the time it didn't seem important. After all, he was a relative. But a police inspector called on Wes and questioned him. Where had he been on the night of the murder? Drinking beer with a couple of guys, he said, and he had also gone to a show. The guys were called Pete and Al, and he couldn't remember the name of the film. But, most significant of all, he insisted that he had not been in or near his uncle's apartment for over six months. The housekeeper later corroborated this.

"So he was taken to headquarters, where he changed his story. He had spent the evening of the murder with a girl at her house. He wouldn't name her—note the pattern—because she was a nice girl and her parents would be horrified to know she had been keeping company with an 'ex con.' Wes likes tough words like 'ex con' and 'stir.' Police told him that a nice girl wouldn't let him hang, so he changed once more—and again we see the pattern—into a married woman with a jealous husband.

"Then after a few hours of that, he abandoned all efforts at realism and produced his conspiracy story, which goes like this: This gang that had framed him was still after him. But he was after them, too. And so was Uncle Edgar. Uncle Edgar had only been pretending to think that Wes was guilty of the theft. In reality, he was ruthlessly tracking them down. The woman witness was the key to the whole thing. She was one of the gang. Uncle Edgar was on her trail, and eventually he would have laid the whole pack of them by the heels.

"However, the brain that runs this gang is pretty crafty. He got one of the gang to call Edgar and warn him to lay off—or else. But you couldn't frighten old Edgar like that. No sir.

"So they worked this frame-up. One of the dolls in this mob picked Wes up and lured him to her apartment, and that's where he spent the evening of the murder. The cunning witch got hold of Wes's key container and slipped in a key to Edgar's apartment, as part of the frame-up. Meanwhile, other members of the gang went to Edgar's place and finished him off. Very well, you say, who was the girl? Where is the apartment?

"But Wes says he was driven to the apartment at night by a roundabout route. He went in by a rear entrance. He can't even guess what *district* it's in. Far from getting the license number of the girl's car, he isn't even sure of the make. The girl's name was Gail—she never told him her last name. Confronted with the evidence of the fingerprints, Wes stumbled a bit, then decided that this gang had invented some subtle photographic process for transferring prints. And so, Wes was charged with murder.

"And now I'll tell you my theory of how it happened. Wes tried every device to win back Edgar's approval, but Edgar, being a blunt fellow, simply rejected him. That rejection so disturbed his emotional balance that he was led to kill his great hero. He probably toyed with the idea for some time. We don't know, for instance, exactly when he obtained a key to the uncle's apartment, or how. On that fatal Friday, everything came to the boil. He went to the apartment and let himself in, and the uncle, watching TV, with his back to the door, did not hear him. Wes may have planned new entreaties; he may have stood there quivering for several minutes before frustration rose in him and nerved him to pick up the blackthorn stick, take two strides and deliver one smashing blow.

"Then, I think, he stood there, reeling with horror at what he had done. It was, of course, an insane act, and I do not think he took the consequences of the act into account at all. As the climax approached, he wasn't even thinking about getting away with it, or possible punishment. It was a blind impulse.

"He knew, of course, that the elderly housekeeper was there. He probably knew that her hearing and eyesight were good for a woman of her age. But he *certainly* knew that she was extremely immobile and very feeble. It takes her a good five minutes to collect her two sticks, pull herself painfully out of bed and make her way to the living room—and longer if she pauses to put her teeth in and find her spectacles, slippers and dressing gown. As I said, he probably took none of this into account; but if he had, if she had appeared to be at all dangerous—if, for instance, the uncle had called out his name—then, I fear, the old lady would have been dealt with quickly and in panic. The same thing would apply if she had succeeded in getting to the living room before he had left the premises. But the fact is that she didn't.

"And, in the circumstances, I believe that Wes's first impulse, when he began to realize what he had done, was to give himself up. I think he went to the telephone, peeled off his gloves—the absence of fingerprints on the murder weapon itself could indicate a degree of premeditation—and, barehanded, started to telephone the police. But then the housekeeper called out, and Wes panicked and departed.

"There is something rather wonderful about what took place after that. The horror of the deed was so great that it was completely blotted out of his memory. He couldn't face it. His mind rejected it, and wove the whole thing into the fantasy which he was already partly living in. This became the work of the gang. The gang had killed his uncle, and Wes and his uncle, shoulder-to-shoulder, had been fighting their villainies. This fantasy allows him to live with himself. He has retired into his dream world, probably forever, and there we plan to leave him. But gentlemen, if proper therapy had been applied at the time of his first arrest, all of this would have been avoided. Now then, the gentleman who had some questions. Let's hear from him."

❄ ❄ ❄

All of the lawyers present were acquainted with Sidney Grant, who was known to his classmates as the "Gargoyle." He looked, they claimed, like some evil figure leering down from a Gothic cathedral. They remembered him best in a characteristic attitude, sitting on the dressing table in the large attic bedroom which he had occupied for years, and frowning down on his guests like some Mephistophelian judge, while he argued endlessly.

The Gargoyle had been called to the bar only a few months before, but, unlike most other young lawyers, he had not gone into an established firm. He had hung up his shingle and commenced the practice of criminal law in the lower courts, where he was already establishing a reputation as a tough battler.

"Okay, Gargoyle, fire away," someone said, and Dr. Heber smiled.

"Question one," Sidney Grant said. "Why such a stiff sentence for a first offense—on the theft charge?"

"Answer one," Dr. Heber said. "The magistrate was like some Fielding character. Wes Beattie broke down in court and made a rather sorry exhibition of himself. He was still trying to lie his way out of it, and he got this old Colonel Blimp magistrate pretty angry, so he threw the book at him."

"Question two," Sidney said. "Why was he tried next day? Why wasn't the case remanded for two weeks so that Beattie could get himself a bit organized? I mean, if he'd pleaded guilty he would simply have got a suspended sentence. If the case had been remanded…"

A beautifully groomed young lawyer stood up at the back of the room. "Dr. Heber," he said, "there is no use trying to protect me any longer. Gargoyle Grant is going to find out all about it, so I will confess. Sidney, I was Wes Beattie's counsel in the magistrate's court, and I have to take a share of the blame."

"James Bellwood!" Sidney said. "What were you doing in the police court anyway? Not your class of client at all."

"Mr. Grant," Bellwood said, "you may go jump in the lake. Our clients get into the magistrates' courts every now and then, usually by mixing alcohol with gasoline. But this case was different. For the visitors I must explain that I am a junior in a very high-class corporation law firm, the sort of firm that my learned and belligerent friend treats with amused contempt. And I will state that if ever one of our clients gets into an action in which Mr. Grant represents the opposition, we will advise him to settle right away, because Mr. Grant is going to be one of our great courtroom lawyers."

"Flattery will get you nowhere, Bellwood," Sidney Grant said with a satanic grin. "Tell us about the Beattie bit."

"Very well. I will have to stick my neck out a bit, but I trust you will regard this confession as being under the seal. My firm has a client called the Superior Trust Company. The secretary of the company is one Ralph L. Paget, who comes out strongly on the side of dignity, propriety and other engaging virtues. One morning at four A.M. Mr. Paget phoned the senior partner of my firm, Mr. Claude Potter, and told him that his nephew, Wes Beattie, was in the cells charged with theft. There was a tremendous flap. Mr. Potter phoned me—I live hell and gone out in Port Credit—and said to come in and bail this kid out and try to hush up the scandal as much as possible. It seems that the kid lived with his granny, old Mrs. Charles Beattie, who had recently lost her husband and was in delicate health. The shock was likely to kill her, because Wes was, quote, the apple of her eye.

"I found the kid in a frightful state. The police had been questioning him—no duress, force, violence or threats, of course. They said he got the bruise on his cheek when he fell downstairs. He'd been caught with the goods on him, so I said there were two things he could do. He could go in and plead guilty, or he could ask for a remand. But meanwhile Mr. Paget had joined me, and he said that a remand would give the papers a chance to get the story and blow it up. I felt that his fears were exaggerated. Wes tearfully tried to tell us some weird story which did not in the least resemble the first statements he had made to the police.

"He said that some Englishman had called him at the bank where he worked, and had offered him a terrific job—as an executive trainee! The man said he represented an English company about to open up a Canadian subsidiary. He wanted Wes to come for an interview to his hotel and told him he would send his secretary to pick Wes up and drive him there. Wes got permission to leave the bank early; the secretary picked him up and drove him to the Midtown Motel, where she parked and walked with him to the rear entrance of the bar. Then she remembered she'd left her handbag in the car and sent Wes back to get it. He must have got confused and taken the wrong handbag from the wrong car, he said. And then, when they looked for the secretary in the bar, she wasn't there. She vanished, he said, into thin air. Mr. Paget got quite angry. He said, 'Wes, I'm sick of your silly lies. You simply get yourself all tangled up in them.'

"Anyway, I talked to the man from the Crown Attorney's office, and he said his witnesses would be in court, and one of them—the woman whose purse had been stolen—was from out of town—Sudbury, I believe. He would be only too happy to proceed, naturally. I met Mr. Potter and Mr. Paget and urged that we get a remand, in the hope that the witness wouldn't show up two weeks later. But Mr. Paget said no, it would be terrible to have this disgrace hanging over the old lady—his mother-in-law, Wes's grandmother. The papers might try to make something of a youth from a prominent family stealing from parked cars.

"So, much to everyone's surprise, the case was heard that morning. Wes pleaded Not Guilty, and tried to tell this silly story of his. The magistrate kept interrupting him, and then, on cross-examination, the prosecutor tore him to shreds. Why had Wes concealed the handbag under his coat? Because, Wes said, he felt silly carrying a woman's purse."

"Which makes good sense," Sidney said. "I dare *you* to carry a woman's purse in that district. You'd be accosted!"

There was much laughter.

"True enough," Bellwood said. "But the owner of the purse was there, she certainly identified her property, and she said that Wes had hung on to the bag even after she claimed it. Wes was asked why, if he was innocent, he had twice tried to break loose, and run away. He said he was frightened and confused. Under fire his features trembled and the tears flowed, and old Cartwright was disgusted. He said Wes was a disgrace to his entire background, et cetera, et cetera, and gave him two months."

"A very pretty mess," Sidney Grant said. "And just what you can expect when you try to hush things up. Damn it, the woman had recovered her property. I'll bet she never would have returned to give evidence if the thing had been remanded."

"I entirely agree with you, Gargoyle," Bellwood said.

"Fine," Sidney Grant said. "But another thing occurs to me. Why, Dr. Heber, don't you simply look this woman witness up, bring her to see Wes Beattie and convince him that she is not a member of a sinister gang? You could show him that his Uncle Edgar wouldn't have had any trouble locating her and that there was no brain to warn his uncle to 'lay off—or else.'"

"My dear Mr.—er—Grant," Dr. Heber said. "We have no interest whatever in exploding this fantasy of Wes's. The moment we question his story he gets wildly hysterical and then withdraws, virtually into a catatonic trance. There is no communicating with him on any other terms than that his story is accepted. We are happy to let him live in this weird world of his."

"Well, how about his counsel in the murder trial— Baldwin Ogilvy? Isn't *he* interested in checking this thing out?"

"Well, no," Dr. Heber said, and smiled. "Please be discreet about this, but Wes's defense will simply be insanity. These delusions will save him from the gallows. The Crown will, I understand, accept the plea of insanity and that will be that."

"I would still like to talk to that woman witness," Sidney Grant said. "Women keep vanishing into thin air. This is one who could be found."

"Then, if it will give you any satisfaction, Mr. Grant, I suggest that you find her and talk to her. Meanwhile, Wes sits in the Psychiatric Hospital on an attorney general's remand warrant, living in his world of fantasy which he will probably never leave again. The reality is too horrible for his mind to contemplate."

"It's a funny thing," Sidney said. "Twice this man has gone through the same routine. 'I was with a nice girl—her parents mustn't know.' Then 'I was with a married woman who has a jealous husband.' Finally 'I was the victim of a vast conspiracy.'"

"That is the way Wes Beattie's mind works," Dr. Heber said. "He has a long history as a chronic liar."

"The boy who cried 'Wolf' too often," Sidney said. "Well, sir, I *am* going to find that woman witness, the one whose handbag was stolen."

"Good for you," the psychiatrist said. "And good luck."

# Chapter Two

The name and address of the woman witness were easy to find. The court office had the information, as well as the Crown Attorney's office, and a stenographer had been sent to the police court from Jim Bellwood's office to take down the proceedings against Wes verbatim, because the magistrates' courts were not themselves equipped with court stenographers.

All sources agreed that the woman whose handbag had been stolen was Mrs. Irene Leduc, of 428 Baylie Circle, Sudbury, Ontario.

So Sidney Grant summoned his secretary, Miss Georgina Semple, an elderly woman with incredible red hair piled high on her head, and dictated a registered letter to Mrs. Leduc, stating simply that he had legal matters of a confidential nature to discuss with her.

His letter was returned by the Sudbury post office, which stated that there was no such address.

"Ha!" he said gleefully, and wrote to a lawyer friend in Sudbury asking him to check on the whole business. Was there any address *like* the one given, or was there a Mrs. Irene Leduc who had been a witness in the Toronto case?

In due course a ribald reply came from the friend, saying that no such woman existed and advising Mr. Grant to be more careful in future when he picked up stray females in bars. Miss Semple, who had large brown eyes and a knowing air, could not suppress her amusement at the reply.

Tracing the woman witness was not, after all, going to be simple routine.

Sidney Grant took the first opportunity to visit the Midtown Motel and examine the register. According to Bellwood's transcript, the woman witness had been a guest at the motel. The manager was inclined to be hostile. He didn't like people, especially lawyers, nosing in his register—but the law was the law. And Sidney discovered that a Mr. and Mrs. G. Leduc, of Sudbury, Ontario, had booked in at the Midtown at 11 A.M. on Thursday, May 11, the day of the theft for which Wes Beattie had served two months in prison. He further learned that the Leducs had checked out at 8 P.M. on the same day.

No doubt all the fuss about the theft had driven them to change hotels, Sidney decided. But, most important, he took down the license number of the Leducs' car, which was noted on the registration card.

Back at the office, he asked Miss Semple to check the car license with the Parliament buildings. It proved to be a black Dodge sedan, belonging to a car rental agency on Dundas Street in Toronto.

"Now what do you make of that, Georgie dear?" Sidney asked Miss Semple.

Miss Semple had spent most of her life in a large law office, from which she had been superannuated. A pillar of virtue herself, she was nevertheless knowing in the ways of the world.

"What do I make of what?" she asked.

"A woman, claiming to be Mrs. Leduc, of Sudbury, rents a car in Toronto, books a motel room at eleven A.M. and gives it up early the same evening."

"The afternoon is a lovely time of day, they say!" Miss Semple said archly.

"This woman had her purse stolen in the motel car park. The thief was caught with the goods on him. *Next* day the woman, using this same name and address, went into court and gave evidence against the thief," Sidney said.

"Well, really!" Miss Semple said. "What some women won't do! I suppose she is a local woman who rented the car and went to this motel with her boyfriend. She rented the car because she knows that motels take down license numbers, and she wanted to pretend she was from out of town. Her husband probably thought she was shopping at Simpson's."

"That's the way it looks," Sidney said. "But if this is a false name, why would she take a chance and appear in court if she didn't have to? She had recovered her property, after all."

"Immoral women can be terrible prudes," Miss Semple asserted. "I mean I knew a notoriously wanton female who was *shocked* if anybody used a bad word. A woman might take a high-and-mighty moral attitude to a sneak thief at the very moment she was being *flagrantly* unfaithful to her husband."

"I suppose so," Sidney said. "But I would certainly love to talk to this woman. In fact, I made a boast that I would. However, she seems to have made herself pretty scarce."

"Why don't you check with the car rental people?" Miss Semple said. "They might have a lead."

"By golly, I will," Sidney said. "First free minute I get." Sidney Grant did not have many free minutes. He spent a great deal of time in the lower courts, working for small fees, and office work filled the rest of his time. He could not even afford the modest luxury of an articled law student.

But nevertheless he managed to get around, being active and wiry, and in due course he got around to the car rental agency, where the manager was proud to show off his record system.

"When we rent a car," he told Sidney, "we open one of these dockets. See? A manila envelope. On the outside we write the details of the vehicle and the renter. Like time of rental, mileage out, mileage in, name, address and driver's license number of the renter. So you tell me the date and all, and maybe I can turn up this rental you're interested in."

"Mrs. Irene Leduc," Sidney said. "Sometime about May tenth or eleventh."

The man disappeared and returned after a short delay with one of the dockets.

"Got it right here," he said. "Now, this vehicle was a black Dodge, and we booked it out at ten A.M. Mrs. Irene Leduc, Sudbury, Ontario. She drove it—holy cow!—she only drove it six point four miles. Boy, it would be a lot cheaper to take taxis! And she brought it back seven P.M. Now here's her driver's license number. You want that? Not checkin' up on the little woman, I hope?"

"Eh?" Sidney said.

"Your wife isn't givin' you trouble, I hope," the man said.

"Definitely not," Sidney said. "She doesn't get the chance. I am a devout bachelor. What is there *inside* the envelope?"

"Well, there won't be anything," the man said. "See, like when the renter buys gas and oil, they pay cash and get a receipt, and we file the receipts in here. Like we refund the money they pay out. And parking tickets or speeding tickets that they hand in—we file them here too, although a lot of creeps just tear their parking tickets up and throw 'em away."

"So there's nothing in this envelope?"

"Well, she'd hardly buy any gas, see? Hold it, though—she did!"

He fished a flimsy receipted bill from the envelope.

"Nope. She had trouble. Fuel pump repairs, a buck fifty, which between you and I is highway robbery. Maybe that's why she brought the car back."

The bill said "Mac's Garage" and was receipted "R. Phelan."

Sidney Grant wrote the details in his notebook, thanked the man for his trouble and returned to the office. "I think we may have a line on the elusive Irma La Douce or Irene Leduc," he told Miss Semple. "Just check this driver's license number out with the Parliament buildings, will you?"

Miss Semple was back in the inner sanctum within three minutes, and she laid a slip of paper in front of her employer. It said: "Mrs. Irene Ledley, 28 Bayview Circle, Toronto."

"Well I'm blowed," Sidney said, and pulled his own driver's license out of his wallet. "Do you suppose she just flashed the license and gave a wrong address, or do you think she actually cooked the license?"

"Very easy to cook it," Miss Semple said. "Look—she could type a four in front of the twenty-eight to make four-two-eight, and she could alter 'Bayview' to Baylie by changing a couple of letters."

"I suppose," Sidney said, "you could erase Toronto and type in Sudbury—both seven letters."

"And you could sign Irene Leduc to make it look like Irene Ledley," she said. "I suppose Mrs. Ledley was having an affair, and she wanted to cover her tracks."

"And then appear in court under her false name," Sidney said. "Tomorrow I am going to visit Bayview Circle. I don't want to phone, but I'd like to catch her when her husband is at the office. Unless I'm wrong, she'll be so scared that she'll tell us anything we want to know."

"Blackmail!" Miss Semple said.

"Persuasion," Sidney corrected.

❄ ❄ ❄

Bayview Circle was in a fashionable suburban area, and Number 28 proved to be a modern split-level house complete with car port, breezeway and Chinese elm hedge.

Mrs. Ledley, however, did not appear to be a typical suburban housewife. She was in her early forties, and there was charm as well as intelligence in her features. She was a little hesitant about admitting a stranger to the house, but Sidney insisted that his business was confidential and could not be conducted on the doorstep.

"Very well, do come in," she said, and led him to the living room.

"Mrs. Ledley," he said, when they were seated, "I have no desire to cause you any embarrassment. But last May somebody rented a car and then rented a unit at the Midtown Motel, using your driver's license as identification."

"*My* driver's license?" she said. "How could that *be?*"

"You were not the person who rented the car?" he asked.

"No! I've never rented a car in my life. What are you implying, Mr.—er—Grant? I don't think I like this."

"I'm implying nothing, Mrs. Ledley. Would you mind showing me your driver's license?"

"Not at all," she said. "Hold on, I'll get my handbag." After a brief search, she found the handbag hanging on a doorknob, and from it produced a small leather folder containing a long plastic envelope. In its compartments were various credit cards and insurance papers and the owner's paper for her car.

But no license.

"Well, that's the oddest thing," she said. "It *couldn't* have fallen out. I wonder what can have happened to it?"

"When did you last have occasion to look for it?" Sidney asked.

"Oh, I don't suppose I've looked at it since I put it in there last March," she said.

"And you wouldn't remember what you were doing in May—around the tenth and eleventh of May?" he asked.

"Heavens, no! We had a holiday in Tobago at Easter. Then in June we went to Ireland. My husband handles diamond drill equipment, and we went to Ireland where there's some drilling on mining properties, and we were there till September, and when that was finished we bought a Peugeot and toured Europe all through September. But May…"

"You have no idea how or when you lost your license?" he said. "I would suggest that you lost it early in May. Is that possible? Nobody stole your purse in May, did they?"

She looked at him in blank bewilderment. "Is this really important, Mr. Grant?" she said.

"Yes, it is. It may be a matter of life and death."

"Well, hold on then. I have a diary in which I write down social engagements. It may give me some clue. Wait a minute, will you?"

"Certainly," Sidney said, and he watched her closely as she left the room.

Was she stalling for time? Had she altered her license and then destroyed it? If so, she was a pretty cool operator. Sidney looked about the room. One split level was much like another to him, but the general arrangements of Mrs. Ledley's house showed quiet good taste, and her manner had a dignity which did not fit in with sordid affairs at motels.

She returned with a diary and a large brochure on coated stock. "We're in luck," she said. "Wednesday, tenth. Mining Awards Dinner. Royal York Hotel. There was a big mining convention on that week, and my husband and I attended several functions. And incidentally, I've just remembered a funny thing. Strange how things come back to you, isn't it?"

"Yes, the human memory is tricky," he agreed.

"Well, anyway, at these conventions a lot of big companies put in hospitality suites—snake rooms, they call them. You know, a big living room with a bar, and a couple of bedrooms opening off it. And people go pub crawling from room to room, having a good old freeload. Well, after this dinner, Ken and I went to several rooms, and I had quite a scare."

"Really?"

"Yes. We were in this suite, and I threw my coat and handbag on the bed in the adjoining bedroom—quite a few women left their coats there. Well, when I went to get my coat, I got a start, because there was my handbag lying on *top* of my coat, and I had left it *under* my coat, and there was over two hundred dollars in it. I felt such a damn fool! My husband would never let me hear the end of it if I lost all that money so stupidly. Well, I quickly pulled it out and counted it, and it was all there.

But do you suppose some woman opened the bag and pinched my license, and I never missed it?"

Sidney looked at her with frank admiration. "That is quite possible," he said. "The timing is right. You said Wednesday, tenth?"

"That's right. Here's the program. Warm-up cocktail party Tuesday evening, and then, for some delegates, the cocktail party continued without interruption until Friday, May twelfth. This dinner was on the Wednesday."

"The night before your license was used to rent a car," Sidney said.

"How very strange!" she exclaimed.

"Now then, Mrs. Ledley," he said, "I'm going to be nasty, just to save time and trouble. The woman who used your license rented a motel room and a car. She appeared in police court as a witness against a young man who stole her handbag. She was seen by lawyers, parking attendants and others. If you are that woman, now is the time to say so, because there are plenty of people who can identify you. And if you *are* that woman, and if you now tell me so, it will go no further. I will promise you full protection."

"I am *not* that woman," she said, calmly, but with a note of anger. "I have told you I'm not. You may take me to all your witnesses and I will defy them to say I am. I have told you the truth, and nothing but the truth, and I resent your insinuations."

"Which I withdraw and apologize for. I wouldn't have bothered you at all if this were not a desperately serious matter. Would you mind letting me have a photograph of you, which I will return in tonight's mail?"

"So you can check up on me with your witnesses?"

"Yes. So that I can positively eliminate you. And I know that that will happen."

"All right," she said, and laughed. "You really don't think I'm the motel affair type, do you?"

"No," he said. "And I wonder if I could keep that convention program."

"Certainly," she said. "It's just junk. It has a complete list of the delegates and registered guests and their wives, broken down by occupations—you know, mining engineers, brokers and so on. Only one thing is missing."

"And what is that?" he asked.

She smiled mischievously. "There is no heading for Call Girls," she said. "And there seemed to be some of them about. Conventions! Heavens!"

Sidney left with the photograph and the convention program, but an hour later he mailed the photograph back. James Bellwood was prepared to state positively that Mrs. Ledley was not the witness who had claimed that Wes had stolen her handbag.

Which left Sidney Grant with a convention program—and a receipted bill for fuel pump repairs. He had spent sufficient time looking for Mrs. Leduc, and for no return at all. But what, he wondered, would Wes Beattie make of it, if he knew how very thoroughly Mrs. Leduc had vanished? There would be fuel for the imagination of a boy with schizophrenic delusions.

Sidney Grant thought about it. What possible explanation could there be for Mrs. Leduc's conduct? Miss Semple had a theory. "Either this woman was married to a very rich man, or her boyfriend was a very rich man," she said. "It was very dangerous for them to meet, which made it all the more exciting. I mean that if her husband was rich and she got caught, he might divorce her with a very poor alimony settlement. So getting this fake driver's license will be a great help to her on other occasions."

"And why did she give evidence in the police court?" Sidney said. "Moral indignation?"

"No, I don't think so, Mr. Grant. The policeman had taken her address and had asked her to show up in court. She was afraid that if she didn't show up, there might be a hue and cry after the stolen driver's license or something like that."

"Uh huh," Sidney said. "Something like that. At any rate, she has covered her tracks with complete success."

# Chapter Three

"Mr. Grant, what on earth are you doing with my handbag?" Miss Semple demanded with a note of outrage.

"What handbag?" Sidney asked innocently, tucking his secretary's purse under his coat.

"Why, my—*Mister* Grant, who steals my purse steals cash. I'd vastly prefer that you robbed me of my reputation."

"Look," Sidney said, "I'm caught with the goods on me. What story should I tell in order to lie out of it?"

"You could say you were a lawyer," Miss Semple said. "Just doing a little experiment to put yourself in a client's position."

"He isn't a client," Sidney said, "but otherwise the story is true, and anybody will believe it, especially in the absence of previous convictions for theft. In other words, I could really be stealing this purse, but get away with it. You caught me red-handed. I laughingly explain and hand the purse back. Now this boy Wes Beattie, who stole this purse..."

"Wes Beattie? Not the one who murdered his uncle? Will we be assisting Mr. Baldwin Ogilvy in his defense?" Miss Semple asked, lighting up like a switchboard.

"No, no, no," Sidney said. "I just got challenged to find a certain woman, the one we've been looking for, Mrs. Leduc, and it made me curious. Now suppose this Wes Beattie wanted to steal that purse. Suppose he opened the car door, airily took it out and carried it openly, swinging it. Would the parking lot attendant challenge him?"

"He might," Miss Semple said. "But the bluff could work."

"Well, suppose he *did* challenge him—'Hey, where are you going with the purse'—the thief could smile and say, 'Just taking it to its owner in the bar.' Martin Luther said 'Sin boldly.' Excellent advice for thieves. Poor young Beattie floundered around looking for some plausible explanation and just got himself all tied up. By the way, keep this all strictly under your hat with your gorgeous curls, Miss Semple," Sidney said.

"Is it necessary to tell *me* that?" Miss Semple said sniffily. "I've worked over forty years in law offices."

"Sorry," Sidney said. "Well, I've still got your purse and I'm walking off with it, sinning boldly. Challenge me."

"Here, you!" she said. "Where are you going with my purse?"

"*Your* purse," Sidney said, looking puzzled. "Oh, for goodness' sake, have I made a mistake?"

"You most certainly have, young man, and I've got a good mind to call the police."

"Oh dear," Sidney said. "It must look really awful. I'm sure you think I'm a crook. Would you please just check the contents and assure yourself that I haven't taken anything?"

"That would work, in all likelihood," Miss Semple said.

"Wes Beattie was just too stupid to change his ground at the instant when the owner of the handbag appeared," Sidney said. "He is what is technically called a crazy mixed-up kid. But I *still* want to talk to Mrs. Leduc and find out why she sent the boy up the river."

"And have you explored every avenue?" Miss Semple asked.

"Aye, and turned every stone," he said. "Except one. It can't possibly get me anything, but damn it, I shall turn it anyway."

All of which led to a futile visit to Mac's Garage, where various mechanics laughed coarsely and told Sidney that he needed to see a headshrinker.

"Listen, bud," one man said, "we might do fifty, sixty little jobs a day. So we should remember fixin' a fuel pump last May? You must be nuts."

"But how about R. Phelan? Is he around? He's the man who receipted this repair bill."

"Rick Phelan? Are you nuts? You expect to find him here during the hockey season?"

Sidney Grant asked for further enlightenment and learned that Rick Phelan was a hockey player who worked only in the summers at the garage. He was, in fact, the greatest prospective defenseman to come down the pike since the late Bill Barilko, and in order to see him Sidney had to catch him when his team was playing in Toronto. This he managed on a Sunday in February, when he found the hockey player in a hotel room not far from the Maple Leaf Gardens.

"Sorry to bug you on a Sunday morning," Sidney said. "And the question may sound exceedingly stupid, but..."

"Stupid questions? I answer dozens," Phelan said. "Fire away."

"Well, last May you did some repair work on a black Dodge," Sidney said. "It was a rented car, and you made out a receipt for a dollar fifty which you gave to the driver. The driver was probably a woman, and she may have had a man with her. The specific trouble was in the fuel pump. Now, is there any chance that you might remember anything at all about such a transaction?"

Phelan shook his head and looked at Sidney Grant sadly. "Boy, you are an optimist," he said. "Now what odds would you offer against me remembering anything about a deal like that?"

"Plenty," Sidney said.

"Sure. Wouldn't anyone? But I'm tellin' you chum, don't do it! You'd lose. The fact is I remember that black Dodge loud and clear, but I'm not sure I ought to tell you anything about it."

"Why not?" Sidney asked.

"Because," Phelan said, "you're not the first guy to come askin' me questions about that Dodge. And if you knew what happened to the first guy that come, maybe you wouldn't be so keen."

"What happened to the first guy?" Sidney asked, and he could feel an old prickling in his calves and a pounding in his temples as he said it, though he asked his question casually enough.

"What happened to him?" Phelan said. "He got murdered. That's what happened to him. No kidding, either."

"Murdered?"

"Yeah. You probably read it in the papers. This guy Edgar Beattie—his cousin or something bashed his skull in. That was the guy that come askin' about the Dodge."

"And you think there was some connection?" Sidney asked.

Phelan laughed. "Hell, no," he said. "Although for a few days it gave me a funny feeling, until they caught this nephew. It kind of made me wonder."

"Tell me about it," Sidney said. "Tell me every detail. This is very, very interesting indeed." He felt faint and giddy, and he had to help himself to a glass of water.

"You mean that? Every detail?" Phelan said. "I don't want to be called L.P. Phelan, but if you really want it I can give you the full treatment."

"I want the full treatment," Sidney said.

"Okay, okay, just like this Mr. Beattie," he said. "And then maybe you'll tell me what this is all about. Anyway, see, this Mr. Beattie came along and just like you he wanted to know about the Dodge. That was early in September. So I told him sorry, you know, what routine job did *you* do last May? Well, he was a very pleasant guy. He said sure, he understood that it wasn't likely, but he asked me would I *think* about it. He also handed me ten bucks, which I didn't like to take. But he said, 'Go on, buy your wife a fur coat.' He said I should get a couple of jugs or a few cases of beer and just think about dames and Dodges and fuel pumps. He said something might come back to me, and he really wanted to get a line on this dame.

"Well, like I said, I hated to take his ten bucks, and I didn't take it very seriously. But then one night I was lying half asleep and something flickered. I remembered making out a receipt. An experienced man can always spot a rented car, so I just automatically made the receipt out. I tried to hand it to the fellow in the car, but he brushed it off and said, 'Just gimme my change.' The dame sort of gave me the eye and reached out and took the receipt and stuck it in her handbag. Well, I thought about that, and then it all started to come back, just like watching a television show. So I phoned this Edgar Beattie and he was tickled pink."

"What all did you tell him?" Sidney asked.

"Well he wanted every detail you could think of, so I told him the whole thing. Like I was servicing this Olds convertible, a very flashy car belonging to a very flashy guy. A guy called 'Bunny,' who used to come in quite a lot, and always wanted to gas about hockey. He was the sort of guy who tries to make out he was once a pretty hot-shot hockey player, and this was strictly from the horse. You can guess which end. For instance, he told me he was on New York Rangers trading list, and if it hadn't been for the war he'd have been in the N.H.L. All that jazz. Well, you know, I'd string him along and ask him did he play for Marlies or St. Mikes maybe, but all he ever played for was his high school team. This all leads up to it, so don't get impatient."

"I'm not," Sidney said. "Just keep right on going."

"Well, anyway, while I was putting new wiper blades on the Olds, this black Dodge pulled in, hopping like a bunny. So, just kidding like, I said, 'Go on, Bunny, see if you can hop like that,' and I offered to bet him five that it was fuel pump trouble. He wouldn't take me. Then this dame, very nicely upholstered, got out of the Dodge and came over, while the guy with her just sat there. She said please could I fix her car in a hurry, and I told her I knew what was wrong and it wouldn't take long. So she went and sat in the car, and I went over to the air pump to check the tires on the Olds, and then this guy from the Dodge came over, steaming mad, and wanted to know how goddamn long

I expected him to wait. I told him just till I finished with the customer I was working on, and I told him to keep his shirt on. He was one of these handsome guys with a kind of ugly expression, and he was just turning around when Bunny jumped out of his car and yelled, 'Hi!' The other guy swung round, and Bunny went up to him holding out both hands and saying, 'Well, well, well, long time no see,' and all that stuff. But the guy from the Dodge gave him the fishy eye and said, 'Hi, Bunny,' and walked off. You know, cold as a Polar bear's nose.

"Well, you should have seen Bunny! He stood there with his mouth open, and he looked like a little boy that didn't hold his hand up soon enough in school. So he turned to me and said, 'How do you like that, Rick? My old pal! What would you do if some old teammate of *yours* gave you that stuff?' I told him in my business the first thing you had to learn was the difference between the rear end of a horse and the rear end of a truck, and that made him laugh, so away he went. So then I fixed the fuel pump and that was it.

"Anyway, Mr. Beattie had said to phone him if ever I remembered anything, so I did, and he was so pleased he slipped me a twenty. I told him to forget it, but he shoved it in the pocket of my dungarees. Only I couldn't remember the last name of this Bunny, although I serviced his Olds quite a bit. Mr. Beattie said would I find out the next time the guy came in, and phone him, but don't tell this Bunny that anyone was asking. He said he was trying to track down this dame, but she'd gone off to Europe or something, and maybe he could find out about her from the guy.

"So next time Bunny came in, I took down the name and address from his credit card and called Mr. Beattie, and I'm telling you, he was a great sport and a big spender. He came down and gave me fifty—which made eighty bucks in all—for nothin'!"

"And can you remember Bunny's name now?" Sidney asked anxiously.

"Sure. Now I can. Peter L. Mayhew. Lives out in Scarborough. Now, do you mind telling me what this is all about?"

"Do you mind very much if I don't?" Sidney said. "I mean, you've been very good, and I hate to give you the brush, but the thing may be dynamite."

"I get it," Phelan said. "Well, I'd sure like to know—I mean this Mr. Beattie was a real nice guy, but..."

"Well, one of these days, if I ever find out the whole story, I'll tell you," Sidney said. "Meantime all I can say is thanks a lot, Rick."

"That's okay, that's okay," Phelan said. "I get the message."

❀ ❀ ❀

"Georgie dear," Sidney Grant greeted his secretary on Monday morning. "We've got hold of something very, very curious. And where it leads to I couldn't guess."

"Have you found Mrs. Leduc?" she asked.

"No ma'am. But this I have discovered. Wes Beattie, who is awaiting trial for murder, has a fantastic story about being the victim of a conspiracy. He claims that his Uncle Edgar, at the time he was murdered, was trying to find this Mrs. Leduc, who had once given evidence against him. And he claimed that Mrs. Leduc had vanished. Well, I have now discovered that Uncle Edgar *was* trying to find the lady and was spending cash on the search. He was really anxious to find her. Nobody believes a word Wes says—but I've proved that two of his claims are true.

"He also says that, when Uncle Edgar got close to the quarry, somebody called him up and warned him to lay off—or else. Maybe that was true as well."

"Will this have any bearing on the murder charge?" Miss Semple asked.

"That is another matter," Sidney said. "They have some pretty solid evidence that would require a lot of shaking. Fingerprints on a telephone. But the suggestion that there was some sort of conspiracy might stir things up a bit. Meanwhile, would you please look up one Peter L. Mayhew in the city directory and find out where his office is?"

Peter L. Mayhew proved to be one of the fifteen vice-presidents in a large advertising agency, and, before heading for the magistrate's court, Sidney ran him to earth behind a desk which consisted simply of a huge sheet of thick plate glass mounted on wrought-iron legs.

Mayhew was fair, with long blond lashes and a thin blond mustache. He wore an expression of amused disdain, and there was an irritating superiority in his speech. "Precisely how can I serve you, Mr. Grant?" he asked.

Sidney outlined the incident at Mac's Garage, as related by Rick Phelan and watched closely at the caution which crept into Mayhew's features as the tale proceeded. When Sidney had finished, Mayhew got up and poured himself a glass of water from a thermos jug on a table behind him.

"Well?" he said.

"Well," Sidney said, "all I want to know is who was this old pal who snubbed you so royally?"

Mayhew laughed lightly. "Nobody," he said. "There was no such incident. This mechanic fellow must have a vivid imagination. Send him around and I'll give him a job in our copy department. We *need* guys with creative imagination."

"You can't remember the incident?"

"No," Mayhew said, "and for the very good reason that it never took place. Look, old boy, if any old chum cut me dead, I'd remember, because under this tough, cynical exterior I am really a very sensitive guy. Was there anything else?"

"Yes," Sidney said. "Is that what you told Edgar Beattie when he came here to ask you about it?"

"Edgar Beattie? Who is Edgar Beattie?"

"A man who came here to ask you about that nonexistent incident," Sidney said.

"Nobody ever came here, I tell you," Mayhew said, the bantering tone yielding to a touch of asperity. "Who *is* this fellow?"

"Oh, come, you haven't heard of Edgar Beattie?" Sidney said. "Get with it."

"Oh, you mean the man who was murdered by his nephew?" Bunny Mayhew said. "Yes, of course I've heard about him, but I never had the ineffable pleasure of making his acquaintance. Now, if you don't mind, I have the odd spot of work to do..."

"Thank you so much for your trouble, Mr. Mayhew," Sidney said.

❈ ❈ ❈

Lunch that day for Sidney Grant consisted of a chicken salad sandwich and a cup of coffee, consumed at his desk, after a frantic morning in court defending various characters of the minor underworld.

"It's true, Miss Semple, it's true," he said between bites. "Someone *did* call Edgar Beattie and tell him to lay off. I'd be prepared to bet heavily on it. Our friend Mr. Mayhew called Mrs. Leduc's boyfriend, and the boyfriend called Edgar. And now, by golly, I am going to find the boyfriend and see what he has to say about it."

"How can you find him?" Miss Semple asked.

"There is a magazine about ad agency people and such like," Sidney said. "I think it's called *Marketing.* I'll bet they have biography files about important people in the ad game, although I don't know if they'd go as low as agency vice-presidents. Anyway, call them up and find out if they've got a file on Mayhew. If so, find out what school he went to. What high school, that is. I've got an idea."

While Sidney finished his coffee, Miss Semple returned to her desk and made the call. She came back with the information neatly written on a slip of paper. "He went to Annette Street Public School and Humberside Collegiate Institute," she said. "Right here in the city."

"Good," he said. "Well, I've already spent a lot of time on this thing, and now I'm going to invest in a cab fare to Humberside for a little historical research. This is a luxury I'm going to allow myself, so, if you will just mind the shop, I'll be on my way."

The school authorities were polite and helpful. The secretary directed Sidney to the library, where the librarian armed him with half a dozen back copies of *Hermes,* the school yearbook, covering the years 1938 to 1943.

Sidney sat down at a long table, where he worked with curious teenagers trying to peer over his shoulder. Each yearbook was crammed with group photographs of teams, and it did not take long to find a hockey-team picture with P. (Bunny) Mayhew in the rear row. Mayhew also appeared with the junior team of the previous year.

Sidney carefully listed the players on both teams. After all, according to Phelan, Mayhew had more or less described the man at the garage as an old teammate. "What would you do if an old teammate gave you that stuff?" or words to that effect. After duplications had been removed, there were fourteen names on the list. A list of war casualties in a later yearbook further reduced the number.

Sidney looked at the short list for several minutes, scratching the whiskers on his chin with his left hand as he did. All that was necessary really was to seize Mayhew, tie him to a polygraph lie detector and read the names to him, but there were obstacles in the way of such a bold scheme. As he stared at the names before him, an idea began to flicker in the back of his head, and the familiar satanic grin slowly spread over his face.

Sidney reached into the briefcase on the floor beside him and pulled out the mining convention program which Mrs. Ledley had given him. Patiently, painstakingly, he went down the columns of names, checking the high school hockey players against the mining people. And then, suddenly, he had it.

But although he had found a duplication, his lawyer's training forced him to continue with the job until he had checked out *all* the names, to make sure that there weren't *two* duplications.

But there was only one. Howie Gadwell had been a defenseman on the Humberside hockey team; Howard G. Gadwell, listed as a "broker-dealer," had been a registered guest at the mining convention.

It was just after five o'clock when a taxi delivered Sidney Grant in a high state of excitement at the building where Bunny Mayhew had his office.

❀ ❀ ❀

"I thought we had finished our business," Mayhew said coldly.

"How wrong you were!" Sidney said. *"Mister* Mayhew, you told me a big, fat fib, and don't attempt to deny it. I've got a good mind to tell your mother."

"Look, before I get mad, I'd advise you to get the hell out of here," Mayhew said.

"Presently, presently," Sidney said. "But first, why didn't you want to tell me that it was Howard Gadwell who snubbed you at Mac's Garage?"

No polygraph was needed to chart Mayhew's reaction. "You're nuts!" he yelled.

"And after Edgar Beattie came to see you, you called Gadwell and warned him that a gent was looking for him, didn't you?"

"Get the hell out of here, you..."

"Easy boy! And did you call Gadwell again today and warn him that *I* was looking for him?"

"Look," Mayhew said, "I told you this morning that there was never any such incident as you described. Now if you want to barge in here and start calling me a liar, you'd better be prepared to take the consequences."

"I'm all prepared," Sidney said. "I'm on my way to see Gadwell to tell him that *you* gave me his name, and you can try to convince him that you didn't."

"Do what you damn well please, but get out of here," Mayhew almost screamed.

"As you say. I'm on my way to Gadwell," Sidney said.

He had his hand on the door when Mayhew called him back, and when Sidney turned around, he found that Mayhew had positively shrunk. "Okay, you win," Mayhew said. "I'd just as soon you didn't go to Gadwell. It was him, all right. Now tell me what it's all about."

"He was with a lady at the garage," Sidney said.

"Sure. Quite a dish," Mayhew said. "Then this burly character came in here, and naturally I took him for a jealous husband."

"Naturally," Sidney said, barely suppressing a smile.

"So I stalled him off. I said I couldn't remember meeting anyone at Mac's. Then I phoned Howie Gadwell and warned him. I said I didn't think much of the way he snubbed his old friends, but all the same, no matter how they act, you've got to stand by your old friends. But in the paper it said this Beattie had been divorced for years."

"What was Gadwell's attitude?" Sidney said.

"Damned rude, actually. He told me it was a good thing for me that I'd kept my mouth shut, and if I valued my health I'd better still keep it shut. Well, then I really let him have it. I said he could be damn well grateful and he'd better lay off that tough talk, so he took the other tack and got all old palsy. He said this dame was dynamite, so please keep quiet, and he'd give me some free shares of some Moose Pasture stock he was promoting.

"Well, when I saw in the paper that Beattie had been murdered, I was pretty scared—I want no part of that stuff. So when I saw that this nephew had murdered him, I was a pretty relieved boy."

"I guess you were," Sidney said. "And now, if you'll give me a rundown on Gadwell, I'll go away and leave you alone. But don't tell him I was asking, if you don't mind."

"Don't worry—I won't," Mayhew said. "What do you want to know?"

"All I can find out about Gadwell—business connections and all that. Love life, et cetera," Sidney said.

"Well, in business, Howie is a sort of minor wheel," Mayhew said. "He owns pieces of things. Radio stations, a commercial film company, a night club. He started out as a phony stock promoter. He operated a boiler room—you know, a room where about twenty salesmen sit phoning to suckers all over the continent, pushing these mining stocks. He's been in trouble with the SEC in the States, and with the Stock Exchange and the Ontario Government securities people here. I haven't met him for years— except that once—but I've sort of followed his career."

"What about women?" Sidney asked.

"Gosh, I haven't got all night," Mayhew said. "His women are innumerable. He's been married about four times, but after his last divorce I think he learned his lesson. He likes girls. And he has this approach, you know; with his studio making TV commercials and all, they say any girl can get a bit to play if she approaches High Grade Howie the right way—like without her clothes. One of his earlier wives was Sharon Willison, the TV singer."

"Did you recognize the girl he was with at Mac's Garage?"

"No, never saw her, but she was quite a dish," Mayhew said. He was a very different man from the superior being who had first welcomed Sidney Grant in the morning, and seemed only too pleased to appease his interrogator in any way he could.

During the days that followed, Sidney Grant did a lot more checking on Howard Gadwell, but he avoided the direct approach. He went back to Mrs. Ledley, who did not know Gadwell, but met her husband, who did. From Mr. Ledley he obtained the names of mining people who knew Gadwell and disliked him—it was a goodly list—and whenever he had a spare minute, he called on them and asked the same question: Who was Howard Gadwell keeping company with at the mining convention last May?

Some of the men were evasive, and some didn't know, but in due course Sidney came upon a mining engineer with an office on Bay Street who knew and was willing to tell. The engineer's name was Val Eckhardt, and he was a big man with a bald dome and a craglike jaw.

"Sure I know who High Grade Howie's girlfriend was," Eckhardt said. "She was the wife of a fellow I know. A geologist from the Kansas School of Mines, and a very nice guy. He brought his wife down to Toronto from northern Quebec for the convention, and she promptly fell for Gadwell."

"And the name?" Sidney said.

"The guy's name is Wicklow, Tex Wicklow, he's called. I don't know the wife's name. Someone he met in Montreal, I believe."

"Do you know," Sidney asked, "if she was an old flame of Gadwell's, or if this was a sudden blooming of love?"

"I couldn't be sure, but I've got an idea they'd met before, and she just decided that Gadwell was the playmate she needed for this week in Toronto."

"Well, that would explain some things," Sidney said. "So Wicklow was busy around this convention, and his wife would be able to slip away to a motel for a few hours of bliss with Gadwell."

"Why slip away?" Eckhardt said. "She had a nice suite all to herself at the hotel."

*"All to herself?"*

"Sure. You see, the first night of this convention there was a warm-up cocktail party, and around eleven Brother Gadwell scooped up six or eight guests and took them for dinner to the Rathskeller, just across Front Street from the hotel. I wasn't in on the party, but I saw it—I was at a nearby table. Madame Wicklow was fairly high and throwing herself all over Gadwell, while poor Tex tried to ignore it and got quietly loaded. On the way back Tex fell behind the main party, and managed to stagger in front of a fastmoving cab. They rushed him to St. Michael's Hospital unconscious, with a suspected skull fracture, and he spent the next ten days being looked after by nuns, just as a contrast to his normal female companionship. Well, his good lady didn't even break stride. She just whooped it up for the rest of the week with High Grade Howie, who was looking pretty prosperous at the time."

"Then there was absolutely no need for them to slip away anywhere else?"

"No—they had a very cozy setup," Eckhardt said.

Eckhardt thought that Wicklow was working at a drill site in far northern Quebec and managed to confirm the fact by means of a telephone call. "They push the drills down into the hard rock, fifteen hundred, two thousand feet," Eckhardt said. "The shaft of the drill is made of hollow pipes, and when they drill a section, they pull up the pipe and take out the hard rock core. Wicklow's job is to examine the drill cores and figure the mineral content. He wouldn't have his wife with him up there—they stake their wives out in Rouyn or Amos, or even Montreal or Toronto."

Getting in touch with Wicklow proved to be difficult. His drill site had two-way radio connections with the air base at Senneterre, Quebec, but mails were slow and irregular. Ken Ledley, when the problem was put to him, suggested that Sidney fly up and interview Wicklow on the spot.

"A nice idea," Sidney said. "But this little investigation is my own. Nobody is paying me, and I just can't afford the time, let alone the money."

"Well, you seem to have some bug in your head about this," Ledley said. "And I'm kind of curious about why somebody would steal my wife's driver's license. I'll bet I can fix it to fly you up there at the company's expense—not my company, but the owner of the mining property."

"How could you work that?" Sidney asked.

"Oh, hell, there are always legal problems," Ledley said. "You aren't a member of the Quebec bar, but there are bound to be papers that have to be notarized or something of the sort. If you put your fee high enough, they'll jump at it. Just leave it to me."

A couple of days later Sidney was summoned to the office of the Capuchin Mining Company, where he was asked to take certain papers to the company's drill site near the shores of James Bay and make some arrangements with the boss of the site. Mr. Ledley had worked well. Sidney could leave on a Friday and return on Sunday, and he would receive a fee of five hundred dollars as well as his traveling expenses.

Miss Semple was terribly worried about his flying off into the wilds among a lot of tough mining men and wanted him to get a complete survival kit, a revolver and a battery-operated electric blanket. Sidney compromised by getting a fur hat with ear flaps and a pair of fleece-lined fur mitts.

He moved off from Malton in a TCA Viscount on the milk run to North Bay, Earlton, Rouyn-Noranda and Val d'Or-Bourlamaque, where, on expert advice, he purchased half a dozen forty-ounce bottles from the Quebec Liquor Commission and went on by taxi over a well-swept road to Senneterre.

It was all very new and wonderful to the city-bred Sidney. The air terminal at Senneterre was set beside a snow-covered frozen lake. It was crowded with all sorts of bush types—prospectors, drillmen, Indians, geologists and engineers—and bush planes of many types were loading up with strange cargoes and winging off into the wilderness.

Sidney embarked in a DeHavilland Beaver, flown by a veteran pilot about nineteen years old, and loaded with machine parts, sleigh dogs and mining men. He was lucky enough to sit beside the pilot and get a superb view of the countryside, which consisted of spruce forest and small lakes stretching off to a far horizon. Fights broke out among the dogs in the rear, and some of the men were airsick.

"Don't worry," the pilot said. "When the men fight and the dogs get airsick, you've got *real* trouble."

They landed on an airstrip bulldozed out of the solid spruce forest, and Sidney finished his strange journey in a caterpillar snowmobile.

He was accommodated, along with the young pilot, in the camp's executive suite, a prefabricated hut with eight bunks, a fat Quebec heater, a two-way radio and a large collection of pinups, records, paperbacks, playing cards, chessmen and cribbage boards. He was given a royal welcome, partly because of the refreshments he had brought.

He had his meals in a cook shack where the drillmen, who spoke a French that was incomprehensible to Sidney, wolfed vast quantities of food amid an obbligato of weird ingestion noises. He had pie for breakfast and heard learned arguments about the specific gravity of the crust. He heard many tall tales of the north, including one about a sample of the cook's pie crust being sent to the assay office by mistake and causing the Capuchin stock to shoot up forty cents a share. The rumor got out that a natural substitute for vinyl floor covering had been discovered. He heard about a diamond drill head breaking off far underground and being drawn fifteen hundred feet to the surface by means of a poultice which contained over two hundred pounds of mustard. He sang songs and drank whisky far into the night with the engineers, in a flimsy shack in the remote bush, with no other human habitation between him and the North Pole.

He completed his legal business with considerable efficiency, and he met Tex Wicklow, a somewhat disenchanted geologist. At first Wicklow got the idea that Sidney was representing his erring wife, and the geologist swore that he wouldn't pay her a cent, not even on a court order, but Sidney convinced him that all he wanted was to locate the lady.

"Well, good luck to you, boy," Wicklow said. "And when you find her, keep her. She left me last September and took everything I owned that wasn't screwed to the walls. All she left really was bills, and plenty of them."

Her maiden name, Wicklow said, was Swann, and she had come originally from Saskatoon. Her mother, a widow who had remarried, still lived in Saskatoon, but Janice Wicklow had not communicated with her for years. Wicklow had met her during a wild furlough in Montreal and had married her on impulse.

"I was bushed," he admitted. "All marriages of guys coming out of the bush ought to be purely provisional for six months. I keep marrying the damnedest women every time I get back to civilization."

Janice had indeed known Gadwell before her marriage and had welcomed him as a long-lost lover when they met in Toronto. "High Grade Howie was in the chips," Wicklow explained. "Money has a fatal attraction for that gal, and this guy Gadwell is quite a hand with the wenches."

Wicklow had not heard a word from his wife since her departure. He suspected that she had gone to join Gadwell. "But that guy won't be nearly as keen on her when it comes to supporting her," he said.

Sidney asked for a picture of Janice Wicklow, and the geologist was able to produce a large selection from the Gladstone bag under his bunk. Janice had been a model in Montreal, and there were shots of her modeling furs, dresses and lingerie. There were even some of her modeling something invisible, like perfume.

"Mrs. Wicklow doesn't appear to have been a prude," Sidney said.

"No, that was never her problem," Wicklow agreed. "Don't let these hyenas see those artistic poses, or they'll want to pin them up."

Sidney picked out half a dozen shots which Wicklow was happy to let him take, and then the two men rejoined the other inhabitants of the executive suite, who were singing to the accompaniment of a five-string banjo.

On Monday morning, somewhat bemused, but back in Toronto, Sidney laid a selection of model photographs, obtained for the purpose, in front of James Bellwood, the lawyer who had defended Wes Beattie on his theft charge. "Identification parade?" Bellwood said, looking the pictures over carefully. "Well, here you are."

He put his finger on a photograph of Janice Swann Wicklow. "That," he said, "is Mrs. Leduc, the witness who said that Wes Beattie stole her purse."

"Well, I'm blowed," Sidney said. "I lightheartedly agreed with Dr. Milton Heber that I would track her down, but I had no idea how elusive she was going to be."

"And now you've done it. Nice work, Gargoyle," Bellwood said.

"No, I haven't found her. But at least I know who she is," Sidney said. "And I can put Missing Persons on the trail, as well as the Canadian Association of Credit Bureaus, so we should be able to interview her soon. If anybody can find her, the credit boys will. She's as addicted to shopping as Lorelei Lee."